her sister's shoes

D1502607

SWEENEY SISTERS SERIES

her sister's shoes

a novel

ASHLEY FARLEY

Cover design: damonza.com
Formatting: damonza.com
Editor: Patricia Peters at A Word Affair LLC
Leisure Time Books, a division of AHF Publishing

ISBN for Paperback: 978-0-9861672-1-8

For my Family

ONE

SAMANTHA

Lovie and Oscar Sweeney had been providing vacationers to the South Carolina coast with fresh-from-the-ocean seafood since opening their doors in May of 1959—and little had changed since then. Not the quality of the service or the layout of the store. The same brass ship's clock still hung on the wall above the door, ticking away the decades. The customers didn't mind the outdated decor so long as the knowledgeable staff served superior product with a friendly smile. The creaking floorboards and dusty shelves welcomed them back year after year, just as the pungent odor of the marsh at low tide greeted them upon arrival in the small inlet town of Prospect.

When it came time to do something about the termites eating away at the floor joists—and to replace the electrical system that was one spark away from a catastrophic fire and the refrigerated display cases that were held together with hope, prayer, and a wad of electrical tape—Samantha Sweeney, the middle daughter of Lovie and Oscar, decided their market was way overdue for an upgrade. Their local customers encouraged Sam to remodel in the same vintage that had brought them success for more than fifty years, but she ignored their advice.

Following her gut instincts, Sam had opted for a radically different approach.

After years of planning and saving, the renovations were nearing completion. With exposed ceiling pipes and pendant lighting, subway tile wainscoting and concrete floors, Sam had envisioned a minimalist style, the seafood being their main event. But as she surveyed the gleaming new showroom, she worried the results were more operating-room sterile than upscale industrial.

Sam suspected her sisters shared her concerns.

Faith turned in circles, contemplating the empty space. "Once the shelves are stocked and the refrigerated cases filled, the place will come to life."

"Why don't we paint the walls?" Jackie whipped her color wheel out of her oversized black patent bag. Sam had hired her older sister, an interior decorator, to offer guidance on trim selections. With mahogany hair styled in a sleek bob, dressed in a tailored black sleeveless top and white pique cropped pants, she embodied the picture of elegance. Jackie thumbed through the color strips, eventually holding out the wheel for Sam to see. "Here we go. I've used this linen color many times before. It's neutral but, at the same time, soft and warm."

Sam barely glanced at the color. "But the painters have already finished. They're out back cleaning up."

"I've never known a painter to turn down more work," Jackie said, tucking the paint wheel under her arm.

Sam and Faith watched their sister glide to the kitchen in the back like a cheetah in search of her prey.

"Don't tell her I said so," Faith whispered to Sam, "but I think she might be right this time."

Sam smiled at her younger sister, who was every bit as pretty as Jackie but in a less sophisticated way.

"She better be. We can't afford another mistake with only two days left before the grand reopening."

Sam took a step back and closed her eyes, trying to imagine

the showroom walls washed in linen. She pictured the wooden wine racks stocked with bottles and specialty dry goods arranged neatly on the metal shelves. She envisioned fresh produce overflowing from baskets on the carts in the front of the store, raw seafood on display in the refrigerated cases in the center of the room, and prepared meals filling the merchandisers along the sidewalls. She imagined customers moseying about, sipping wine from little plastic cups while the staff offered advice on the best practices for grilling tuna.

Sam drew in a deep breath of confidence and exhaled any leftover feelings of doubt. She respected her sister's taste. If Jackie thought linen-colored walls were the finishing touch the room needed, then who was she to argue?

Jackie returned with a self-satisfied smirk on her face. "The painters promised to have everything wrapped up by noon tomorrow. There's hardly any wall space to paint, considering the pass-through to the kitchen in the back and all the windows out here."

Sam ran through her mental checklist. "Noon tomorrow means we'll lose half a day of cleaning and stocking. We'll have to work around the clock in order to open on time on Saturday."

"Why don't you hire someone?" Jackie said with a flippant wave of her hand, as though a strong-bodied person might materialize from thin air.

"What about the twins?" Sam asked. "They're always looking for a way to earn extra spending money."

Jackie's sixteen-year-old sons, Cooper and Sean, often showed up at the market, late in the afternoon, peddling fish and shrimp and crabs—anything they could catch with a net, a trap, or a fishing rod. Sam paid them the same amount she would a wholesaler—even more when their product was fresher, which it usually was.

"You'll have to find someone else." Jackie busied herself with gathering up tile and concrete samples that were scattered across the wine-tasting table. "The boys are busy getting ready to leave for camp on Saturday."

"Today is only Wednesday," Sam said. "Since when does it take a teenager two days to pack?"

"They're not just packing, Samantha. They've made plans with friends."

"Ask them anyway. I'm sure they'll want to help. They already talked to me about working at the market when they get home from camp."

"They'll be busy with football practice when they get home from camp." Jackie flung her bag over her shoulder. "This may come as a surprise to you, but I have higher aspirations for my boys than running a seafood market."

Even if that smelly seafood market provided you all the luxuries you felt entitled to when we were growing up, Sam thought. "I'm not talking about a full-time career, Jackie. The boys just want to earn some money while they have a little fun."

"They will have plenty of fun at camp, and they'll get paid this year, as junior counselors."

"Why do you send them off to camp, anyway, when we live ten minutes from the beach?" Sam asked.

"Not that it's any of your business, but having them tucked away in the mountains keeps them out of trouble."

"And out of your hair," Sam mumbled.

Jackie's face turned red. "Don't you have enough to worry about with your own son without worrying about mine?"

Sam's eyes narrowed and her back stiffened. She was preparing for battle with her older sister when Faith intervened. "Curtis can help with stocking the showroom. He's looking for work."

"I take that to mean the job at the brick plant didn't work out," Jackie said.

Faith picked at a hangnail. "Turns out they hired too many

people. Since Curtis was the last one hired, he was the first one they fired."

"He'll find something else soon, I'm sure. In the meantime, I can definitely put him to work around here. At least for the next couple of days," Sam said, thinking how her brother-in-law's physical strength made up for his lack of brainpower. "I'll work out the details with him when I see him at the party tonight."

"Speaking of the party, I've gotta run." Jackie positioned her designer sunglasses on her face, the dark frames in contrast to her pale unblemished skin. "Can one of you pick up Mom?"

"Since when does Mom need a driver?" Sam asked.

"Since she's been acting so forgetful lately," Jackie said. "Surely you've noticed."

"Of course she's forgetful," Sam said. "She's eighty-two years old."

Jackie slid her sunglasses down and peered at Sam over the top of her bug-eyed lenses. "She's not just forgetful. She's downright demented. I can hardly have a conversation with her anymore. She asks the same questions over and over again." Jackie turned toward Faith. "You know what I'm talking about, don't you?"

Faith shook her head, her eyes wide with concern. "I haven't seen much of Mama since we started the renovations."

"Well . . ." Jackie repositioned her sunglasses on her nose. "I've invited some important people to my party. I don't want Mom embarrassing herself."

Sam glanced at the ship's clock above the door. "Okay, look. It's already five o'clock. Clearly this is something we need to talk about later."

"I agree," Jackie said. "Let's just get through tonight first."

Sam turned to Faith. "I might be running a few minutes late by the time I pick Jamie up from physical therapy and help him get changed. If you can bring Mom to the party, I'll take her home."

"I can do that," Faith said.

"Perfect." Jackie leaned over and kissed Faith's cheek, then Sam's. "In case I forget to tell you both later, happy birthday."

Sam locked the front door and stepped back, admiring the new logo painted in seaweed green across both windows, the interlocking Ss announcing that Captain Sweeney's Seafood Market was open for business.

Sweeney's was located at the T-intersection of Main Street and Creekside Drive. Sam's parents had chosen well when they leased the corner property in 1959. Creekside had always been a thoroughfare to South Carolina's most popular beaches, but Main Street had only recently become the home for many outdoor cafes and novelty boutiques.

Sam heard someone calling her name from across Creekside Drive at the Inlet View Marina. She shielded her eyes against the late-afternoon sun and waved at Captain Mack Bowman, her father's oldest and dearest friend. With his frizzy gray hair and scruffy beard, cigar stub dangling from his lower lip, Captain Mack was an old salt of a man, his body scarred from his many adventures at sea.

Mack cupped his hands around his mouth and shouted across the noisy street, "Will you be ready for a mess of fish tomorrow around this time?"

"Bring 'em on," she hollered back.

He gave her a thumbs-up, and she blew him a kiss in return.

Sam watched his tall frame lumber back down to the dock, where a long line of charter and commercial fishing boats were coming in from a long day of fishing in the Gulf Stream. Mack Bowman and Oscar Sweeney had spent most of their adult lives floating alongside each other in the ocean. Neither of their commercial fishing boats—the *Miss May* and *My Three Gulls*, named after the women in their lives—was ever seen coming in or going out of the inlet without the other on her stern.

Oscar Sweeney was no more than eight when his family immigrated to the United States from Ireland. His father, Sam's grandfather, worked as a lobsterman in a small New England seaside village. Away from the confines of the streets of Dublin, Oscar developed a passion for outdoor living, but his extreme hatred for the endless, bitterly cold Maine winters eventually drove him south. The day after his eighteenth birthday, with his life savings sewn securely in the lining of his coat, Oscar embarked on a journey. He hopped from one fishing vessel to another until he found himself in the small town of Prospect, deep in the heart of South Carolina's Lowcountry. Three weeks later, he spotted Sam's mother window-shopping the boutiques on Main Street and set out to make her his bride.

Back in those days, young ladies from prominent families weren't allowed to marry fishermen with orange hair and thick Irish brogues. But over time, Louvenia's parents grew to appreciate Oscar's gentlemanly nature and his deep belly laugh. They even took to calling her Lovie, Oscar's nickname for his petite china doll.

Determined to see his son-in-law a success, Lovie's father lent Oscar the money he needed to start his own business, a retail shop or perhaps a small cafe. Instead, Oscar partnered up with Captain Mack, the born-and-raised South Carolinian he'd met while working a shrimping boat, and together they bought the *Dreamer*, the fifty-foot commercial boat they fished in together for the next ten years.

Desperate to pay her parents back, Lovie set up shop under an umbrella in the parking lot of the Inlet View Marina. By the end of the second summer, the money she'd earned selling fresh fish and homemade baked goods to the vacationers who traveled through town every Saturday was enough to sign a lease on the empty building across the street. When her lease ran out five years later, she convinced the building's owner to sell her the property. By scrimping and saving and operating the business on a tight budget, she was able to pay off the bank loan in less than ten years.

A cool breeze tickled Sam's skin, raising the hairs on her arm. She untied the sweater from around her waist, slipped it on, and headed for the parking lot. She hopped in her red Jeep Wrangler, buckled her seat belt, and turned up the volume on the classic rock station. She was waiting for a break in the traffic to make a right-hand turn onto Creekside Drive when a silver Audi convertible, with vanity plates DR HART, blew by her, headed in the opposite direction. She recognized the handsome driver as her brother-in-law, the illustrious cardiologist, but the female passenger in the pink scarf with the hot-pink lips was definitely not her sister. Not only was it logistically impossible, considering Jackie had left the market only ten minutes ago, but her sister would never be caught dead in any shade of pink.

The traffic cleared, miraculously, like the parting of the Red Sea, and Sam whipped into the lane behind the Audi, following them through town at a discreet distance. She racked her brain as to why her brother-in-law was driving around town with a beautiful woman riding shotgun. The woman was wearing a sundress and not a uniform, which ruled out the likelihood that he was giving one of his nurses a ride home. Maybe she was a patient, although that seemed unlikely since the glamour girl superglued to Bill's right arm was no damsel in distress. She was too old to be a student intern and too young to be one of those volunteers from the women's auxiliary at church who looked for local professionals to donate their services to the needy.

Jackie had never given Sam any reason to believe her marriage was anything less than perfect. Then again, Sam and Jackie didn't confide in each other the way most sisters did. From Sam's perspective, they appeared the perfect couple—Bill the doting husband and Jackie the devoted wife.

Three or four miles on the outskirts of town, Bill made a sudden, sharp right turn into Water's Edge, a new community of three- and four-story houses built on pilings on tiny parcels of land. After several blocks, he pulled into a driveway with the familiarity of a well-traveled path and screeched to a halt.

Sam eased up to the curb alongside the house next door, hopped out of the Wrangler, and crept up to the giant magnolia tree that separated the properties. She peered through the branches and watched her brother-in-law help his passenger from the car. To Sam's dismay, Bill kissed the woman passionately, in the middle of the driveway for the entire world to see. The woman then pulled away and led him by the hand around the back of the house.

Sam made her way over to Bill's convertible. When she noticed the keys in the ignition, she entertained the idea of driving off in his car. She would love to see his face when he discovered his most prized possession missing. She imagined him pacing up and down the driveway, ranting and raving to the police when he called to report it stolen.

Sam collapsed against the hood of the car. She didn't see Bill as the cheating type. She'd never felt especially close to him, and aside from family occasions, their paths had rarely crossed socially. Not that Sam even had much of a social life. But Bill had always been supportive of her son. He took Jamie hunting and fishing on a regular basis, and he came to as many of his sporting events as he could manage with his busy schedule. He was the best kind of father to Cooper and Sean, and they worshiped him in return. A divorce would devastate them.

Sam stared at her watch, counting the minutes as they ticked away toward party time. The idea of barging in on the couple in bed, with Bill's mistress pulling the sheets up to cover her naked body, held no appeal for Sam. But she couldn't leave until she had a chance to confront the cheating bastard.

Five minutes later, Bill emerged from the house alone. He stopped dead in his tracks when he saw Sam leaning against his car.

"She doesn't look sick, so I'm guessing she's not your patient. Should I assume she's one of your nurses? She appeared skilled in giving you mouth-to-mouth resuscitation."

Bill smiled at Sam, the warm smile she imagined he used when delivering bad news to his patients. "She's actually the widow of one of my patients."

Sam stared at him, mouth agape.

"Is there any chance I can convince you to keep this between the two of us?" he asked, his tone hopeful.

Sam pushed herself off the car and stood face-to-face with him. "You're kidding, right?"

He held her gaze. "Actually, I'm not."

"If you wanted to keep your little love affair a secret, why were you flaunting your glamour girl through the middle of town like a beauty queen in the Fourth of July parade?"

His shoulders sagged. "I wasn't thinking."

"You were thinking, all right. Just not with the head on your shoulders. Are you going to tell my sister or should I?"

He slumped back against the car. "I should be the one to tell her. Although I think I should wait until after the party tonight."

"That's awfully big of you, considering it's her fiftieth birthday and she's been planning this party for months."

"You never have liked me much, have you, Sam?"

She smacked him on the back. "Don't take it personally, Bill. Aside from my father and Captain Mack, I've never met a man I could trust."

TWO

SAMANTHA

By the time she arrived at the office complex at the hospital, Sam was nearly thirty minutes late to pick up her son. She slid into the closest handicapped-parking place and ran inside. She found Jamie waiting in the lobby, hunched over in his wheelchair, watching a baseball game on ESPN.

"You're late," he said, his eyes glued to the television.

She bent down to kiss the top of his dark head. "I know, honey. I'm sorry. Something important came up."

"Moses wants to see you. He's waiting for you in his office."

Sam glanced at her watch. They were due at Jackie's in an hour. "Okay. Wait here and I'll be right back."

"Seriously? Like, where else would I go?"

Sam dashed down the hall to the physical therapist's office and burst in without knocking. "I'm so sorry, Moses. I had a family emergency."

"Nothing serious, I hope." He came from behind his desk to greet her. He towered over her as he took her hand in his. Although she'd gotten to know the therapist well over the past six months, Moses's size always amazed her. Jamie referred to the framed articles on the walls and the trophies lining the shelves as his shrine, a tribute to his time playing tight end for the Georgia Bulldogs.

Sam let out a deep breath she didn't realize she'd been holding. Revealing family secrets was not in her nature, but Moses had proven his trustworthiness many times. "I caught my brother-in-law Bill in a rather embarrassing situation this afternoon."

Moses's chocolate-brown eyes grew large. "Uncle Bill, the brother-in-law who's married to the sister with the twins?"

"Exactly. Cooper and Sean."

"That's too bad," he said, shaking his head.

"I probably shouldn't be telling you this, but I thought you should have a heads-up about the situation. The last thing Jamie needs right now is more drama, but considering his close relationship with the twins, he's likely to get mixed up in the fallout from the divorce."

"Calm down, Sam. You're snapping the ball before the quarterback calls the play. Millions of men and women have extramarital affairs. Not all of them end in divorce. Hopefully, for the twins' sake, your sister and her husband can work out their problems."

Sam paused, letting that thought sink in. She couldn't imagine Jackie letting Bill off the hook for something as big as an affair, but she'd given up on second-guessing her older sister a long time ago. "Maybe you're right."

Moses took Sam by the elbow and guided her to the door. "I have to meet another patient in a few minutes. Do you have time to walk with me to the recreation room? I'd like to talk to you about Jamie's progress."

"Of course." Sam followed him out of the office and into the hall.

"I spoke with Jamie's neurologist this afternoon about his recent MRI. Apparently Dr. Mitchell has been trying to reach you."

Sam increased her pace to keep up with Moses's long legs. "We've been playing phone tag for the last few days. Did Mitchell have good news?"

"Good and bad," Moses said. "I'll give you the good first. The MRI showed the bone has healed and the swelling is gone."

"And the bad news?"

"The obvious. Jamie should be walking by now and he's not." Moses took her elbow and drew her to a halt. "Your son's problem is no longer physical, Sam. Dr. Mitchell believes, and I am in agreement, that his paralysis has become psychosomatic."

"Yo, Mo!" A bald-headed man, his muscles bulging from his navy scrub top, approached them. "Can I have a quick word with you about a patient?" He pulled Moses aside, leaving Sam to stand alone in the hallway.

The prognosis for Jamie's recovery had always been good. A team of doctors at MUSC had inserted a rod and repaired the damage to his lower spinal cord, an injury sustained in an ATV accident at his best friend's house. But that was five months ago, and Jamie had yet to take his first step.

"Sorry for the interruption." Moses rejoined her, and they started walking again in the direction of the lobby. "As I was saying. I know Jamie had several sessions with a psychiatrist on staff while he was in the hospital. Has he seen anyone since then?"

"No. He refuses to talk about the accident. He says it only makes things worse."

"And I empathize with him," Moses said. "What your son experienced would be tough for anyone to handle, especially an eighteen-year-old kid. Jamie is a very angry boy, Sam. He is grieving, and he is carrying a load of guilt. He has hit a wall. I'm afraid he won't walk again until his heart gives his body permission to do so."

None of this was news to Sam. Her hope was that time would

heal all her son's wounds, both physical and emotional. "What can I do to help him?"

Moses handed her a business card.

Sam read the card. "Dr. Patrice Baker, MD, Psychiatrist."

"Patrice is a close friend of my older sister's. She's helped many of my clients before."

She dropped the card in her handbag. "I trust you, Moses. I'm willing to give her a chance. I only hope I can convince Jamie to do the same."

When Sam returned to the waiting room, she saw Jamie deep in conversation with a police officer. Panic gripped her chest as she approached them. "Is my son in some kind of trouble, Officer?"

Jamie's head jerked up, surprised to see his mother standing over them. "Right, Mom. What could I possibly have done wrong, drive my wheelchair over the speed limit?"

The officer chuckled. "That's a good one, speed limit for a wheelchair. I'll have to remember that." He stood to greet Sam and offered his hand. "I'm Eli Marshall. Your son and I have just been discussing batting averages. I'm impressed with his knowledge."

Sergeant Marshall, according to his name badge, was about the same size as Jamie, medium height and stocky build. Judging by the crow's feet around his eyes and the dark curly hair graying at his temples, Sam guessed him to be in his midforties.

She accepted his callused hand, a workingman's hand. "Sam Sweeney. Nice to meet you."

"Jamie was telling me about his recent trip to Turner Field."

Sam followed the officer's eyes to the television. "Aha. The Atlanta Braves. Jamie's uncle was good enough to invite him along when he took his boys to Atlanta last summer," she said, reminded of Bill's more generous qualities. "But did Jamie also tell you his true devotion lies with the Red Sox?"

Eli smiled. "He may have mentioned that."

Sam ignored her son's glare. "I bet Jamie didn't tell you he's been offered a scholarship to play shortstop for USC."

Eli's gray eyes grew wide. "Wow! The Gamecocks are huge. Congratulations."

"That's all in the past, Mom. The sooner you realize that, the better."

"Baseball is your future, Jamie. The sooner you realize that, the sooner you'll get out of that wheelchair."

Eli placed a hand on Jamie's shoulder. "I don't know what your situation is, buddy, but never give up on your dreams no matter how many bumps in the road you encounter. Trust what you feel in your heart and everything else will work out."

"That's the problem," Jamie said under his breath. "I don't feel anything in my heart anymore." He spun his chair around and wheeled toward the door.

Sam watched him go, and then turned to Eli. "I apologize for my son's rudeness. He's really not himself these days."

Eli held up his hand. "No apology necessary. He's a good kid with a lot on his mind."

Sam shook the officer's hand again before following Jamie to the parking lot. When she caught up with him, Jamie was struggling to hoist himself up into the Wrangler. Refusing her help, he managed to lift his body onto the passenger seat. She folded the wheelchair and stowed it away on the special rack she'd had installed on the back of the Jeep.

"You were pretty rude to that policeman," she said, climbing into her seat. "I know you're hurting, but you have to at least try. Having a positive attitude is the most important step toward your recovery."

He rolled his eyes. "Can we please not start this again?"

Sam knew she sounded like a nag, but she had no idea how

else to reach her son. She held three fingers up Boy Scout–style. "I promise. No negative talk tonight. We have a party to go to." She started the car and weaved her way out of the parking lot.

She thought about the long night ahead of her, of being forced to watch Bill make nice to her sister for the sake of the party. She would have to be careful not to let the secret slip to her sister and her mother. If only she had her son back to confide in. Sam missed their camaraderie, but mostly, she missed his humor. The old Jamie had always taken a light-hearted approach to life's difficulties. But there's nothing funny about being confined to a wheelchair. And no place for humor when you are mourning the loss of your best friend.

"Did you get a chance to enjoy the nice weather today?" Sam asked.

His eyebrows shot up. "Since when is hundred-degree heat nice weather? I took your suggestion and wheeled my way over for my appointment this afternoon. I was dripping with sweat when I got there." He lifted his arm and smelled his armpit. "I smell like shit."

"Come on, Jamie. It couldn't have been that bad. The hospital is only five blocks from our house, downhill all the way."

"I'd like to see you try it."

Sam waited for the traffic to clear before turning right onto Main Street. "I'm sorry, honey. I wanted you to see that you can still have some independence. Prospect is a small town. You can wheel yourself over to a friend's house who can drive you places. My schedule is going to be busy after the market reopens this weekend. I'm not always going to be around to take you where you need to go."

"You don't need to worry about me, Mom. I'm fine at home. I just want to be left alone."

"Staying cooped up at home in front of the Xbox is not good for you. You should be out and about, enjoying your summer."

A group of Jamie's friends from school pulled up next to

them at a red light. The driver motioned for him to roll down his window, but Jamie ignored him. The boy shouted at Jamie through the closed window, "Beach Week wasn't the same without you, dude."

Sam felt a sick feeling in the pit of her stomach. Jamie had never mentioned going to Beach Week.

The light turned green, and Jamie flashed his friends the peace sign before they sped off.

Mother and son rode the rest of the way home in silence.

Fifteen years ago, Sam bought her little yellow cottage from Captain Mack when his wife died after a long battle with breast cancer. He couldn't stand to live in the house surrounded by all the memories of the good times they'd shared. Without children to consider, Mack made Sam an offer she couldn't refuse and moved to the old houseboat he kept on a wooded property he owned. The property was on the inlet outside of town.

Built in the early 1940s, the cozy one-story Cape Cod offered everything a mother and her young son needed—front porch and back deck, three bedrooms and two baths, sitting room, dining room, and kitchen. The fenced-in yard had given Jamie plenty of room to run around in when he was little, and the detached garage had provided storage space for all his hunting and sporting equipment as he got older.

Sam drove in the driveway and parked in front of the garage. She shifted in her seat to face him. "I had a nice chat with Moses today. He's convinced you will walk again."

"What does Moses know?" Jamie stared out the window. "All he does is work my worthless muscles."

"I have never known you to shy away from a challenge. You are a strong, gifted athlete." She grabbed his chin and turned his head toward her. "You just need to work a little harder, push yourself a little more. You've always been a fighter. You set your goals high and go after them with gusto. That's who you are."

"This isn't a baseball game, Mom. I'm not trying to lift more weight or reach a certain speed. In case you haven't noticed, I am paralyzed. Translated, I can't walk."

"There's a difference between can't and won't."

He opened the door to escape, then realized he couldn't get far without his wheelchair. He closed the door again. "I'm the one who got screwed here. I get to spend the rest of my life in a wheelchair while Corey gets to fish for eternity in the great big ocean up in heaven."

"What happened to Corey is not your fault."

"How can you say that? I was driving the Gator."

"On Corey's family's property. His parents were responsible for making sure the trail was cleared. If anyone is to blame, they are. Look,"—she tilted his chin toward her—"I understand you are still coping with a lot emotionally. I think talking to someone might help. Moses gave me the name of a doctor—"

"How many times do I have to tell you, I don't need a damn shrink?" He drew his fist back and punched the dashboard. He winced in pain and his eyes filled with tears. "Will you please just get my chair?"

Her son reminded Sam so much of his father with hair and eyes as black as coal. Until now, he'd never exhibited any signs of Allen's dark moods. He'd always been a happy boy, but lately, she'd sensed a storm brewing beneath the surface.

Sam glanced at the clock on the dashboard. "We will table the discussion for now. But only because we've got to get ready for the party."

Sam helped Jamie into his chair and pushed him up the wheelchair ramp, through the back door, and into the kitchen. "Aunt Jackie is expecting us to be on time. Can I help you get cleaned up?"

"I'm not going to her stupid party."

"Of course you're going. It's her fiftieth birthday."

"Seriously, Mom. I'm not in the mood to have everyone

staring at me, the poor pitiful cripple. Please, will you just go without me?"

Sam squatted down beside his chair. "We are family, honey. We have to go and support Aunt Jackie." She ran her hand down his unshaven cheek. "Besides, Cooper and Sean are counting on you to come. After you make polite conversation for a few minutes with the adults, the three of you can go off and do your own thing."

"You make me sound like a little kid. My legs are paralyzed, not my brain. I'm capable of having an intelligent conversation." He rolled off toward his room.

"Can I help you with anything?" she called.

He slammed his bedroom door in response.

She tapped lightly on his door. "Don't forget to shave. And wear a collared shirt."

Sam headed down the hall to the smaller bedroom on the front of the house.

After the accident, she gave up her master bedroom so Jamie would have easy access to the en suite bath. Even with the special sink and shower her handyman had installed, it took Jamie a long time to carry out his routine. He'd begun to let his hygiene slip. His hair hung in greasy strands to his shoulders. Angry pimples covered his forehead, the result of not using his cleanser. He hardly ever shaved. His facial hair grew in patches, giving him a bedraggled appearance rather than the outdoorsy scruffy look popular among his friends. A sour odor emanated from his body, a combination of dirty hair and sweat.

Sam showered, towel-dried her short hair, and rummaged through her closet, wishing she hadn't loaned Faith her favorite black dress. She settled on a pair of white jeans and a pale-blue sleeveless silk top. Grabbing her straw clutch, she went to the kitchen and dumped the contents of her everyday bag onto the counter. She retrieved Dr. Baker's business card from the pile and created a contact with the doctor's numbers in her cell phone, then tore the business card into little pieces, depositing them in the trash can. She didn't want to risk another confrontation with Jamie if he happened to find the card.

Time was running out, and Sam was desperate for help. She would drag her son to see Patrice Baker if she had to. If Jamie didn't walk again soon, she would have to make some hard decisions about his future.

Last spring, during Jamie's junior year in high school, the University of South Carolina offered him a partial scholarship to play baseball. When the head coach learned of his accident, he consented to hold the spot open for several months in light of the speedy recovery the doctors had promised. But when spring arrived and Jamie showed no signs of improvement, the coach withdrew his offer, claiming he had a long list of healthy recruits to choose from. Sam remained optimistic the coach would consider Jamie for the team when he recovered. She was thrilled when the university offered him the same amount of money based on his academic merit.

After several knock-down-drag-outs, the subject of college had become the elephant in the room that neither mother nor son dared to mention. Sam viewed the academic scholarship as an opportunity for Jamie to get an education she could not afford otherwise, while Jamie viewed the money as a consolation prize. He refused to consider leaving home for reasons he would not discuss.

Moses was right. Jamie had hit a wall. He had given up.

THREE

FAITH

Curtis whistled when he saw Faith wearing her sister's simply cut, form-fitting black dress. "Why are you so dolled up?"

He lay, sprawled out in his boxers and undershirt, with one leg thrown across the back of the couch, while their six-year-old daughter, Bitsy, sat on the floor next to him, busily coloring at the coffee table.

Faith had told her husband countless times about the party. She'd even affixed the invitation to the refrigerator so as to remind him every time he got a beer.

"Stop messing around, Curtis." She nudged him with the toe of her worn-out ballet flat. "We're gonna be late if you don't get dressed."

He spit tobacco juice into an empty can in his right hand and took a sip from the full beer in his left. "Late to what?"

"Aunt Jackie's birthday party is tonight, Daddy," Bitsy said without looking up from her coloring. "Do you think they'll put fifty candles on her cake?"

"I ain't going to no party with no stuck-up rich people." He

21

wiped his stringy brown hair out of his face. "Besides, I already made plans."

"Then unmake them. Jackie has been planning this party for months." Faith pulled Bitsy to her feet. "Don't sit on the floor like that, honey. You'll wrinkle your dress." She smoothed her hand along the bottom of her daughter's dress, hoping no one would notice the crease in the fabric where she'd let out several inches of hem. "Go get your hairbrush out of the bathroom," she said, patting her daughter's bottom.

"Come on, Curtis." Faith picked his foot up off the couch and let it drop to the floor. "We're supposed to pick Mama up in ten minutes."

"Aw, hell, nah." He drained the rest of his beer and crumbled the can. "I'm not going anywhere with that crazy old bitch. I'm supposed to meet the gang later."

Faith placed her hands on her hips. "It won't kill you to come to the party, at least for a little while."

His eyes narrowed. "I don't remember you ever asking me if I wanted to go."

"I shouldn't have to ask you to go to my sister's fiftieth birthday party. Sometimes you have to do things for your family, whether you want to or not."

He struggled to sit up. "I guess I could stop by for some grub on the way to meet the fellas. But she better have some real meat, like barbecue ribs. Those fancy little bite-size things you pop in your mouth ain't food."

Bitsy returned with her hairbrush and a ribbon, handing them both to her mother.

"Oh . . . I almost forgot. Sam needs you to help stock the showroom tomorrow and Friday."

"Fine, as long as she pays me."

Faith experienced a pang of guilt. "Haven't you already been paid enough?" She secured Bitsy's ponytail with a hairband, tied the pink ribbon in a big bow, and set the hairbrush down on the coffee table.

"My going rate is twenty an hour. Take it or leave it." Curtis hauled himself up off the couch. He picked Bitsy up by her shoulders, planted a big kiss on her cheek, then set her back down and turned to Faith. "Damn, woman, you're looking downright hot tonight. Where'd you get the money to buy the new dress?" His face was so close to hers she could smell the stale tobacco juice on his breath.

"I didn't buy it. I borrowed it from Sam."

He lifted a lock of Faith's hair and sniffed it. Fingering the pearls around her neck, he said, "I haven't seen you wear these in a while. They'd fetch a pretty penny down at Hank's."

Faith swatted his hand away. "Daddy gave me these pearls, Curtis. They belong to me. And one day I will give them to our daughter." She opened the door and escorted her daughter out before her husband got any more ideas about pawning her pearls.

She stood for a moment on the front steps. The refreshing evening air offered a welcome relief from the stuffy trailer and the heated exchange with her husband.

"Why is Daddy mad at you, Mama?" Bitsy skipped along beside Faith as they walked across the driveway to her rusty old pickup truck.

Once white, the paint on the truck had yellowed with age. The tires were bald and the starter was shot, but Faith loved the truck just the same. Her father had given her the pearls on her sixteenth birthday and the truck when she graduated from high school—the only two items of value she owned.

"He's not mad, honey. He's just in a bad mood." Faith scooped her daughter up and gave her a big hug before sliding her into her car seat in the back.

"But he's always in a bad mood," Bitsy insisted as Faith was fastening her in.

"Not always, baby. It just seems like it lately. That happens sometimes when grown-ups have a lot on their mind." Faith kissed the tip of Bitsy's nose. "But that's nothing for you to worry about."

For the past two years, Curtis had been in and out of numerous jobs. He'd been fired from the job at the brick plant after only three days. The longer Curtis went without a job, the meaner he got and the more he drank. Most nights he came in drunk. She only wished he spent as much time looking for a job as he did hanging out with his biker friends.

Faith, saying a silent prayer that the truck would start, turned the key several times before the engine finally caught. "We're not gonna let Daddy's bad mood spoil our fun, now are we?" she asked, looking at Bitsy in the rearview mirror.

"No, we're not!" Bitsy said, bouncing in her seat. "Mommy, will they have a cake for you and Aunt Sam tonight, too?"

"No, sweetie. We decided to let Aunt Jackie have the spotlight this year since she's turning fifty." Bitsy's disappointed face prompted her to add, "But I'll tell you what. After the grand reopening on Saturday, I'll let you buy me an ice cream sundae at Sandy's to celebrate my birthday."

She stuck her lower lip out in a pout. "But I don't have any money to buy ice cream."

Faith smiled. "How about if I loan you the money and you can pay me back in kisses and hugs?"

Bitsy beamed as she bobbed her head up and down.

Faith turned the truck around and headed down the long dirt driveway toward the highway. Moving their double-wide to the woods in the middle of nowhere had been Curtis's idea. He loved to kill squirrels with his shotgun and scratch his privates on the front steps without anyone around to see. Faith dreamed of having neighbors, a friend to drink coffee with in the mornings, children for Bitsy to play with in the afternoons. She envied her sisters their proximity to town, especially Jackie, whose expansive property fronted on the water.

Faith wasn't smart like Sam or creative like Jackie. Instead of going off to college like her sisters, she'd chosen to stay home and attend classes at the regional community college. All she'd ever really wanted was to be a mom. But one child was all she and Curtis were destined to have. After several miscarriages and a difficult pregnancy, she was lucky to carry Bitsy until the thirtieth week. She'd never forget the chaos in the delivery room that day—the emergency cesarean section, her baby's blue face as the nurses rushed her off to the neonatal nursery, her husband's pale face when the doctors told him the baby was a girl and there'd be no more. For one whole month, Faith never left the side of the incubator. The baby had problems eating and breathing, and a little problem with her heart that eventually worked itself out. Faith named the baby Elizabeth after Curtis's great aunt, but Lovie called her Bitsy from the start. "Such an itsy-bitsy thing, fighting for her life."

Mother and daughter sang along together, very loud and very off-key, to Brad Paisley all the way to town. Faith turned left onto Creekside Drive, drove four blocks, then turned right into the complex where her mom lived in the last townhouse in a row of ten. The corner unit afforded her two hundred more square feet than the others, plus a first-floor master suite and a large deck out back.

Faith pulled up in front of the townhouse and blew the horn, a honking noise that sounded like a wounded goose flying in for a landing.

Her mama appeared at the door. Lovie was not a fancy dresser. Shorts in the summer, jeans in the winter, and the same red knit dress on Sundays to church. She'd shrunk two inches in the past few years, now measuring in at exactly five feet. Today's outfit—a pale-blue silk nightgown cinched with a zebra-skinned belt and topped with a furry vest—made her look like a little girl playing dress-up.

Bitsy giggled from the backseat. "What is Lovie wearing, Mama?"

"I don't know, sweetie, but we'd better go find out."

Once freed from her car seat, Bitsy ran over and wrapped her arms around her grandmother. Faith could hardly believe her mom was only six months shy of her eighty-third birthday. She'd always been the youngest-acting of all her friends' moms. She'd insisted her grandchildren call her Lovie, claiming it made her sound like a hip grandmother instead of some old lady granny.

Jackie had mentioned their mother's memory slipping, but she hadn't said anything about strange behavior.

Faith ran her hand down the back of Lovie's vest. "Is this real?"

Lovie beamed. "Jacqueline gave it to me two Christmases ago. Mink isn't exactly my taste, but I thought I'd wear it in honor of her birthday."

"It's kinda cool tonight, but I think you might get hot," Faith said.

Lovie reached for the door handle on the truck. "We don't have time for me to change now."

"At least put on a slip. I can see right through your nightgown."

"My nightgown?" Lovie looked down, apparently realizing for the first time what she was wearing. She rubbed the silky fabric between her fingers. "I guess you're right. This is kind of a strange outfit. I never could figure out how to wear this silly old vest." She rummaged through her pocketbook for her house keys. "It won't take me but a minute to change."

Faith glanced at her watch. "Take your time. We don't have to be there until seven." Faith knew Jackie would prefer for them to skip the party than arrive with their mom in her nightgown. She took the key from Lovie and unlocked the front door. "Come on, we'll help you find something to wear."

Once inside, Faith glimpsed the mess in the living room as

they passed by, but the chaos in Lovie's bedroom caught her by surprise. Clothes lay strewn across the floor and every piece of furniture as though a tornado had ripped through her closet and dresser. Her mama had always insisted they keep their rooms tidy when they were young. They had shared two tiny rooms between the three of them, but they had always kept their underwear folded in their drawers and their dresses hung in neat rows in the closets.

"What happened in here?" Faith asked. "Hurricane season is still weeks away."

"There's a method to this madness." Lovie dug through the pile of clothes on her bed until she found her navy slacks. "All my pants are here. And my blouses over there." She found a white silky blouse from the mountain of clothes heaped on top of the rocking chair.

While Lovie changed into her new outfit, Faith began to straighten the room. When she went to hang her mom's robe on the back of the bathroom door, she found cosmetics scattered across the counter and clumps of dried toothpaste in the sink. Wet towels were piled up in the corner and the wastebasket over-flowed with lipstick-blotted tissues.

"What time are we supposed to be at Jackie's?" Lovie asked.

"Seven o'clock, Mama." She'd told her mom that not ten minutes ago.

Lovie glanced nervously at her bedside table, where three different alarm clocks were set to the same time. "Oh Lordy. It's already six thirty."

"Relax. We've got plenty of time. What's with all the clocks, Mom?"

"They help me keep my appointments straight. Each night before I go to bed, I write my appointments for the next day on those little sticky notes next to the clocks. Then, I set a different alarm for each appointment, fifteen minutes before I'm supposed to be there."

Faith glanced over at Bitsy, who was listening attentively, as though her grandmama's system was the most brilliant idea ever. One of the alarms sounded, a loud beeping noise, and the three of them jumped. Lovie removed the sticky note attached to the clock and held it up for Faith to read. "See, Jacqueline's party. You told me a fib. We're supposed to be there at six forty-five, not seven o'clock. Which means we better get going." She stuffed a wad of tissues in her bag and started toward the door.

"Shouldn't you put on shoes first?"

Lovie looked down. "Oops." She slid her feet into gold sandals and then motioned to Faith and Bitsy to follow. "Come on. We're going to be late."

As she passed down the hallway, Faith studied the disarray in the other rooms. Stacks of newspapers and catalogs cluttered the floor and furniture in the living room, and dirty dishes filled the kitchen sink.

"Why don't I come over on Sunday and help you clean up?" Faith said.

"Don't be ridiculous. I can do it myself. I've been so busy lately, I haven't had time."

Busy? Doing what? The market had been closed for remodeling for more than six weeks. Lovie didn't belong to a bridge club or a book club or any groups at church. Other than taking meals to sick friends and looking after her family, her mom's life had always revolved around the seafood market.

Lovie asked Faith five more times during the ten-minute drive what time the party started. When they passed their old driveway, next door to Jackie's, Lovie smacked her hand on the dashboard and shouted, "Where on earth are you going, Faith? You missed the turn."

Faith hesitated. Did her mom think they still lived in the cottage next door, or was she simply confused about whose driveway was whose?

"I know it's hard to see with the sun glaring through the

windshield, but that's our old driveway." Faith pulled up next to the mailbox at the end of her sister's driveway. "This is Jackie's."

"Oh right," Lovie mumbled. "Of course."

Her mama popped the top off a Maybelline tube and smeared lipstick across her lips. Lovie had always worn the same shade of cherry-red lipstick, but the woman who grinned over at her looked like a clown with penciled-on eyebrows, flushed cheeks, and bright orange lips.

FOUR

JACQUELINE

From the balcony off her second-floor kitchen, Jackie watched the party preparations taking place on the terrace below. The band members tuned their instruments and tested their microphones. The bartenders iced down beer and opened bottles of wine. The caterers placed trays of sushi and bowls of shrimp on the tables while the wait staff stood ready to offer the guests fried oysters on Ritz crackers with a dab of remoulade sauce.

The late afternoon sun was inching toward the horizon. A full moon would soon rise over the high tide, bringing with it the promise of a lovely summer's eve. Tiki torches illuminated the path leading down to the dock, which was outlined by strands of hundreds of little white lights. The stage was set for Jackie's guests to dance the night away.

That is, if anyone actually showed up.

She felt a bit guilty for not sharing her birthday with her sisters. All three of them were born during the first week of June —the first, the second, and the fourth—Jackie, Sam, and Faith, respectively. Sam was two years younger than Jackie, and Faith was six years younger than Sam. When they were little, the girls always celebrated their birthdays with one great big party on June 3, the one nonbirthday, neutral day of the week.

The parties were chaotic affairs, usually set up on the lawn with games of Pin the Tail on the Donkey and Musical Chairs. After a peanut-butter-and-jelly lunch, the three girls would blow out the candles on a full-size vanilla sheet cake. Next came the required thirty minutes of rest to allow their food to digest. Then children and grown-ups migrated down to the dock for an afternoon of swimming. It's a wonder no one ever drowned, with kids of all ages diving and cannonballing from the dock.

The parties grew smaller as the girls grew older. In recent years, the burden of hosting the party had fallen on Jackie. For as long as she could remember, she'd thrown a dinner party on June 3 for the whole family—husbands, children, and Lovie—complete with a catering staff to execute her elaborate themes. She'd planned everything from the traditional hamburgers-and-hotdogs-on-the-grill cookout to a festive Hawaiian luau. One year, she'd surprised Sam on her fortieth by inviting all her friends to a sixties throwback party. As the first to reach the midcentury mark, Jackie had declared a new rule—each sister reserved the right to have her own birthday party when she turned fifty.

She watched a pelican swoop in and settle on the railing of the dock, the bird's large throat pouch reminding Jackie of her own thickening neck. Her father, inspired by his love of seagulls, had always referred to his three daughters as his gulls, but Jackie preferred to think of herself as a blue heron, tall and elegant and lean. For her fortieth birthday, her husband had given her a four-foot bronze heron. She'd named the statue Grace and positioned it on the terrace at the edge of the walkway to the dock, where she could see it from every room on the waterside of her house. She placed a wreath and red bow around the heron's neck at Christmas and hung a basket of colored eggs from its beak at Easter. Tonight, for the occasion of

Jackie's fiftieth, Grace sported a lei of white dendrobium orchids.

Jackie heard a screen door slam at the cottage next door, then saw ten-year-old Rebecca Griffin flying across the lawn toward their dock. "Happy birthday, Miss Jackie," the child called, waving up at her.

Jackie waved back. "The boys are expecting you to come over later for cake."

Rebecca flashed a mouth full of metal before continuing on her mission. When she got to the end of the dock, she untied a rope from one of the cleats and hoisted a crab trap out of the water. Jackie was too far away to count the crabs in the trap, but the little girl's squeal signaled a successful catch.

Rebecca reminded Jackie of Sam at that age: long tanned legs and freckles splattered across her cheeks. When she wasn't fishing or shrimping or mud-hole punching, Sam had followed their father around from one home improvement project to another.

How could three sisters with the same parents, the same set of genetics, be so different?

The girls were nine, seven, and one when they moved into the house next door. With three tiny bedrooms, two baths, and a sweeping view of the inlet, the rundown shack had been their parents' dream home, the only waterfront property they'd ever be able to afford. Looking past the peeling paint and rotten floorboards, their parents combined their life savings and devoted the next five years to weekend work projects. Oscar became proficient with a hammer and a saw while Lovie developed a knack for turning flea-market trash into treasures. Jackie and Sam, dressed in matching overalls, appointed themselves the painters. Naturally, Sam was better with a brush and roller, while Jackie fancied herself the color consultant. The sisters had argued over which color to paint their room—Jackie's purple against Sam's green— until Jackie finally convinced Sam they should paint one side a subtle shade of moss green and the other a pale-lavender hue.

The most impressive of the family's accomplishments was the large screened-in porch they built across the front of the cottage. They ate dinner together on the porch every night during the summer, gathered around the old wooden picnic table the girls had painted a high-gloss fire-engine red. After dinner, they'd camped out, reading and talking and listening to country music, rocking back and forth in the rocking chairs, and taking turns swinging in the hammock.

Despite their best efforts at remodeling, their charming quarters paled in comparison to the elegant plantation house next door—Moss Creek Farm—that Jackie now called home.

Built in 1850, the main house was the only structure on an old cotton plantation that survived the Civil War. In the property's one-mile stretch along the waterfront, the remnants of an ancient concrete dock still occupied the bank about five hundred yards past the house. Prior to development of the area, families traveling from their summer cottages on the beaches had used the landing as their point of entry to their permanent homes inland.

While the house had been renovated many times since, the integrity of the building remained intact. With stately columns and wraparound porches, the three-story Georgian had endured Yankee occupation and weathered countless hurricanes, providing five different families a safe haven for more than 150 years.

The sweet scent of Ligustrum from the hedge that separated the two properties drifted toward her, bringing with it her earliest memory of the women who would one day cause her downfall.

⁊

On a warm Saturday in late May, six months after Jackie and her family moved into the cottage, she was daydreaming the afternoon away, perched atop one of the upper branches of the sprawling live oak in their side yard. When she heard voices and soft music drifting over the Ligustrum hedge from the house next door, she hopped down from her perch and climbed into the hedge, deep enough to stay hidden while she spied on the party.

Mimi Motte and her daughter, Julia, were hosting a garden tea party for several women and little girls. Dressed in matching floral sundresses, with blonde manes and backs ramrod straight, Jackie watched in envy as mother and daughter moved from table to table socializing with their friends.

A bee swarmed Jackie's head, then another and another. She swatted at them, but that only made them mad. When the bees attacked her full on, she lost her balance and tumbled from the hedge. She landed on her fanny only feet away from where Julia sat visiting with her friends.

"Oh no!" Julia set her lemonade down and rushed to Jackie's side. "Are you okay?" she asked, helping Jackie to her feet.

"I'm fine." Jackie brushed the grass off the back of her shorts. "A swarm of bees attacked me."

"Did they sting you?"

Jackie searched her arms and legs for stings. "I don't think so. My name is Jackie."

"And I'm Julia. Why don't you come sit down a minute? You need some refreshments." Julia took Jackie by the hand and led her over to the table, gently pushing her down to the one empty chair. She summoned one of the maids in gray uniform, who rushed over with a tray of sweets. The maid set an empty plate in front of Jackie and used small silver tongs to load the plate with three small iced squares.

Jackie appeared skeptical.

"You'll like them, I promise. Mama calls them petit fours, but I call them tea cakes."

Jackie took a tentative bite. "It's delicious."

"These are my friends." Julia pointed to each of the six girls, quickly introducing them. Jackie caught only two of their names, both of them Donna.

Julia's mom appeared at her daughter's side. "Who's your new friend, sweetheart?"

"Mimi, this is Jackie. Jackie, this is my mom," Julia said with a flick of her hand back and forth. "But you can call her Mimi. Everyone else does."

"Is Jackie short for Jacqueline?" Mrs. Motte asked.

"Yes, ma'am."

"And what is your last name, dear?"

"Sweeney. I live next door."

"Oh. I see." Julia's mother turned to her daughter. "I didn't realize you'd invited the neighbors to the party."

"She didn't invite me, Mrs. Motte. A swarm of bees chased me into your yard. Julia was nice enough to give me some cake and lemonade."

Another mother approached the table and cupped Jackie's chin in her hand, turning her head first one way then another. "And who is this stunning creature?" she asked.

Jackie sensed evil lurking behind this woman's attempt at kindness. While her smile was wide, her pointy canine teeth showed like vampire fangs when she parted her bloodred lips.

"Ethel, this is Jacqueline Sweeney. From next door. Jacqueline, this is Ethel Bennett, Donna Bennett's mother."

Mrs. Bennett's hand fell from Jackie's chin as though she'd been scalded. "Sweeney?" she asked, her perfectly plucked eyebrow raised in an arc. "You mean the family who runs the seafood market?"

Jackie hung her head. "Yes, ma'am."

The woman moved to the Donnas' side of the table, placing a hand on the shoulder of the Donna with the smug look on her face. "One of our reporters—our family owns the *Prospect Weekly*, you see—did an article on your parents a while back. We named your mom and dad the most hard-working couple in town."

Jackie's face reddened. She did see—and perfectly clearly. In

Mrs. Bennett's book, being named the hardest-working people in town was anything but an honor.

Jackie stood to go. "I should get home now. My parents are expecting me for dinner," she said, even though it was only three o'clock.

Julia walked Jackie to the end of the hedge where a narrow passageway allowed her room to slip through. "Would you like to come over tomorrow afternoon?" Julia asked.

"Sure . . . but shouldn't you ask your mom?"

"She won't care. She pretty much gives me anything I want. We have to go to church first and then brunch at the club. I'll come over and get you around two."

Jackie half expected her new friend not to show up, but to her great delight, Julia appeared at two o'clock sharp. Together, the girls crawled back through the hedge, leaving a hole that would eventually become a permanent passageway between their two houses.

"Jackie, dear, how lovely to see you," Mimi said when the girls sought her out in her rose garden to ask permission to go swimming.

Jackie could tell Julia's mother was neither expecting her nor glad to see her, but she refused to let that ruin her afternoon. Instead, she set about proving herself worthy of Julia's friendship. Aware of Mrs. Motte's eyes watching her every move, she made certain she used her very best manners.

Over time, Mimi softened toward her. Julia and Jackie spent hours playing dress-up in Mimi's closet, or decorator with her discontinued fabric and carpet samples. They seldom fought and would've spent every waking hour together, if Mimi hadn't insisted Julia continue her relationships with her other friends. Whenever Julia had one or both of the Donnas over, Jackie resumed her perch in the tree and spied on them over the hedge. On the rare occasion when Julia invited her to join them, Jackie usually declined, preferring solitude to spending time with the Donnas.

Jackie had been obsessing over plans for her birthday party since before Christmas. But now, hearing voices coming down the driveway, she wanted nothing more than to put on her silk pajamas and crawl in bed with her book. She listened carefully, hoping to hear Julia's slow Southern drawl, but all she heard was the sound of her mother's cackling laughter.

Julia had responded a week ago to the party invitation. "I'll try and stop by before I go to Donnas' supper club. You know I can't miss their supper club. It's the biggest event of the year."

She was all too aware of the Donnas' supper club, a party they held every year on the second Wednesday in June. The Donnas claimed they had a conflict with the annual wildlife benefit for the second Wednesday, but Jackie had a hunch they'd moved their supper club up a week, to the night of her birthday, to get under her skin.

Jackie and Bill had been invited to the supper club every year until now, but she wasn't surprised when their invitation never arrived in the mail, considering the chilly way the Donnas had been acting toward her of late.

"It's because of Caroline," Julia had said when Jackie confronted her about the Donnas' behavior a few weeks back. Caroline was Corey's mom, the boy who was killed in the Gator accident with Jamie. "The Donnas feel it would be awkward for Caroline to be around you right now."

"That's funny. I've been to see Caroline many times. She's the only one in this town who doesn't blame Jamie for the accident."

Julia gave her hand a little squeeze. "Caroline is overcome with grief. One minute she says one thing, the next another. She just needs a little time. You understand, don't you?"

Jackie understood perfectly. Her friends were using Caroline as an excuse to get Jackie out of the way so they could talk openly about Bill's affair with his dead patient's wife.

Two weeks ago, Jackie had spotted Bill and a woman she'd never seen huddled together in the back booth of the Inlet Coffee Shop, with two caffe lattes and a blueberry muffin on their table. Jackie assumed the woman was a pharmaceutical sales rep until she saw her husband gently brush a blonde wisp of hair off the woman's forehead. Jackie had started paying attention after that. She found smudged pink lipstick stains on his button-down collars and unexplained charges from Victoria's Secret on their American Express card.

Worse than his act of betrayal and the public humiliation was the knowledge that she had failed him as a wife. Theirs was never an overly passionate marriage. They had some spark in the beginning, a dim flame that lasted until she got pregnant with the twins. Jackie's waddling around with two babies in her belly, carrying an extra fifty pounds, twenty of it in her ass, wasn't exactly a turn-on for her super fit husband.

She couldn't deny that Bill had been a good provider. Three years after they were married, when Mimi decided to build her six-thousand-square-foot dream house on a peninsula of land overlooking the marsh ten miles outside of town, she came to Jackie and Bill with an offer for them to buy Moss Creek Farm. Bill accepted with very little negotiation. "Anything to make my bride happy," he'd told Mimi.

Jackie had wanted to live at the farm all her life, but she'd learned that having your dreams come true didn't always make you happy.

If she had to pick a date that marked the beginning of the end of their marriage, it would be Christmas Eve of 1998. The twins were seven months old and still not sleeping through the night. Bill had come home midday from deer hunting and found her in the kitchen, Christmas wrapping paper spread across the pine table, a baby on one hip, a burned piecrust in the opposite hand, and Gerber sweet potatoes congealed in her hair.

He gave her a perfunctory kiss on the top of her head. "You look tired."

"What the hell do you expect?" She slammed the piecrust down on the counter. "I haven't gotten a decent night's sleep since the babies were born. And now, with shopping and decorating and cooking for the holidays, you're damn right I'm tired."

"Have you ever thought of getting a nanny?"

Jackie had never considered hiring someone to look after her children, but she realized that might be the solution to restoring some sense of normalcy. Two weeks later, she hired Carlotta, the sister of a mate on Captain Mack's fishing boat. By the end of January, the twins were sleeping through the night, the house was organized in a way it had never been, and Bill was getting hot meals for dinner. Having Carlotta in charge of all the domestic affairs left little for Jackie to do. Within the month, she'd returned to work and begun once again to focus on her social life. She often felt like a stranger in her own home, but Jackie didn't mind. She considered the quiet woman who worked behind-the-scene miracles a godsend.

Jackie and Bill nurtured their boys over the years, but they failed to nurture their marriage. Lately, she sensed Bill gathering courage to ask for a divorce. He'd even started the conversation a couple of times—"Jack, we need to talk"—only to be interrupted by one of the boys, or the ringing or text dinging of his cell phone. She would give him his divorce, but not before she made him grovel. Jackie was prepared to fight for the house, the kids, and full control of their brokerage account.

Bill snuck up behind her and gave her a little peck on the cheek. "Happy birthday, Jack."

When was the last time he'd given her a real kiss?

"Speak of the devil, I was just thinking of you."

"All good thoughts I hope." He flashed a smile, but she didn't smile back. "Your guests are beginning to arrive."

She leaned over the balcony railing, hoping to catch a glimpse of Julia's blonde curls. But the only people in the driveway were Sam, Faith, and the kids.

"Sam and Faith aren't guests. They're family. You can count on us having plenty to eat and drink, because I doubt anyone else will show up."

"Don't be ridiculous. I saw your guest list on the counter in the kitchen. Plenty of people have responded that they're coming. It's still early."

"Julia promised to stop by on her way to supper club with the Donnas."

Bill leaned back against the railing. "So this is about Julia, is it?"

Jackie bit back tears. Although Julia was part of it, Jackie's fragile emotional state was about so much more than her best friend acting cold toward her. She hated her husband for cheating on her, but she couldn't bring herself to kick him out. Letting him go meant a lifestyle change she wasn't ready to face.

He turned her chin toward him. "Let me offer you a little advice. Turning fifty is a big deal, Jack. Look at it as an opportunity to make a major change in your life if so warranted."

"And what do you suggest I change?" Her heart pounded. Surely he wasn't about to ask her for a divorce before the start of the most monumental birthday party of her life.

"You need to stop settling for mediocre. You deserve to have better friends than these selfish women who don't feel the same about you as you feel about them. It's time to clean house, rid your life of everything that causes you heartache. Take a chance on something new, maybe a new career, or even the same career but with a boss who appreciates you."

Jackie glared at him. "And what big change did you make last year on your fiftieth birthday?"

His face softened in sorrow and regret. "Jack, I—"

She held her hand up to stop him. She'd opened the door for him to confess his infidelity, then realized she wasn't ready for the truth. "You know what, save it. I don't want to hear it. Not tonight. Not on my birthday."

The band picked up their tempo from the soft background music they'd been playing, and Sam waved from the terrace below.

"They're playing Van Morrison for you, Jackie," Sam called. "Come join the crowd. 'It's a marvelous night for a moondance.'"

Jackie closed her eyes and tried to clear her mind of unpleasant thoughts. As the music took over her body, her feet began to move. She vowed not to let anyone ruin her party—not her husband or her backstabbing friends. Tonight she would dance with someone young and handsome, and first thing tomorrow morning, she would start cleaning her house by taking out the trash. Tomorrow morning she would kick her philandering husband out on the street.

FIVE

SAMANTHA

Sam and Faith had parked at the end of the driveway, blocking others from pulling up close to the house. The vacant field across the street provided sufficient parking for guests.

Jamie refused Sam's offer of help and struggled to maneuver his chair over the bumpy cobblestoned driveway. Bitsy skipped alongside him, babbling on about balloons and birthday cake, while Faith and Lovie followed close behind. When they reached the end of the tunnel of live oak trees, Jackie's majestic old plantation home stood before them, decked out for the party in all her glory. Not a blade of grass was out of place on the manicured lawn. Pink roses and white hydrangeas bloomed in the flower beds adorning the terrace. The shutters sported a fresh coat of black paint, and the original blown-glass windows gleamed against the late-afternoon sun.

Linen-draped tables surrounded the parquet dance floor under an enormous circus tent. With a generous variety of liquor and wine at hand, three bartenders stood ready to fulfill any request. Waiters, dressed in black and white, presented champagne in glass flutes to guests as they arrived. The scene was classic, a party that could have taken place during the sixties, the seventies, or even the roaring twenties. The funk band wore traditional attire—no-frills tuxedos for the men and a black sequined dress for the female lead singer.

The twins came out to the driveway offering hugs for their grandmother and aunts, high fives for Jamie, and whistles for Bitsy when she twirled her dress for their approval. With their good looks and easygoing personalities, Cooper and Sean were teenage heartthrobs in the making. For now, though, hunting and fishing and football occupied their attention.

With their auburn hair, freckled faces, and ocean-blue eyes, the two brothers reminded Sam so much of her father that she often choked up when she saw them. Much to Oscar's delight, Jackie had named the twins after his older brothers, Cooper and Sean Sweeney, who had been killed in the same boating accident when they were in their early twenties.

"Where's the birthday girl?" Lovie asked her grandsons.

"She hasn't come down yet." Older than his twin by ten minutes, Cooper was quicker to respond to a question—the first to do many things, actually. He thrived on being in control, while Sean seemed content to let his brother take the lead.

Sam leaned over and whispered in her mom's ear. "The princess would never miss an opportunity to make a grand entrance."

"Oh hush you, Sammie." Lovie swatted her daughter with her handbag.

Sam reached over and removed two plastic curlers dangling from Lovie's hair just above her collar. She'd never known her mother to let her hair grow so long.

Two Labrador retrievers, one yellow and one black, Max and Felix, bounded over for attention, tongues licking and tails wagging. Cooper turned to his brother. "Help me lock these beasts in their kennel before they slobber all over everyone's clothes."

The twins dragged the dogs off, and returned a minute later.

"We caught a mess of flounder for you today, Aunt Sam," Cooper said.

Sam winked. "Big ones, I hope?"

"Yep." Sean spread his arms wide. "Over the legal limit by a mile. They're cleaned and waiting in the downstairs refrigerator. We'll bring them to you tomorrow if you want."

"We should be ready for them by tomorrow afternoon. We'll take whatever you catch, " Sam said. "You can count on the going rate, same as always. I'll pay a premium if you can bring me a bushel of those jumbo Jimmys like you caught last summer."

Locking eyes, the twins said in unison, "Our secret hole."

"We can set our traps first thing in the morning," Cooper said. With any luck, we'll have a mess of crabs by late afternoon. We're saving our money to buy a car."

"We've got our eye on an old Land Cruiser like the one Pops used to drive," Sean added with a grin that revealed perfectly straight, post-braces teeth.

Cooper puffed up. "Early '90s model, fully restored. Old Oscar would be proud."

"That sounds cool," Jamie said. "I might even consider riding with y'all . . . but only if Cooper drives." Everyone laughed.

They heard the voices of other guests arriving down the driveway. Cooper held out his hand to Bitsy. "Carlotta is waiting for you in the kitchen with a big plate of chicken nuggets and a stack of Disney movies."

Bitsy looked at her mother uncertainly. "But I don't want to miss the cake."

"You won't," Cooper said. "Carlotta is in charge of the cake. You can help her light the candles."

Faith kissed her daughter's head. "You'd be bored down here with all the grown-ups, anyway."

Sean turned to Jamie. "What do you say we go inside and play a little Xbox? Cooper just bought the new edition of MLB."

"That's the only kind of baseball I can play anymore," Jamie mumbled.

Cooper and Bitsy entered the house through the side door of the garage while Sean wheeled Jamie to the terrace. Sam pretended not to notice when Sean stopped at the bar and discreetly removed two icy Bud Lights from the cooler. He dumped the cans into Jamie's lap, spun the wheelchair around, and disappeared through the french doors to the game room.

Sam didn't approve of underage drinking any more than she approved of the twenty-one-year-old drinking age. In her view, if our government trusted a young man to vote, be responsible for his own health care, and defend our country at war, why shouldn't we trust him enough to drink a beer? If all went as planned, Jamie would be off to college soon, where he'd undoubtedly be exposed to plenty of alcohol. Who better for him to experiment with than the cousins he loved and trusted?

Sam and Faith guided their mother toward the bar. While standing in line for a drink, Sam noticed her mother's blouse was inside out and drew Faith's attention to it.

Faith's eyes narrowed as she zeroed in on the tag. "That's nothing. You should've seen the first outfit she was wearing when I went to pick her up." She held her finger to her lips, and they stepped back so Lovie couldn't hear them. "I'm really worried about Mama. Her house is a disaster, with dirty plates in the sink and clothes thrown all over the place. She has three alarm clocks on her bedside table with little reminder notes stuck to them."

Sam sighed. "I guess Jackie was right. Something weird is going on with her. I've been too wrapped up in Jamie's recovery and the renovations at the market . . ."

"At least you have a legitimate excuse. I realize now that I've been neglecting her."

"Not on purpose," Sam said. "We are used to seeing her every day at work. Once the renovations started, we failed to reach out to her because it wasn't our habit."

"However lame that excuse is, it's the truth," Faith said.

Once the bartender served them their drinks—a glass of Pinot Grigio for the sisters and tonic water straight up with a lime for Mom—Sam and Faith took Lovie inside to straighten out her blouse.

When Faith went upstairs to check on Bitsy and Sam was waiting for Lovie to finish in the powder room, Bill appeared.

"Are you stalking me?" Sam asked.

He chuckled. "I guess I am, if you want to put it that way. I was hoping for the opportunity to tell you how sorry I am about today."

Sam nearly choked on her wine. "Cheaters are never sorry for their actions. They're only sorry they got caught."

"Ouch. That hurt. But I guess I deserve it. I promise I'll tell her tonight after the party."

Sam struggled to keep her voice down. "In case you haven't noticed, Jackie has worked damn hard on planning this party. Her memories from tonight should not include her husband asking her for a divorce."

He hesitated, then said, "I guess it won't hurt to wait until the morning."

Sam and Faith stationed themselves with their mother along the edge of the dance floor. When the boys made their obligatory appearance, undoubtedly prompted by Bill, Sam took the opportunity to dance with each of the twins while Jamie gobbled down a loaded plate of food, the most appetite she had seen from him in months. Afterward, the three boys greeted several adults before snatching another beer from the cooler and disappearing back inside their man cave.

The band had left the stage for their first break when Curtis stumbled into the party. Sam caught up with him at the food table. "Faith volunteered your services at the market tomorrow. I hope that works for you?"

He stuffed a whole ham biscuit into his mouth at once. "Volunteer, hell. I expect to get paid," he said with a mouthful of food.

"Maybe 'volunteer' was the wrong choice of words. Of course I'm going to pay you, Curtis. But only what you're worth."

He stopped chewing, and an expression Sam interpreted as guilty crossed his face.

"What's that supposed to mean?" he asked.

"It means you better take it easy on the booze tonight. There's a lot of work that needs to be done. I'm not going to pay you if you're hungover."

His body relaxed, visibly relieved. What was her brother-in-law up to?

"Don't worry, Sexy Sammie. You can always count on me. Call me anytime, day or night." He pinched her cheek, his fingers lingering long enough to make her uncomfortable.

She smacked his hand away. "Just don't be late." Sam turned her back on him, anxious to escape.

She headed across the dance floor toward Jackie, who was surrounded by a group of younger women Sam had never seen. She waited off to the side while the group chatted about summer vacation plans. When the band returned to the stage and launched into a repertoire of Motown from the early seventies, Sam grabbed the birthday girl by the hand and led her out to the middle of the dance floor, where they carried on like they were little girls again, bouncing on beds and singing into hairbrushes.

It was close to ten o'clock by the time Carlotta, Bitsy, and the boys wheeled a gigantic round cake onto the dance floor. After the crowd finished singing "Happy Birthday," it took Jackie several tries to blow out the blaze of candles.

Sam was helping cut the cake when Carlotta leaned over and whispered, "I have some bad news I need to tell Miss Jacqueline, but I'm not sure how to do it."

Sam set down the knife. "What sort of bad news, Carlotta?"

"I'm handing in my notice."

Dread settled over Sam like humidity on a sweltering summer day. "My sister will be lost without you. I'm sure if it's more money you need or less hours . . ."

Carlotta's dark eyes opened wide. "Oh no, Miss Sam. It's nothing like that. My sister has breast cancer, a bad case of it according to the doctors. I'm moving to Florida to help out with her children while she goes through her treatments."

"Oh, Carlotta, I'm so sorry to hear that. Is there anything I can do to help?"

"Pray?" she said.

"That goes without saying," Sam replied.

Sam would also be praying for Jackie tomorrow when both her husband and her right-hand woman dropped atomic bombs on her at once. Jackie would survive the divorce, but no way could she keep her life together without Carlotta.

Sam handed Carlotta a piece of cake. "You know my sister better than anyone. The most important thing in delivering bad news is picking the right time. Who knows, she might surprise you."

"I hope so. Miss Jacqueline always frets over the small stuff but never breaks a sweat over the things that really matter."

Sam tried to suppress her surprise. All these years, her sister had fooled Carlotta. Jackie never broke a sweat over the big things because she held her emotions in until she exploded.

Fifteen minutes later, Sam was dancing up front with the band when Faith approached, flustered and out of breath. "I can't find Mama anywhere."

"What do you mean you can't find her?"

"After she finished eating her cake, she went inside to use the powder room, but she never came back. I've searched the house. She's nowhere to be found."

Sam climbed onto a nearby chair and scanned the crowd. "I don't see her anywhere." She hopped down. "Round up the kids and get them to help you look out here, down the driveway and on the dock, while I go search the house again."

"Jackie's gonna freak out."

"That's why we're not going to tell her. Don't worry. I'm sure Mom just crawled into an empty bed and is taking a nap," Sam called over her shoulder as she headed inside.

Sam started on the ground floor and made her way up, looking under beds and in closets. No one had seen her. Not Carlotta, who was cleaning up the kitchen, or Bill, who was in his study talking softly into his cell phone. While checking the bedrooms on the third floor, she noticed light streaming from under the attic door. She opened the door and tiptoed to the top of the stairs. Someone, presumably Lovie, had ransacked Jackie's perfectly organized attic. Ripped-open cardboard boxes and brown packing paper littered the floor. An artificial tree lay toppled on its side, and one of the hurricane lanterns had fallen off a shelf, shattering into a million pieces on the floor. At the far end of the attic, Lovie was digging through an old steamer trunk, tossing out items left and right—a black feather boa, a pair of red satin heels, and a black beaded evening bag.

Faith arrived on the scene. "What's she doing?"

"I don't know," Sam whispered. "She looks like a starving homeless woman digging through a dumpster for a leftover doughnut."

Sam and Faith tiptoed across the wooden floor and eased up beside the trunk, careful not to startle their mother. "What are you doing up here, Mom?" Sam asked.

Lovie sat back on her knees. "What does it look like I'm doing? I'm trying to find something." She tossed a brimmed sun hat at Sam like a Frisbee, then returned her attention to the trunk.

Sam caught the hat and set it down on top of the battered dresser beside her. "We can see that, Mom. But what, exactly, are you looking for?"

Lovie's eyes darted around the room. "I'm not sure."

Sam took her mother's arm, gently helped her up, and guided her over to an old wing chair. "Do you know where you are, Mom?"

"Of course," Lovie said with a blank expression on her face. She reached into her pocket and removed an antique key attached to a silver chain.

"What does the key fit, Mama?" Faith asked.

"I don't know."

Over their mother's head, Sam and Faith exchanged a look of concern. "Just sit there and rest a minute," Faith said, rubbing her mother's back.

Lovie took several deep breaths, then tried to get up out of the chair.

Sam pushed her back down. "Not so fast. Where do you think you're going?"

"To find my pocketbook. I need my car keys."

Sam spotted Lovie's silver quilted bag on the floor next to the trunk. "Here's your bag, Mom. But your car is not here. Faith drove you to the party, and I'm taking you home."

Lovie knitted her brows in confusion. "What party?"

Sam cut her eyes at Faith. "Jackie's birthday party. But it's almost over now. Time to go home."

Sam and Faith each took one of their mother's arms, and escorted her down the stairs and outside. Lovie shuffled, as though her feet were encased in concrete blocks, all the way down the driveway. Curtis had parked his motorcycle behind their cars, blocking them in. They settled Lovie on the wooden bench under the magnolia tree beside the mailbox.

Sam was headed back to find Curtis when he stumbled up with the children on his heels.

Jamie wheeled up beside his mother. "Where'd you find her?" he asked, his cheeks rosy and his words slightly slurred. He'd obviously had more than a couple of beers.

"I'll explain later. Talk to her while we decide what to do." Sam pulled Faith and Curtis aside.

"What's wrong with your mama?" Curtis asked. "Has she finally gone and lost her mind?"

"Shut up, Curtis." Faith elbowed him in the ribs. "This is serious."

"Do you want me to go find the high and mighty Doctor Bill?" Curtis asked.

"No. There's no sense in ruining Jackie's party. I'll call Bill from the hospital." Sam turned to Faith. "I need to get Jamie settled in at home. Why don't I meet you and Mom at the emergency room?"

"What about Bitsy? I can't let her ride home on the back of the motorcycle with him." Faith aimed her thumb at her husband, whose head was bobbing back and forth as he tried to follow their conversation.

"You have a point." Sam grabbed Curtis by the elbow. "Come on. I'll take you and Bitsy out to your house, then drop Jamie at home."

"Hell, nah. I'm not leaving my bike here." He jerked his arm away and stumbled off toward his motorcycle.

Sam waited for Faith to go after him. When she didn't, Sam said, "You're not seriously going to let him drive in that condition, are you?"

Tears glistened in Faith's eyes. "I can't stop him."

"Don't worry." Sam pulled a wadded-up cocktail napkin out of her pocket and handed it to her sister. "I'll follow behind him to make sure he gets home."

Faith dabbed at her tears. "I don't want Bitsy to be afraid.

Will you please make sure she gets her pajamas on and brushes her teeth?"

"Of course." Placing her hand on Faith's back, Sam urged her sister toward her truck. "But you need to get Mom to the hospital. She's acting so strange. What if she's had a stroke? Every second counts. I'll get there as soon as I can."

SIX

FAITH

S am headed south on Creekside Drive while Faith drove north toward town. She tried not to think about her husband. She didn't care if Curtis bashed his own stupid brain in as long as he didn't hurt anyone else. She envisioned Bitsy kneeling on the pavement beside Curtis's mangled body, knowing Bitsy would never get over the trauma of seeing her daddy killed right before her eyes.

Next to her in the passenger seat, Lovie stared out of the truck window into the dark night. If only Faith knew what was going on inside her mother's scrambled mind.

"Did you get a piece of cake at the party, Mama?" Faith asked.

Lovie thought about it for a minute before answering, "I suppose so. It was chocolate, wasn't it?"

"No, carrot cake with cream cheese frosting. Jackie's favorite. She had it shipped down from Confections, her favorite bakery in Charleston."

"I remember now," Lovie said, but Faith was sure she didn't.

"Your grandchildren were all there. Can you name them?"

"What kind of silly question is that? Of course I can—Jamie,

Cooper, Sean, and Bitsy." She ticked them off on her fingers. "Where's your father? Did we leave him at the party?"

Faith's skin prickled with fear. How do I tell my mother her husband has been dead for more than five years?

Faith crossed her fingers. "We'll meet up with him later, Mama." *In heaven.*

Mother and daughter rode on for the next few miles in silence, Faith's concern growing with each mile. Her daddy's painful battle with pancreatic cancer had at least been short. She didn't know what she'd do if she lost her mother. Lovie was Faith's rock. All her life, her mother had cleaned up after Faith when she'd made mistakes and encouraged her to try things she wasn't brave enough to attempt on her own. Like going out for cheerleading her junior year in high school. Without an ounce of athleticism in her body, Faith hadn't made the squad, but knowing she'd tried something new, and survived, gave her the courage she needed to join the yearbook staff. As her problems with Curtis worsened, she needed Lovie, her rock, more than ever —not this emotionless zombie sitting next to her.

"Where are you going?" Lovie asked when Faith made a left-hand turn onto Main Street instead of going straight. "Aren't you taking me home?"

Surprised to hear the bossiness back in her voice, Faith glanced over at her mother. She saw that Lovie's eyes once again sparkled with life.

"Do you remember where we've been?" Faith asked.

"What do you mean, do I remember where we've been? We've been at Jackie's birthday party."

Just like that, as though a hypnotist had snapped his fingers and brought her mother out of her spell. Five minutes ago she didn't remember what kind of cake she'd eaten at the party. Five minutes ago she thought her father was still alive.

Faith ignored her mother's question and drove on. Sam would know what to do.

"Where are we going, Faith? I'm tired and ready for my bed."

Faith let out a sigh. "We're meeting Sam at the hospital."

"The hospital? Did someone get sick at the party?"

"Yes, Mama. You. You're the one who got sick at the party."

"That's ridiculous. I feel perfectly fine. Now take me home."

Faith pulled into the hospital parking lot and found a spot close to the emergency room entrance. She turned the key in the ignition. The engine sputtered a couple of times before dying. "If you can tell me what you were looking for in Jackie's attic, I'll take you home."

Her mother's face paled. "I don't remember being in Jackie's attic."

"Really, Mama? You tore her attic apart like you were Hurricane Lovie."

"Was I looking for something?"

"That's what we all wanna know. You told us you were looking for something, but you couldn't tell us what it was."

Lovie fingered the antique key she now wore on a chain around her neck.

"You probably had some kind of spell." Faith wiped away an orange lipstick smudge from the side of her mother's mouth. "I'm sure everything is fine, but we'd all feel better if the doctor checked you out."

Lovie gathered her belongings and reached for the door handle. "I suppose you're right."

After providing insurance information and a brief description of the evening's events to the woman at the admission's desk, a willowy young nurse named Bridget whisked Lovie back to an examining room. "We don't waste any time when someone presents with your symptoms."

Bridget handed Lovie a gown, and Faith helped her mother pull her blouse up over her head. "She seems perfectly fine now, but an hour ago my mama was a walking, talking zombie who barely even knew her own name. Do you think it's strange that she doesn't seem to remember anything that happened tonight?"

"I've seen stranger things in here." Bridget strapped a blood pressure cuff on Lovie's arm. "But we'll get to the bottom of it, whatever it is." Bridget repeated the blood pressure test three times with the same result—150 over 100.

"Isn't that really high?" Faith asked.

"I've seen higher," Bridget said. "A lot of times a patient's blood pressure will spike at the thought of being in the hospital. We call it the White Coat Syndrome."

Faith took a seat and watched Bridget perform an EKG on her mother's heart and insert an IV in her arm.

The doctor arrived a few minutes later. She guessed him to be about her age, with sandy-colored hair receding at his temples and thinning across the top. He carried a little extra weight around his middle and in his face, but Faith appreciated a guy who filled out his jeans. Unlike Curtis, who didn't have enough meat on his bones to hold up his pants.

After introducing himself as Dr. Mike Neilson, he turned his attention to the patient, using his stethoscope to listen to her heart and lungs. He asked Lovie simple questions, which she answered correctly. She named the president of the United States and stated the current month and year. But when he asked her about the events of the night, she barely remembered being at Jackie's party.

"To give you an idea of how confused my mom was earlier," Faith said, "in the car on the way over here, she asked me why we left my daddy at the party. He's been dead for five years."

"Mmm-hmm," he said, but he didn't appear too alarmed. He checked for other symptoms that might indicate a stroke—drooping face, difficulty speaking, weakness in the arm—none of which she presented.

He studied her EKG. "Your lungs are clear, and your heart appears healthy. But I am concerned about your blood pressure and the confusion. Oftentimes these brief losses of memory are unexplainable, but I wouldn't rule out the possibility of a TIA."

"A TI who?" Lovie asked.

"A TIA, which is an acronym for Transient Ischemic Attack, otherwise known as a ministroke."

Lovie's eyes filled with tears.

The doctor patted her arm. "Millions of people have TIAs every day, most of them undetected. The danger, however, is that a major stroke will follow. With your permission, I'd like to keep you overnight so that we can monitor your vitals and run some additional tests in the morning."

Lovie smiled. "Whatever you think is best, Doctor."

He patted her arm again. "I'll be back in a minute. I'm going to check on the availability of a room for you."

Faith followed him into the hall.

"Excuse me, Dr. Neilson. Can I talk to you for a minute in private?"

"Certainly." He took her by the elbow, pulling her aside as a team of EMTs rushed past with an elderly woman on a gurney. "I'm sorry. I didn't catch your name."

"I'm Faith."

"Faith." The single syllable rolled off his tongue in a lazy Southern drawl. "I find inspiration in names like Hope and Faith," he said, as he fixed his pale-blue eyes on her.

Faith's left thumb searched for her missing wedding band. Her engagement ring with the diamond chip and matching wedding band had provided groceries for a week with enough left over for Curtis to buy booze for a three-day bender.

"Mama's been acting kind of strange lately, and I'm worried it might be related to this spell she had tonight."

"Can you give me some examples of this out-of-character behavior?"

"Well . . . my mom is kind of a neat freak, and I haven't been to her townhouse in weeks, but earlier this evening, when I picked her up for the party, I found the place a shambles." Faith paused, taking in a deep breath. "And, not only that, she keeps asking the same questions over and over again. We tell her the answers, then three minutes later, she asks the question again."

"Many people her age experience short-term memory loss. The tests I've ordered might give us some indication of what's going on. Our neurologist, Dr. Baugh, is not on call tonight, but I'll pass your mother's case on to him first thing in the morning and have him stop in to see her on his early rounds."

When he saw her look of frustration, he added, "Doctors have a process to go through, Faith. We eliminate possibilities, then consider others. Sometimes it takes weeks, maybe even months. Other times we get it right the first go-around."

"I understand. Thank you for taking care of her."

"Don't you worry. Your mother is in good hands," Dr. Neilson said before heading to the nurses' station.

Sam appeared suddenly at her side. "How's Mom?"

"Better." Faith filled her sister in on the latest developments, about how their mother had snapped out of her spell and about everything the doctor had said.

"Why don't you go on home? I'll stay here with Mom. When I left your trailer, Curtis was passed out on the sofa."

"In that case, I should get home to Bitsy. But first, let me go in and say goodbye to Mama."

The sisters crowded around their mother's bed. "How're you feeling, Mom?" Sam asked.

"Like I'm ready to go home," Lovie said, her eyes bright with hope.

"You heard the doctor," Faith said. "You have to stay here overnight, so they can finish running their tests. I'm going home to check on Bitsy, but Sam's going to stay with you."

"You should both go home." Lovie smiled over at her nurse, who was typing something on a laptop computer. "Bridget will take care of me."

Bridget looked up from the laptop. "At least until they move you to your room. They'll assign you another nurse upstairs. She'll attend to you during the night."

Lovie appeared frightened, and Sam said, "I'm not going anywhere, Mom, until I know you're settled in your room."

Faith kissed her mother on the forehead and gave Sam a quick hug before wending through the maze of corridors to the lobby. According to the clock above the main entrance, she had five more minutes until she turned into a pumpkin.

Faith seldom went out at night, and hardly ever alone. Driving down her long dark driveway, she imagined shadows in the trees waiting to jump out at her. Curtis's bike wasn't in its usual place in front of the trailer, and for the second time that night, goose pimples broke out all over her body. Surely her husband wouldn't leave their daughter alone.

Faith unlocked the door and entered the dark trailer, tripping over the coffee table as she groped for the lamp.

She heard what sounded like muffled cries coming from her daughter's room. She found Bitsy trembling under the covers in her bed, her teeth chattering. Faith wrapped the child in her arms and held her tight. "Hush now, baby. Mama's here."

Bitsy sobbed even louder.

"Shh, now. Try to take a deep breath."

Whimpering, the tiny girl buried her face in her mother's chest. "I got up to go to the potty, and you weren't here."

"I know, baby." Faith stroked her daughter's hair. "Remember, I had to take your grandmama to the hospital."

Bitsy pushed away so she could see her mother's face. "Is Lovie going to be okay?"

Faith wiped a damp strand of hair out of the child's eyes. "She's better already, much more herself."

"Why'd you leave me alone?" Bitsy asked, her lip quivering.

Faith reached for the lamp on her bedside table. "Daddy's here with you, isn't he?" she asked, already knowing the answer.

Bitsy shook her head. "He was asleep on the sofa when I went to bed, but now he's gone."

Faith imagined Bitsy in the dark house, going from room to room and window to window looking for her mama and daddy. Anger boiled inside of her. What kind of man leaves his six-year-old daughter in the middle of the woods in a trailer alone?

Faith held her daughter close and rocked her back and forth. "I'm so sorry, sweetheart. I promise it will never happen again."

When Bitsy finally dropped off to sleep, Faith tucked her daughter in tight and turned out the light. Removing the shotgun from the closet in their bedroom, she loaded two shells in the barrel and settled on the sofa to wait for Curtis.

Her father had tried to teach his three daughters to hunt. Sam took to it right away, eventually becoming their daddy's favorite hunting partner. Although Jackie and Faith had never demonstrated much interest in killing birds, they'd learned to shoot a gun—a skill Faith never thought would pay off.

Nothing had turned out like Faith had hoped. She and Curtis once had dreams of buying a house on the creek. Faith wanted Bitsy to experience growing up on the water, to watch sunrises and sunsets, to learn to ski and sail and drive a boat. None of it was likely to happen with Curtis constantly out of work. She was stuck in a backwoods shack with a no-good husband. To make matters worse, she'd let Curtis force her into doing criminal acts that were morally wrong just so they could make ends meet. Even if no one ever found out, she'd never be able to forgive herself.

Curtis had never hit her, because she'd always avoided his temper. He lost his cool over the smallest things—when she was late fixing his dinner or she hadn't washed his favorite Harley T-shirt. She'd seen him provoke fights in bars with beastly men four times his size. But tonight she didn't care. Tonight she was angry enough to put a bullet in him.

Her husband came staggering in around three. Faith switched on the lamp beside the sofa, nearly blinding him with the bright light.

"Damn, woman." His hand clutched his chest and he stumbled backward. "You scared the hell out of me."

She aimed his shotgun at him. "If you ever leave my daughter at home alone again, I will shoot you dead."

His eyes were slow to focus on the gun. "You don't even know how to load that gun, you dumb bitch."

When he took a tentative step forward, Faith pumped the gun, loading the shells into firing position. "You forget who my daddy was."

He held his hands up. "Just calm down now, Faith. I would not have left Bits alone if I didn't think she was safe. Nothing's gonna happen to her way out here in the woods."

When he tried to grab the gun, Faith rammed it in his belly.

He jumped back, crying, "All right, already. Just put the gun down. I won't ever leave her alone again. I promise."

"Consider this a warning, Curtis. I will not give you a second chance."

SEVEN

JACQUELINE

At half past midnight, only two couples remained on the dance floor, swinging to what the band promised would be the last song. The caterers cleared tables and the bartenders packed up their glasses while Jackie reveled in the success of the evening.

Even though Julia had failed to show, the crowd of nearly a hundred, based on Jackie's estimate, seemed to enjoy themselves. The wannabes in attendance—the younger women on Jackie's new tennis team and their tanned, broad-shouldered, golf-club-swinging husbands—would make sure the word spread. Jacqueline Hart's fiftieth birthday party rocked.

The song ended, but when the lead singer saw Jackie standing on the edge of the dance floor, he launched into a slow, sexy version of "Happy Birthday."

"I thought the song you just played was the last song," Jackie shouted.

The music tapered off and the lead singer made a grand bowing gesture. "One more special song for you, pretty lady." He signaled to his musicians who began playing Jackie's favorite classic melody, "The Way You Look Tonight."

Bill appeared from nowhere on the dance floor. "May I have the last dance?" he asked, holding his hand out to her.

She took a tentative step, realizing it would not only be the last dance of the evening but their last dance as a couple. This was their song. They'd danced to it on their first date, and they'd danced to it at their wedding reception. They'd made a stunning couple back then, with their bodies molded together, perfectly in sync.

Resting her chin on his shoulder, Jackie thought back to all the dances they'd shared over the years—their friends' weddings, the endless benefits they'd attended, drunken New Year's Eve parties at Julia's. Now all those good times were coming to an end. Yet, as mad as she was at her husband for sleeping with another woman, Jackie knew she'd forgive him if he got on his hands and knees and begged. For the sake of their family, she would sacrifice her own feelings, demand he go to a marriage counselor, and find a way to move on with their lives. Not only to save face but to avoid having to face the future alone.

The song ended, and she blew the band a kiss.

"Let's walk out on the dock," Bill said. "I hate to waste a minute of this full moon."

She allowed him to take her by the hand and lead her down the gravel path. They walked to the end of the dock and leaned against the railing, staring up at the moon. If the sick feeling in her gut was any kind of premonition, the moment she'd been dreading for weeks had come.

"You outdid yourself tonight, Jack. Everyone seemed to have a good time."

"Everyone except my family. They left without saying goodbye."

"That's because of . . ."

She turned to face him. "Because of what?"

"Sam didn't want to spoil your party, but I think you have a right to know. Your sisters took your mother to the emergency room. The doctors have reason to believe she may have suffered a ministroke."

"Oh no." Jackie's hand went to her mouth. "I hope they are keeping her for observation." As a cardiologist's wife, Jackie understood the risk of a major stroke following a TIA.

"They are. And to run some tests in the morning."

"Why didn't you tell me sooner?"

Bill placed his hand on Jackie's. "Sam and I decided not to spoil your evening."

She snatched her hand away. His bedside manner no longer worked on her. "Why would Sam call you and not me? Lovie is my mother, not yours."

"For obvious reasons, honey. I'm a cardiologist. Sam asked me to speak to the doctor on call, to make certain they are doing everything they can for Lovie. Which they are."

"I should probably go to the hospital," she said, making no move to leave.

"There's no reason to go rushing over there tonight, Jack. Sam is with your mother. She will call us if she needs us."

He sat down on the wooden bench, pulling Jackie down beside him. "I need to talk to you about my trip to the mountains."

A chill that had nothing to do with the damp night air traveled Jackie's spine.

"What about it?" Their plan had been in place for weeks. Bill would drive up with the boys on Saturday, spend the night in Asheville, and return Sunday after he delivered them to camp.

"The boys and I have decided to head up first thing in the morning. I want to spend a couple of days with them, alone, before I drop them off at camp."

"But they haven't finished packing." She'd hardly seen Cooper and Sean since they'd gotten out of school. Selfishly, she was looking forward to spending the next two days with them before they headed off for three weeks.

"They're doing that now. Carlotta is helping them."

"But they had plans to go fishing with friends tomorrow."

"Trust me, they are excited about going up early. I've made arrangements with a fly-fishing guide for Friday."

"Well . . . I suppose, since you've got it all worked out . . ."

"I was going to wait until tomorrow to tell you"—Bill glanced at his watch—"but what the hell? Technically, it is tomorrow." He leaned forward, propping his elbows on his knees and burying his face in his hands. "I won't be coming home from the mountains, Jack. I mean, I'll be coming back to Prospect. I just won't be coming back here. To this house."

Jackie wrapped her shawl tighter around her shoulders, surprised at how calm she felt. She'd anticipated the moment for so long, she'd practiced over and over what she would say. "What you really mean is, you will be coming back to your new home, the one you've created with your blonde bimbo."

He lifted his head and stared at her, his mouth agape. "You mean, you knew?"

She sat up tall and smiled smugly. "Of course I know about your little mistress, you bastard. I saw the two of you cuddled up together in the back corner of the Inlet Coffee Shop. You really should be more discreet. I'd hate for your sons to see you parading your mistress around town."

He furrowed his brow.

"You haven't thought about that, have you?"

"Of course I have. That's why I decided to go up to the mountains early, so I can tell them at dinner Friday night."

"Liar. You are too much of a coward to tell the boys. You will save that unpleasant task for me."

"You think you know me so well, don't you?"

"Better than you know yourself."

"That's just it, Jackie. You don't really know me at all. You see the bad. It's almost like you expect it. But you never acknowledge the good."

A part of her knew he was right. When had she started jumping to the wrong conclusion without giving him the benefit of the doubt?

Around the time he started disappointing her on a regular basis with his broken promises.

"You are having an affair with another woman, Bill," she said softly. "Where's the good in that?"

"I've been a good provider and a good father, and you know it." He slumped back against the bench.

"Maybe in the past, but you blew it this time."

They sat in silence for a minute. "I suggest we see how the separation goes before we tell the boys," he said.

"This woman, your mistress, is a person, Bill, not a new suit. You can't just try her on for size, then come running back to me when she doesn't fit into your life."

"That's not at all what I'm suggesting."

"Then what are you suggesting?"

"I'm suggesting we wait until the boys get home. What's the point in ruining their time at camp? This is about so much more than my affair with Daisy."

"Daisy? You're having an affair with a woman named Daisy?"

"Her name is Daisy Calhoun. But that's really beside the point. As I was saying . . . our problems started long before my affair. I just need a little time to figure a few things out."

She sprang to her feet. "Here's a news flash for you, Bill. I have no intention of sitting around here, waiting for you while you're off playing doctor with your nurse."

"Can't you at least give me a little time, after all I've given you?" He stood up and faced the house, his arms spread wide. "I just want to feel like me again."

Placing both hands on his chest, Jackie pushed him back down to the bench and leaned over him, exposing a good portion of her creamy bosom. She grabbed his necktie and twisted it around her hand. "Listen, Bill, and listen good. You are a grown man, not a college kid asking his parents to send him to Europe for the summer to find himself. I will not grant you a trial separation. You made a vow. 'Till death do us part.' You broke that promise, and now you will pay. First thing tomorrow morning, after you leave for the mountains with the boys, I plan to call my attorney and file for divorce. Do you understand?"

He held both hands up. "I get it."

She loosened her grip, smoothed out the tie, and pinched his cheek. "Good."

He grabbed a handful of her hair and pulled her close to him, his lips on hers. "I miss that spunk. Why have you been hiding it from me for all these years?"

She wanted to smack the dimples right off his handsome face. What a fool she'd been, falling for the man because of his good looks. She slapped his hand away, then turned and sauntered up the dock. When she felt his eyes on her backside, she winked at him over her shoulder. "You're missing out on a whole lot more than spunk."

EIGHT

SAMANTHA

S am hadn't planned to spend the night at the hospital, but once they got her mother moved to a private room on the third floor and they were waiting for the nurse to bring her a sleeping pill, Sam had dozed off sitting straight up in the lounge chair in the corner. At some point during the night, someone had reclined her chair, stuffed a pillow under her head, and covered her with a blanket.

If rest was such a vital component for recovery, why didn't the doctors and nurses ever let the patient sleep?

According to the clock, it was only half past six, but the nurses at the nurses' station across the hall were laughing and chatting about the disastrous blind date one of them had been on the night before.

Lovie blinked open her eyes. "Morning, Mom. How do you feel?"

"Groggy." Her mother closed her eyes again. "I'm not used to taking sleeping pills."

"You had a big night. Just lie there awhile and rest," Sam said as she tucked the covers under Lovie's chin.

Sam splashed water on her face at the sink in the corner and

"Inside, unpacking boxes. You might want to make sure he's putting everything where you want it."

Sam stacked several boxes on a dolly and wheeled it over to the back entrance to the market. The painters had nearly finished in the showroom, and she was thrilled with the effect of the linen-colored walls. Soft and warm, clean and subtle. Not dramatic, just the right amount of contrast against the white trim. She imagined their new logo on the empty wall above the wine section—the seaweed-green interlocking *S*s.

The paint foreman waved to Sam. "What you think, Miss Sam? It's pretty, yes?" Lou bobbed his head enthusiastically. Although he'd come to the United States from Mexico ten years ago, his English was still broken.

She gave him a thumbs-up. "It's perfect, Lou."

He beamed. "You lucky. Looks like we'll only need one coat."

Sam caught a whiff of alcohol and realized the smell was coming from Curtis, who was unpacking boxes as fast as he could, slamming items around, and arranging them in a haphazard fashion on the metal shelves behind her.

"Hey, take it easy there, Curtis." She took a jar of tartar sauce out of his hand and placed it gently on the shelf. "You might chip the glass." She noticed his chest, bare and glistening with perspiration. Spotting his T-shirt draped on top of one of the boxes, she threw it to him. "The health department requires all workers be fully clothed when handling food."

He struggled into his T-shirt. "This ain't the kind of food they mean, but whatever."

Sam ran her finger along the edge of the metal shelf. "Did you think to wipe the shelves down before you loaded them up?"

His angry eyes bore a hole through her. "Faith didn't say nothing 'bout cleaning no shelves!"

"There's a layer of construction dust on everything." She held up her dirty finger as evidence. "The whole showroom needs to be cleaned."

Curtis swept his arm across the shelf, sending several packages of stone-ground grits into the box on the ground. He got in Sam's face. "What're you gonna do about that, Sexy Sammie?"

She smelled his sour breath. Whether he was hungover or not, she needed his help. "I'm going to let the cleaning service dust the shelves when they get here. In the meantime, there's plenty for you to do in the kitchen. Come on, I'll get you started."

Once the two of them were alone in the kitchen, Curtis turned on her. "I don't appreciate you dissing me in front of them Mexicans." He grabbed Sam's wrist and twisted it behind her.

"I wasn't dissing you, Curtis, and you know it." She took a deep breath and counted to ten, reminding herself to be patient. "Look, this is my fault. I should have given Faith some instructions. Let's just put our feelings aside and get back to work?"

"Feelings?" He released her arm and brushed a strand of hair off her forehead. "So you're finally ready to admit you have feelings for me?"

"Don't be ridiculous, Curtis."

When she turned her back on him and started to walk away, he forced himself on her, pinning her from behind against the stainless steel counter. "Admit it. You've always been jealous that I married your sister instead of you."

The bulge of his erection against her backside sent chills down her spine. She elbowed him in the gut and snatched a butcher knife from the wooden block on the counter. She turned on him, pointing the knife at his chin. "If you ever touch me again, I'll slice your nuts off and feed them to the crabs." She raised the knife so the tip was touching his skin. "And just so we're clear: the only thing I've ever felt for you was pity."

On a bitterly cold Christmas Eve in 1997, the Sweeney

family gathered around the mahogany table in their tiny dining room to celebrate the holiday and the recent engagement of their youngest member.

"I'd like to propose a toast to my baby girl." Oscar Sweeney raised his glass of champagne to his youngest daughter.

Lovie clinked her glass against Faith's. "May all your days be merry and bright."

Oscar turned to his soon-to-be son-in-law. "As for you, Curtis, if you hurt a hair on my daughter's head, you'll have to answer to me."

Everyone laughed. Everyone, that is, except Curtis. Oscar's size alone was enough to scare all the young men in town. His reputation as the sharpest shooter in the eastern part of the state only terrified them more.

"Yes, sir!" Curtis downed his champagne in one gulp. "As long as she promises to obey me." His comment fell short of funny.

Oscar's lips formed a tight smile. "Marriage is a two-way street, my young friend. It would benefit you to remember that."

"How'd he pop the question?" Sam asked Faith, hoping to break the tension at the table.

Faith stared dreamily at her small diamond engagement ring. "He took me out to dinner to our favorite restaurant."

"Dinner out at a special place is always a good choice," Bill said.

"Even if that special place is the Pelican's Roost," Jackie added, her lip curled up in disgust.

Bill reached for his wife's glass. "I think you've had enough of that. Alcohol isn't good for the babies."

Jackie grabbed the glass back. "A little bit isn't going to hurt them. It might even calm them down enough for me to get some sleep."

"Hang in there." Bill rubbed her swollen tummy. "Not too much longer."

Jackie brushed his hand away. "Easy for you to say. I have to listen to you snoring peacefully night after night while I flop around like a beached whale hoping for just a few minutes of sleep."

"Have you set a date yet, Faith?" Sam asked. She refused to let Jackie bitch about her pregnancy and spoil the moment for their younger sister.

"Give a guy a break, Sammie." Curtis filled his glass to the rim with champagne. "We only got engaged last night. I need to let the idea of marriage sink in."

"What's the point in waiting?" Jackie asked. "You've been dating since high school and living together for more than two years."

"Give them some time. Curtis and Faith will make their plans when they're ready," Oscar said.

"Just think, Daddy,"—Jackie ignored her father's warning glare—"now that Faith is taken care of—if you call living in a seedy apartment above a filthy garage where her husband works being taken care of—you can focus your attention on finding a home for Sam and Jamie. Then you and Mom can finally enjoy your empty nest."

"That's it." Bill pushed back from the table. "You've had enough."

Bill helped Jackie out of her chair and into her coat. Happy to be going home, she didn't protest. After a round of hugs and kisses and best wishes for a Merry Christmas, the soon-to-be parents left the others to clean up from dinner.

When all the dishes were put away, they settled in the family room with big slices of red velvet cake and steaming cups of decaf coffee.

Snuggled together in the La-Z-Boy, Faith lay her head on her fiancé's shoulder. "The sooner we get married, the sooner we can have a baby." She looked longingly at Jamie, who was sound asleep, nestled between his grandparents on the sofa.

glared over her tortoiseshell readers. "Commercial decorating isn't really our style, dear. Taking on this project will make the company appear desperate."

In all the years Jackie had worked for her, Mimi had never tried to hide her distaste for their family business. Commoners were beneath her social status, and retail merchants who peddled a product as smelly as seafood sat on the bottom rung.

"We are talking easy money, Mimi," Jackie had argued. "Sam already knows what she wants. All we have to do is execute her plan."

Mimi had reluctantly agreed to let Jackie continue with the Sweeney's venture, but she'd never inquired about their progress or asked to see the designs, and she'd excluded Jackie from staff meetings and planning sessions on all their other projects.

She could take a hint. Time for her to find a new job.

Bill's words echoed in her mind. Take a chance on something new, maybe a new career, or even the same career but with a boss who appreciates you.

Jackie had landed some big accounts for Motte Interiors over the years, clients who were still loyal to her for all their decorating needs.

"I'll take my clients and start my own firm. What do you think about that?" she called out to the blue heron ambling near the edge of the water.

The heron craned its long neck to get a good look at her before flying off.

Jackie's body slumped. Maybe she should take up golf.

She slammed her coffee mug down on the railing, suddenly struck with a brilliant idea. She would focus her attention on the boys, make up for all the extracurricular activities and sporting events she missed out on while she was working. Might as well make the most of these last two years before the twins left for college. If she hired a housekeeping service to do the basic cleaning, she could take over the shopping and cooking herself. After all, she had a folder full of recipes she'd been dying to try. She imagined a pot of chili, a fire crackling in the fireplace, yellow ginkgo leaves blowing across the front walk where a row of carved jack-o-lanterns waited to welcome the boys home from football practice.

Who was she kidding? The boys wouldn't notice if she painted the walls of the living room black. And they hated it when she tried out new recipes. They shoveled food in their mouths so fast they hardly tasted it.

She would simply have to find a better use of her time.

Jackie glanced down at her new floral sundress. She'd taken extra care with her appearance that morning in the hopes that Julia would invite her to lunch to celebrate her birthday and apologize for not showing up for her party on Wednesday night. But it was already close to noon, and her cell phone remained silent.

She contemplated changing into her bathing suit, grabbing the new Dot Frank novel she'd picked up from the bookstore, and going down to the dock for an afternoon of sunning. Then she remembered the hours she spent at the dermatologist's office, reversing the damage she'd done to her skin in her youth.

She should support her family and attend the market's reopening. She needed to check on her mother, anyway, to find out how she'd been feeling since she got out of the hospital two days ago. But she lacked the energy to spar with Sam or answer Lovie's relentless questions.

No children, no husband, no housekeeper, no best friend. Alone. All dressed up with no place to go. She could either pour herself another cup of coffee and sit around feeling sorry for herself, or do what she always did when she felt depressed—go to Charleston for some much-needed retail therapy.

With the top rolled back on Bill's midlife-crisis mobile and Whitney Houston blaring from the radio, Jackie passed the long line of Saturday beachcombers entering the city limits as she headed in the opposite direction. Just thinking about maxing out Bill's credit cards improved her mood. She would start at one end of King Street and work her way to the other, searching the galleries for any ultra-modern work of art and trendy knickknack she could find.

Bill always preached, "Don't buy on a whim. Buy things of value that will last, things that will never go out of style."

His knowledge of antiques was impressive. Unfortunately, he lacked the taste to compliment his collection. With her husband out of the picture, she could hire herself to redecorate Moss Creek Farm. And, since Bill would be paying the bills, she could use her exorbitant consulting fees to buy everything she'd ever wanted.

By the time she'd driven forty miles to Charleston and fought the traffic leading into downtown, her caffeine buzz had transitioned into a headache, dampening her spirits. She merged onto East Bay Street and headed south toward the Battery. Parking on Murray Boulevard, she got out of the car and strolled up and down the promenade, refreshed by the cool salt air on her face. She wove in and out of the residential streets, admiring the restored antebellum homes, peeking through iron gates at hidden gardens, admiring the massive planters overflowing with summer annuals. Exhausted and sweaty, her Tory Burch sandals rubbing a blister between her toes, she found a park bench under a shady oak in Battery Park to rest. Starving, she searched her bag and found a crumbled, partially melted protein bar, which she choked down with half a bottle of warm water.

Stretching her legs out in front of her, Jackie watched a family with identical twin sons and a daughter who climbed on the Civil War cannons. She estimated the boys to be a couple of years older than their sister. When the little girl slid off the cannon and landed on her bottom, the boys rushed to help her to her feet and brush the dirt from her shorts. Jackie imagined the dynamics of her own family if she'd had a third child, a baby girl. She would have called her daughter Annabella, so soft and feminine, the syllables rolling off her tongue. Would Annabella have been a priss pot like Jackie or a tomboy like Sam? Would Annabella's presence have annoyed Cooper and Sean, or would they have been protective of her like the children playing on the cannons?

If only she hadn't gone back to work so soon after the twins were born. If only her marriage had been happier. When had her life become one great big *if only*? Sadly, the time had long since come and gone for her to do anything about any of it.

The melody from *Swan Lake* drifted across the street and caught Jackie's attention. A little girl about eight years old glided across the side porch of her stately home on the toes of her ballet slippers. Tall and lean in a pale-pink leotard and matching tights, with her blonde hair pulled tight in a high bun, the child reminded Jackie of herself at that age. Out of nowhere, two boys appeared in the garden below and began shooting at the little girl with their water guns. The girl stuck her tongue out at the boys and spread her arms wide, welcoming their assault. She curtsied, and they squirted her some more, but when one of them threw a pebble at her, she stomped her foot. "Moommm, Christopher's throwing rocks at me."

An adult version of the little girl appeared—simple and elegant in green Capri pants and a white cotton tee. Held in place with a barrette at the base of her neck, her hair was the same white blonde as her daughter's.

"Leave Lilly alone and let her practice. Y'all have been here long enough. Why don't you go on down to Scooter's for a while? If you ask nicely, I bet his mom will make you a grilled cheese."

The boys dropped their guns and took off running down the sidewalk.

The mother went back inside, leaving her daughter to continue with her practice. Lilly glided and leaped, pirouetted and pliéed, unaware of the stranger watching her from across the street.

Jackie hadn't danced like that since her single days, when she rented a carriage house several blocks from where she now sat. She had treasured her time in the little cottage, the only space that had ever belonged solely to her. She converted the guest bedroom into a dance studio and used her free afternoons to choreograph long, intricate pieces of modern ballet.

Jackie had lost all sense of self when she moved out of that carriage house. When she gave everything up for love.

She'd never forget the day she'd made her choice. Late on a stormy Sunday afternoon during the summer of 1993, she and Bill were sprawled out on her queen-size brass bed, spent from hours of making love.

"What's this?" she asked when he placed a black velvet ring box on her naked chest.

He grinned like a naughty little boy. "What do you think it is?"

She picked up the box, turning it one way, then another, imagining the size and cut without opening the lid. "But why now, when I'm getting ready to move to New York?"

"Isn't it obvious? I don't want you to go."

The window unit clicked on, blowing cold air across their naked bodies. She pulled the covers up to her chin and set the black box down on top of her chest. "Why don't you come to New York with me? There are plenty of hospitals. You could have your choice."

"I've spent most of my life trying to get away from big cities, Jackie. You know that. First Boston, now Charleston."

She rolled her eyes. "I wouldn't exactly call Charleston a big city."

"I'm a big-fish-in-a-small-pond kind of guy. I've accepted an offer with an established practice in Prospect."

"Prospect?" She turned over in bed to face him. "You mean, my Prospect, my hometown?"

"I'm not aware of any other Prospects. At least not around here."

"But what about MUSC?"

He shook his head. "They're fully staffed at the moment. With no openings in sight. Or so they say." He wrapped a stray strand of her hair around his index finger. "Seriously, Jack. All my life I've struggled to keep up. First at prep school, then Harvard, then UVA medical school. I don't want to be that guy anymore. I can make something of myself in Prospect. I can be a successful doctor but still have a life outside of my practice, playing golf and hunting and fishing, doing all the things I enjoy."

He picked up the black velvet box. "Marry me, and I'll give you everything you've ever wanted." He flipped open the box and showed her the brilliant-cut solitaire diamond.

The light from the bedside table lamp hit the prisms, casting rays of color around the room. Her breath caught and her eyes brimmed with tears. "It's the most beautiful ring I've ever seen."

"And I'll buy you a great big house on the water to go with it. We'll wake up every morning with our two children and our golden retriever and stare out across the creek. We'll swing open the french doors and breathe in the healthy salt air."

"I want more than two children. And Labs make better hunting dogs."

"We can have all the children you want, but we'll have to discuss the breed. Retrievers are equally as good hunters."

"But this is my big chance. How can I possibly say no to one of the top design firms in New York?"

"At least try it on." He removed the ring from the box, and she held out her hand while he slid it on her finger. "Do you like it? The stone was my grandmother's. I had it reset."

She nodded, not trusting herself to speak. The ring was a perfect fit, a two-carat symbol of his everlasting love for her.

In that moment, Jackie had forgotten about everything else. Her career. New York. She'd given everything up. For him.

She leaned her head back against the park bench and closed her eyes, savoring the warmth of the sun streaming through the trees onto her face. She imagined Lilly's father, tall and handsome with blond curls cropped close to his head, arriving home from work with a bottle of wine in one hand and a bouquet of pink lilies in the other, kissing his wife on the lips and his daughter on her forehead before going outside to throw the baseball with his son.

For Lilly's family's sake, Jackie hoped her father never lost that look of adoration for her mother.

Jackie tugged off her engagement ring and wedding band and dropped them in her bag. "Never trust a man, Lilly," she said out loud to the little girl across the street who couldn't hear her.

TEN

SAMANTHA

Throngs of beachgoers arrived at Sweeney's first thing on Saturday morning. They came in their Suburbans, packed to the roof with floats and grills and beach chairs. A few of them complimented the remodeling. Most of them seemed impressed with the selection of prepared foods. All of them were relieved to see the high quality of fresh seafood had returned.

With the exception of Curtis, whose services were no longer needed, and Jamie, who couldn't be cajoled away from the television, all hands were on deck. Lovie seemed her old self in every way. She worked the fish counter all morning, welcoming their patrons and offering to share her latest recipe—lemongrass and ginger grilled shrimp.

Sam couldn't have kept her mom away from Sweeney's even if she wanted to. Lovie was still the sole proprietor, even though she took only enough money out of the business to support her modest living. Faith and Sam were her employees, salaried workers with pay grades based on their responsibilities. Sam managed the personnel and the purchasing while Faith looked after the books. Sam worked the storefront more than Faith, giving her the flexibility to attend to Bitsy's needs.

"We've run out of the little crab cakes, Sam. Do you want me to get some off the shelf?" Faith gestured toward the plastic containers stacked high in their refrigerated section.

"Why don't we try something different? Maybe a dollop of tuna salad on a cracker?"

"Good thing we're closed on Sundays," Faith whispered.

Sam nodded. "It'll give Roberto a chance to catch up before Monday."

"I appreciate the business from the beachgoers, but I haven't seen one local person all day."

The moment the words slid off Faith's tongue, the front door swung open and Prospect's Prima Donnas—Donna Bennett and Donna Berry—sashayed in, followed by Julia Motte. As they entered, Bitsy offered to pour them a cup of lemonade. With barely a glance in the child's direction, Donna Bennett dismissed the offer with a rude flick of her hand.

How could Jackie consider these tacky women her friends?

As much as Sam wanted to backhand the smug look off Donna Bennett's face, she knew it would mean suicide, the death of Sweeney's. Donna Bennett's family ran the only local paper— the *Prospect Weekly*—which offered fishing reports and news from the high-school sports teams, the general goings-on of Prospect's citizens. The townsfolk used to wait in anticipation for the Monday paper to arrive in their mailbox, but since Donna's father passed away three years ago, the quality of newsworthy items had diminished.

"Those weren't the locals I had in mind," Faith said under her breath.

"Be nice. Remember we need their support if we want to survive the winter." Sam pointed at their mom, who was leering at the Prima Donnas from behind the fish counter. "That goes for you, too."

"I don't know what Jackie sees in them." Faith grabbed a pint of tuna salad from the cold case and scurried off to prepare her samples.

"Afternoon, ladies." Sam greeted the man-eating lionesses with a forced smile. "Nice of you to stop by."

Donna Bennett glanced around the empty showroom. "From the looks of things, I'd say you are desperate for our business."

"Actually, this is the first lull we've had all day," Sam said. "The beachgoers have been lined up waiting to get in the front door for most of the morning."

"We're not planning to buy anything, of course." Donna Berry's wicked grin revealed a smudge of red lipstick on her front tooth. "We just stopped in to have a look around."

"Help yourselves. We've run out of our bite-size crab cakes, but Faith should be out with tuna samples soon."

Placing a hand across her chest, Donna Bennett sucked in her breath. "We're hardly the sampling kind of gals."

"But thanks anyway." Julia smiled at Sam, her apology for her ill-mannered friends.

The three women wandered around the store, careful not to touch anything as if fearful of contamination.

Donna Bennett pointed at a container of shrimp scampi. "That just looks gross."

"Looks like the key lime pie they sell in the freezer section at Harris Teeter," Donna Berry said about their display of pies.

When the Donnas burst into laughter, Julia's face turned pink. "The place looks nice, Samantha. I understand from Jacqueline that the design was mostly yours."

Donna Bennett elbowed Julia in the ribs. "You didn't tell me that. What do you call this design, warehouse chic?"

Donna Berry whispered to Julia, loud enough for Sam to overhear, "I can't believe your mother put her pristine reputation on the line for this project."

"What choice did she have?" Donna Bennett whispered in

the same loud tone. "She could hardly say no to Jacqueline considering Samantha is her sister."

Julia turned her back on her friends, but she did not come to Jackie's defense.

"Speak of the devil, where is Jacqueline?" Donna Bennett wandered to the back of the market and stuck her head in the kitchen pass-through. "Is she hiding out back here, too embarrassed to face the public?"

Sam glanced over at her mother. Lovie's face was flushed red with anger, irritated as much by her daughter's rude friends as she was disappointed that Jackie had been a no-show for the ribbon-cutting ceremony. Sam understood her sister's need to lick her wounds in private, like an injured animal, but answering their mother's endless questions about Jackie's whereabouts was growing tiresome.

Donna Berry pointed at the ceiling. "Oh look, Samantha. They forgot to finish your ceiling."

Sam's temper boiled. She gave her mother the nod. Sound the bells. Let the fight begin. To hell with Donna Bennett's tacky tabloid. If she wanted to give Sweeney's a bad review, then bring it on.

Lovie came out from behind the fish counter, and Bitsy scampered across the showroom and darted behind the produce cart.

"Girls. I'm so pleased you approve of our new look." Lovie's voice was full of sarcasm. She turned her attention to Donna Bennett. "Warehouse chic, I believe you called it?"

An angry scowl settled on Donna Bennett's face.

"Chic, as in elegant and stylish," Lovie said. "And to think Sam and Jackie managed it all on their own, without any help from Mimi."

All eyes turned to Julia. "Oh no. It wasn't like that at all," Julia said, appearing flustered. "Mimi would've helped them if they'd needed it. They seemed to know what they were doing."

Donna Bennett started in again. "Mrs. Sweeney, you must be

so proud of Sam for moving on with her life so soon after the accident. Poor Caroline is having the hardest time getting over Corey's death."

"I don't imagine you ever get over losing a child," Sam said.

"No, I don't suppose you do." Donna Bennett shook her head in feigned sorrow. "Lucky for you, your son was spared."

"You're right, Donna. I thank God every day my son is alive. But I wouldn't go so far as to say he was spared. He's in a wheelchair, but I'm pretty sure you already know that."

Donna Bennett nodded. "I can't imagine how he lives with the guilt of knowing he caused the accident that killed—"

Lovie wagged her finger in Donna's face. "Now you listen here. My grandson is mourning the loss of his best friend. Even if Jamie is able to walk again one day, his life will never be the same."

Faith arrived on the scene, holding a tray of tuna salad samples out to their guests. She sniffed. "Something smells fishy, Sammie. The tuna is fresh, so it must be the company."

"Well, I never," said Donna Bennett, placing her hand over her chest.

A crowd of beachgoers entered noisily through the front door, bringing with them a wave of hot air. "Please excuse us while we help the customers who can afford to pay," Sam said and turned her back on the Prima Donnas.

"You are finished in this town, Samantha Sweeney." Donna Bennett spun around and stalked off in a huff with Donna Berry and Julia on her heels.

As Faith approached the new customers with her tray of samples, Bitsy crawled out from her hiding place under the produce cart. She sprinted over to Sam, who lifted the little girl into her arms and hugged her tight. "Did those mean old ladies scare you?" Sam whispered.

"Yes," Bitsy said, burrowing her face in Sam's neck. She could feel her niece's heart pounding against her chest.

Faith returned with an empty tray. "Don't you pay any attention to them," she whispered to her daughter. "They're nothing but a bunch of old windbags."

Bitsy giggled, her breath tickling Sam's neck.

"You forget that one of those windbags rules this town with her newspaper," Sam said. "We'll be lucky to get any local business after that cat fight."

Lovie snorted. "Let her print whatever she wants. No one takes that girl seriously since her father died."

"I'll remind you of that when she destroys us in Monday's paper," Sam said.

ELEVEN

SAMANTHA

When Jackie called early Monday morning and insisted the three sisters meet at noon for lunch at the Pelican's Roost, Sam assumed she wanted to break the news about her divorce. No one had heard from Jackie since her birthday party— no calls or texts to congratulate them on a successful grand reopening, or to check on their mother's health. While she knew her sister needed time to adjust to the changes in her life, Sam was tired of covering for her.

"Shall I bring Mom?" Sam asked.

"No! Let's just keep this between us." Her response was quick and curt. Too quick and curt.

The Pelican's Roost sat atop the Inlet View Marina store, offering panoramic views in all directions. Sam and Faith requested a table overlooking the parking lot, so they could keep an eye on the market across the street. Irritated at her sister for keeping them waiting, Sam was ready to walk out of the restaurant when Jackie arrived.

"You are twenty minutes late, Jackie. We don't have all day. We have a business to run, remember?"

"I'm sorry. I got tied up on the phone," Jackie said as she sat next to Faith.

Sam leered at her. "That excuse became obsolete when they invented cell phones."

"We should probably go ahead and order." Faith signaled the old gray-haired waitress who'd worked at the Pelican's Roost for years.

Sam and Faith ordered grilled chicken sandwiches and sweet potato fries, while Jackie asked for a small mixed green salad with vinaigrette dressing on the side. Then she turned to her sisters.

"We need to talk about finding a retirement home for Mom."

Sam nearly choked on her diet Coke, sending carbonation bubbles up her nose. "Mom doesn't need a nursing home, Jackie," she said, wiping her nose with a napkin. "The doctor granted her a clean bill of health. If you'd taken the time to call her, you'd know that already."

"I'm not talking about a nursing home, Sam. I'm talking about a retirement home."

"What's the difference?" Faith asked.

"There's a big difference. A retirement home is for people like Mom who are capable of taking care of themselves. They live independently, in an on-site cottage or condo, with twenty-four-hour access to medical help when they need it. A nursing home provides round-the-clock care. The retirement home offers those services as well, of course, but not until their residents need them."

"Thanks for making the distinction," Sam said. "But Mom doesn't need either."

Jackie let out an exasperated sigh. "If you'll just hear me out for a minute. The nicer places have long waiting lists. We need to start the process now so we will have a spot when she's ready."

"And who is going to pay for this nice retirement home?" Sam asked.

"Bill will, of course," she said.

Sam's jaw dropped. Did Jackie seriously expect Bill to dish out hundreds of thousands of dollars to pay for his ex-mother-in-law's retirement home? She studied Jackie's face for signs of distress, swollen eyes or dark circles, but her older sister appeared as stunningly beautiful and put together as ever. Which could only mean one thing—Jackie was in denial. She would not confess her grievances until she was ready, whether in a day or a month. To confront her would only send her deeper underground.

"I don't think Mama will go for that," Faith said in the soft voice she used when tiptoeing around Jackie's temper. "You know how stubborn she is about paying her own way."

"That's why we're not going to give her a choice in the matter," Jackie said.

An image of Jackie dragging their mother by the hair, kicking and screaming, into a retirement home flashed through Sam's mind. "Good luck with that."

"It's all in the way you handle her, Samantha. Haven't you figured that out by now?"

"Okay." Sam placed her hands on the table, palms down, fingers splayed. "Let's assume for a minute that you coerce Mom into going into a retirement home. Where exactly are you planning to find a place like that? All the nursing homes around here are dumps."

"There are several to choose from in Charleston," Jackie said.

"Charleston? Mama doesn't even know anyone in Charleston. She won't be happy that far away from home," Faith said.

"It's a forty-five-minute drive, Faith. I wouldn't exactly call that a long way from home."

Sam patted Faith's hand. "Don't worry. Jackie is getting way ahead of herself. The test results—"

Jackie struck the table with her fist, causing her sisters to flinch. "The test results are inconclusive. I don't need a doctor to tell me something's wrong with Mom. She hasn't been herself in weeks."

Sam took a deep breath and silently counted to ten. *Consider her feelings*, she reminded herself. *She's volatile right now.*

"Listen, Jackie," Sam said in a calm voice. "Mom has been staying with me since she got out of the hospital. She seems totally fine. In fact, she's manning the market as we speak."

"You left her over there alone?" Jackie pushed her chair away from the table, preparing to get up. "She might slip and fall carrying one of those heavy trays you let her carry."

Sam grabbed Jackie's wrist and pulled her back down to her chair. "First of all, we purchased carts to replace those trays. Secondly, she's not alone. Roberto is with her. Thirdly, we're right across the street if something happens. Lastly, and sadly, business has been slow all morning." Sam pointed out the window. "I'm keeping an eye on things. If a mob of customers suddenly appears, I'll run across the street and help her."

Jackie jerked her hand away. "If that's supposed to make me feel better, it doesn't. She could just as easily trip over a cart. Women her age don't always recover from broken hips. And I'm still not convinced she's in her right mind."

"Well I am," Sam said. "If you're so convinced otherwise, feel free to take her to MUSC for a full psychological exam."

"Can I say something, please?" Faith raised her hand like an elementary-school student vying for her teacher's attention. "I've given this a lot of thought, and I'm pretty sure I know what Mama's problem is."

"By all means." Sam held her hands wide open.

"Well . . ." Faith took a deep breath. "Mama doesn't play bridge or belong to any prayer groups at church. She doesn't knit or do any type of needlework. Her life has always revolved around the seafood market."

"She likes to cook," Sam reminded her.

"True, but she can't cook all the time, especially when she's only cooking for one," Jackie said.

"Let me finish, please." Her sisters quieted down, and Faith continued, "When we closed for remodeling, Mama didn't know what to do with all that free time, with no workplace to go to during the day. My guess is, she went a little nutty trying to keep herself busy."

Jackie gave a reluctant nod. "You may be on to something, Faith."

"Now that the market has reopened, things should get back to normal for her," Faith said.

"Still, it wouldn't hurt to keep a close eye on her," Jackie said.

"I agree," Sam said. "We can take turns checking in with her on her days off and at night."

"But we have to promise to tell each other if anything strange happens," Faith added.

"Sounds like we have a plan," Sam said. "Do we all agree?"

Faith said, "Yes," and Jackie mumbled, "I guess. But I still think we need to make arrangements for her retirement."

Excusing herself, Sam got up from the table and made her way to the ladies' room. She ran her finger over the seagull carved into the restroom door. *Gulls* for women, *Buoys* for men. She remembered her father's thick Irish brogue when he called the daughters his three gulls. The sisters all knew they controlled his heart. They also knew how much he loved seagulls, his constant companions during the day. They greeted him at the crack of dawn on the dock, flew beside him on his way out of the inlet, then guided him to the fish in the Gulf Stream.

Sam would trade anything to hear her father call her his gull one more time.

Her sandwich was waiting when Sam returned from the restroom. While they ate, Jackie filled Faith and Sam in on Carlotta's sad and sudden departure from her life.

"Are you looking for someone to take her place?" Faith asked.

"Not right away. At least not a full-time housekeeper like Carlotta. I called Happy Maids this morning. They're going to take care of my basic cleaning for now."

"We missed you at the reopening," Sam said, disappointed that Jackie hadn't bothered to ask how their customers perceived the renovations.

Jackie reached in her oversize black bag and pulled out the *Point Pleasant Weekly*, unfolding it and holding it open to reveal the headlines: SWEENEY'S NEW SEAFOOD MARKET. TOO UPTOWN FOR SMALL TOWN.

Jackie handed Sam the paper. With Faith peering over her shoulder, they read the scorching review. Donna Bennett reiterated everything she'd said on Saturday, including her comment about the unfinished ceiling. "The Prima Donnas at their finest," Sam said when she was finished reading.

"Sounds like I missed the big showdown. What happened?" Jackie asked.

Sam filled Jackie in on the details of their confrontation.

"It takes guts to accuse the Donnas of smelling like fish," Jackie said to her youngest sister.

Faith beamed red. "I'm sorry, Jackie. I know they're your friends."

Sam gave the paper back to Jackie. "Where'd you get this, anyway? I certainly hope you didn't pay for it."

"Believe it or not, someone left it on my door stoop this morning."

Sam rolled her eyes. "I can only imagine who that someone was."

Jackie crumbled up the newspaper and stuffed it in her bag. "For the record, Sammie, I think you have given the market a fresh face with a vibrant young vibe. I have no doubt Sweeney's will be a success, especially with the out-of-towners. People around here don't respond well to change. Just give them a little time."

While encouraged by her sister's rare vote of confidence, Sam remained skeptical. "I hope you're right, because we can't survive without the locals."

Jackie sat back in her chair. "In any case, I wanted the two of you to be the first to know, in case you hear it on the street . . ."

Sam held her breath, waiting for the news of Jackie's divorce to follow.

"I mailed in my resignation to Mimi this morning. I no longer work for Motte Interiors."

TWELVE

FAITH

All the talk about putting their mama in a retirement home had given Faith a headache, the kind where the pressure built behind her left eye socket until she vomited from the pain. The only relief was a cold washcloth in a darkened room.

As they were crossing the street on the way back to the market, Faith said, "I'm pretty much caught up in the office. If you don't mind, I'm gonna call it a day. I'm coming down with one of my headaches."

"Having lunch with Jackie is enough to give anyone a headache." Sam held the door open for her, and they entered the empty showroom. "From the looks of things, we won't need you on the floor this afternoon, anyway."

They had no idea what to expect from their first weekday of business in their newly refurbished home. Mondays had always been a slow day for them. For a brief time, about four or five years ago, they closed the market on Saturday night and didn't reopen until Tuesday morning.

"How was lunch?" Lovie asked. "It does my heart good to see you girls getting along so well."

"We didn't kill each other, if that's what you want to know. I take it business was slow while we were gone?" Sam said.

"Not a single soul has crossed the threshold."

"We need to advertise to the local working crowd, to get the word out about our lunch specials," Sam said.

"Why don't I make up some fliers?" Faith volunteered, wincing from the pain in her skull.

Lovie looked closely at her youngest daughter. "Headache?"

"A bad one," Faith said.

Her mother withdrew a large bottle of Advil from beneath the checkout counter. She shook out three capsules and handed them to Faith, who popped the pills into her mouth and swallowed them without water.

"Why don't you go on home?" Sam draped her arm around her shoulders and escorted her to the kitchen. "Do you need me to drive you?"

"No, I'll be fine," Faith said as she headed toward the back door.

Faith had organized activities for Bitsy for most of the summer—Bible school and backyard camps run by teenagers. She'd even sprung for a week of adventure camp, sponsored by the local forestry service. But she hadn't found any affordable programs for the first two weeks of the summer break. Since Curtis was currently unemployed, Faith considered it his responsibility to take care of their child while she worked. But when she drove up in front of the trailer and noticed his bike missing, the throbbing in her head worsened. Surely he wouldn't be stupid enough to leave Bitsy alone again after she'd threatened him with a shotgun the other night.

"Where's your daddy?" Faith asked her daughter, who was curled up on the sofa watching *SpongeBob*.

Bitsy shrugged, her eyes glued to the television. "He said he was gonna get some lunch and come right back."

Faith experienced the first wave of nausea. "How long ago was that?"

"I don't know. I got hungry, though. I couldn't wait." She gestured toward a can of Vienna sausages on the coffee table. "I cut my finger on the rim." She held her index finger up for Faith to see. The cut was short but deep with a bit of blood oozing out.

"Come here, honey." Faith pulled Bitsy to her feet and led her to the kitchen. She lifted her daughter onto the counter, rinsed her cut in the sink, and wrapped a princess Band-Aid around it.

"Listen, Bits, this is very important. I need to know how long Daddy's been gone."

Bitsy stared at her wide-eyed.

"Have you been watching *SpongeBob* the whole time?"

The little girl nodded.

Faith scooped Bitsy in her arms and carried her back to the den and over to the antique clock. "It's two o'clock now. See, the big hand is on the twelve and the little hand is on the two. Do you know where the little hand was when Daddy left?"

Bitsy studied the clock. "On the twelve, I think."

She pointed at the twelve. "You mean both hands were here."

"Yes."

Faith's skin crawled. Curtis had left their daughter alone for two hours. "That means you watched four different episodes of *SpongeBob*."

"There was nothing else to do. Am I in trouble?"

"Not at all, sweetie." She kissed her daughter's forehead. "How would you like to go down to the docks later to see what the fishermen caught?"

Bitsy clasped her hands together. "Do you think Captain Mack will be there?"

"I certainly hope so." Faith set Bitsy down. "In the meantime, let's you and I go have a little rest in my bed."

Bitsy stared up at her mother. "But I'm not tired."

"Then you can read one of your books while I close my eyes for a while."

Bitsy skipped over to the basket of books on the coffee table and dug through them until she found the ones she wanted—*The Diary of a Wimpy Kid* and a Dr. Seuss, Faith's favorite, *Green Eggs and Ham.*

Nestled together in bed, Faith closed her eyes and immediately dozed off. It was nearing four o'clock when she woke up, headache free, with Bitsy sleeping soundly beside her. Faith sensed the stillness in the trailer. Curtis had still not come home.

Anger pulsed through her body. She'd told Curtis not to expect her until dinner. If she hadn't come home early from work, their six-year-old would've spent the afternoon in the trailer, in the middle of the woods. Alone.

"Hey, Sleeping Beauty." She gently nudged Bitsy awake. "Are you ready to go down to the docks?"

Bitsy's eyes shot open. "Can we get a hotdog for supper?"

"You bet."

Bitsy hopped to her feet and began jumping up and down on the bed. "Can we go to Sandy's for ice cream afterward?"

"Only if you brush your hair and teeth before we go."

"Yippee!" Bitsy jumped one last time, then leaped from the bed and dashed to the bathroom.

With Bitsy tucked into her car seat behind her, Faith rolled down the truck windows and turned up the radio. She refused to let Curtis spoil their outing. She planned to confront him later, but first, she needed more information about her husband's habits.

She waited until Taylor Swift had finished serenading them about her "Love Story" before she sought out Bitsy's yellow green eyes in the rearview mirror. "Did Daddy leave you at home alone last week while I was at work?"

Bitsy chewed on her lower lip. "I don't like it when his friends

He grabbed a fistful of her shirt and pulled her to him, so close she could smell the beer and stale tobacco on his breath. "If you don't find some money from somewhere, we're gonna be sleeping on the streets."

"Sleeping on the streets? What do you mean? What've you done?" she asked.

"Let's just say I got dealt a bad hand, kind of like when I married you."

He pushed her down on the bed and whipped off his belt. Cowering back against the headboard, Faith saw hatred in his bloodshot eyes. He was preparing to strike, with his belt in the air, when a tiny gasped stopped him.

Bitsy stood in the doorway with her thumb stuck in her mouth. "Is Mama getting a spanking, too, Daddy?"

Faith remembered her daughter's words from earlier. *Stay in your room or else.* Was his belt the *or else?*

She choked back her fury. "No, sweetheart. Daddy is just getting undressed. Go on back to your room. I'll be there to read to you in a minute."

"Okay, Mama," she said and scampered off.

Faith drew her leg up to her chest for leverage and kicked Curtis in the gut as hard as she could. As he staggered backward, he tripped over his own feet and fell to the ground.

She snatched the belt away from him. "How dare you beat my child."

He clutched at his stomach. "How else is she going to learn to obey?"

Faith folded the belt in half and snapped it loudly. "If you ever touch her again, I'll beat you till your skin bleeds." She tossed the belt on the bed and ran to Bitsy's room, slamming the door and pushing the bureau behind it to create a barricade.

"What's wrong, Mama?" Bitsy whimpered. "Did Daddy send you to my room, too?"

"No, honey. We're playing hide-and-seek." Faith turned off

the bedside table lamp so her daughter couldn't see her tears. "He won't be able to find us in the dark."

Heart pounding, Faith crawled into bed and wrapped her arms around Bitsy, holding her tight. She lay awake long after Bitsy had fallen asleep, imagining the horrors her daughter had experienced at the hands of that lunatic. How long had the brutality been going on? He'd had plenty of opportunity. He looked after Bitsy every Saturday during the school year while Faith worked at the market. She'd never seen any bruises or marks on her daughter, but that didn't mean they didn't exist.

Sometime around midnight, she got up and crammed some of Bitsy's clothes in her pink school backpack. She pushed the bureau away from the door and slowly turned the knob, praying the hinges wouldn't squeak. She gathered their necessities from the bathroom and tossed them into an empty pillowcase. She tiptoed into her bedroom. As she was reaching for her underwear drawer, Curtis shined a flashlight in her face.

"Just where do you think you're going?" he asked.

Faith gathered an armful of underwear and opened the drawer below. "To Sam's. You and I need some time to cool off." Her arms full of clothes, she turned toward the door.

"You better think twice before you go crying to Sister Sammy."

The warning tone in his voice stopped her dead in her tracks. "I'm not going to cry to her. I'm just going to stay with her for a few days."

"I wouldn't do that if I were you."

Chill bumps crawled across her skin. "Is that some kind of threat?"

"You tell me, Faith. Do you have anything to feel guilty about?"

She turned around to face him, her courage fueled by her anger. "You wouldn't."

"Hell yes I would. If you leave this house, I'll be forced to tell

Sam about your extracurricular activities at work. Be mighty embarrassing for you to get caught with your hand in Sweeney's cookie jar."

"But you forced me . . ."

"Do you seriously think Sam will care whether or not I forced you? What you did was illegal."

Faith knew she was trapped. She dropped the load of clothes in the middle of the floor and went back to bed in Bitsy's room. She was still staring at the ceiling, the hopelessness of her situation sinking in, when the sun peeked through the blinds the following morning.

THIRTEEN

SAMANTHA

Late Tuesday afternoon, Lovie announced as the market was closing that it was time for her to go home. "Tomorrow is my day off, and I'd like to use my free time getting settled, doing chores, and running errands. I miss having my own car."

Sam switched off the overhead lights, then locked the door behind them and headed to the parking lot. "Are you sure you should be driving?"

"I'm tired of all the fuss, Sammie. I'm perfectly capable of taking care of myself."

Sam couldn't argue. She'd been watching her mother closely for the past few days, and Lovie seemed like her old self in every way, aside from being a little forgetful. But what eighty-two-year-old woman didn't have trouble remembering things at times? She'd even noticed her own short-term memory wasn't as sharp as it once was.

Sam jumped in the driver's seat beside Lovie and started the engine. "Then let's go get your things from my house. I'm sure Jamie could use some fresh air. We'll make him ride with us to take you home."

It took longer for Sam to rouse Jamie from his resting place on the sofa than it took for Lovie to pack up her belongings.

"I don't understand why I have to go with you," Jamie said.

Sam parked the wheelchair beside the sofa and waited while Jamie climbed in. "Because you haven't been out of the house all day. You need some fresh air."

She thought her son needed a bath, too, but she wasn't going to push her luck.

They stopped by the Harris Teeter for milk and juice and a few items for their respective dinners. Jamie stayed in the car while they went inside. When they returned, the air in the car smelled sour from his body odor.

"Let's help Lovie with her bags," Sam said to Jamie as they pulled up in front of her mother's townhouse.

"Seriously, Mom, like how do you expect me to carry her bags?"

"You can at least come inside while I help your grandmother get unpacked."

"No thanks. It's not worth the effort of getting up those stairs." He aimed his thumb at the three steps leading to Lovie's front door.

Lovie winked at Sam, a plea for Sam not to upset Jamie. "I can manage myself, sweetheart. You've already done enough."

Sam acquiesced. "I can at least help you get your bags inside."

Lovie shifted in her seat to face her grandson. "You be nice to your mama now, you hear? She loves you very much."

The corners of Jamie's mouth lifted a fraction. "I'll try, Lovie. Are you sure you're going to be okay alone?"

"Don't you worry about me, sweet boy. You just concentrate on getting yourself better."

Sam carried her mother's overnight bags to her bedroom and returned to the kitchen, where Lovie was unloading her groceries. When Sam began stowing the perishable items in the refrigerator, Lovie said, "Go home, Sam. Your son needs you more than I do."

Much to Sam's surprise, tears sprang to her eyes. She couldn't remember the last time she'd cried.

"Oh, honey." Lovie drew Sam in for a warm embrace. "You don't have to handle this by yourself. Jamie is a very angry boy right now. And understandably so. He needs someone to talk to, someone other than you or me. I've never had much use for them myself, but now might be a good time to consult with a psychiatrist."

Sam pulled away to tear a sheet from the paper towels by the sink and wipe her eyes. "He has an appointment to see one on Thursday. I have no idea how I'm going to get Jamie to agree to meet with her."

"You'll find a way." Lovie placed her hand at the small of Sam's back and nudged her toward the front door. "But for now, take him home and feed him, and for goodness' sake, make him take a bath."

As hard as she tried, Sam couldn't get a word out of Jamie on the drive home. She longed for those days when he shared so much with her—gossip about a friend or the results from a test, who chose whom for kickball during recess.

He refused Sam's help getting out of the Wrangler when they arrived and somehow wormed his way into his wheelchair. She grabbed her grocery bags and walked alongside him. "We're having brats for dinner," she said, fumbling with her keys. "Do you want to cook them on the grill?"

Jamie loved to cook. They used to spend their Sunday after-noons trying out new recipes, from Mexican to Thai to Italian. Jamie was no longer interested in eating, let alone cooking, but that didn't stop Sam from trying.

"Can't you cook them on the stove? It's hot out here."

She held the door open while Jamie wheeled his chair inside. "I can do that, but only if you make your secret-recipe cornbread to go with them." She ignored him when he grumbled he wasn't in the mood to cook. "Why don't you go shower while I start the oven?" When he wheeled off, she called after him, "And bring your dirty laundry when you come back."

Jamie returned thirty minutes later balancing his laundry basket on his lap. He set the basket on top of the washing machine and went to the refrigerator for eggs, milk, and butter, setting them one at a time on the island. He wheeled his chair onto the platform Sam had built to allow him easy access to the island and the sink counter. He placed a stick of butter in a small baking dish and set it in the microwave.

"Good news!" Sam said, forcing a happy tone. "I was able to get an appointment for you to see Dr. Baker on Thursday at four o'clock, after your physical therapy session."

Jamie cracked an egg and dumped its contents into a glass bowl. "Then cancel it, because I'm not going."

Sam turned to him. "Jamie, you need to talk to someone about the accident. I'm worried about you. You seem so angry."

"I'm not angry." He cracked another egg on the side of the bowl, the force of the blow crushing the egg in his hand. "Well, maybe I am a little angry. But I'm dealing with it." He pitched the mutilated egg in the sink.

"That's the thing, honey. I don't think you are dealing with it."

"I'd like to see you walk in my shoes, Mom. Oh wait, I forgot. I can't walk anymore." He hurled the whole bowl in the sink, splattering egg goo everywhere, and wheeled off toward his bedroom, slamming the door behind him.

Sam leaned back against the counter. She'd failed to reach him once again. Her eyes homed in on the case of wine her distributor had given her, abandoned beside the backdoor where she'd left it last week. She'd never been much of a drinker, but she'd brought it home because she wanted to develop her tastes in order to make qualified recommendations to her customers. She flipped open the lid and inspected the labels before deciding on a Shiraz, one with a screw cap, since she didn't own a corkscrew.

She located a dusty wine glass in the back of a cabinet, which she rinsed. Pouring a small amount, she sniffed and sipped the wine like she'd seen people do in restaurants. She had no idea what she was supposed to smell, but she liked the rich, warm taste. She kicked back the rest and poured herself a full glass.

Glass in hand, she walked down the hall to Jamie's bedroom and tapped lightly on the door. "I'm sorry, Jamie. I didn't mean to upset you. I'm trying, but obviously I'm not doing a very good job of it. This thing is bigger than either of us can handle. That's why I think we need some help."

By way of response, he cranked his music to a near-deafening level.

Back in the kitchen, she sipped on her wine while she cleaned up the egg mess, popped a frozen container of macaroni and cheese in the microwave, and threw together a Caesar salad.

This time, when she knocked on Jamie's door to inform him that dinner was ready, he shouted, "Go away. I'm not hungry."

Sam poured another glass of wine and settled in at the island to eat. She nibbled at her food, but mostly she drank. Another glass, and then another, until the bottle was nearly empty.

She covered Jamie's plate in foil and left it on the kitchen counter, like she'd done more nights than not during the past months. She felt certain she'd find it untouched in the morning.

Using the walls in the hall for support, she made her way to the front of the house to her bedroom. Fully clothed, without washing her face or brushing her teeth, she lay down on her queen-size bed, letting the fluffy duvet and mound of pillows swallow her up. When the room began to spin, she rolled over on her side and passed out.

FOURTEEN

JACQUELINE

J ackie's plan was spur of the moment. At least the part of the plan that involved her mother. Jackie had been plotting and scheming about buying a new car since Bill returned the Suburban to her and drove off in his sleek convertible. She'd become attached to the modern conveniences of a newer-model car—Sirius radio, backup camera, and navigation, for starters. She liked the idea of connecting her phone to the music system and listening to her audiobooks on her frequent trips to Charleston.

She drove to Lovie's, expecting to find her baking a cake or tending her potted herb garden on the back deck—not decorating her pre-lit artificial Christmas tree.

"What on earth are you doing, Mom? Please tell me you're not planning to celebrate Christmas in July."

"Of course not. It's only June." Lovie cast a quick glance at her daughter, then went back to hanging ornaments. "I was searching for something in the storage room this morning and I came across the tree. I decided to get an early start this year."

"'Early' is definitely the operative word." Jackie removed a glass ball from the box and inspected the hand-painted seagulls. "Where'd you get this one?"

Lovie placed her hand over her heart. "Your father bought that for me the Christmas Faith was born. His three gulls, he always called you girls. That ornament was his favorite. Hang it right there." Lovie pointed to an empty branch on the tree.

Jackie hung the ornament, and the two of them stepped back to admire it. "Did you find what you were looking for?"

"Looking for where, honey?" Lovie asked, still marveling at the ornament.

"In your storage room. You said you were searching for something. Did you find it?"

Lovie considered the question. "You know, I can't even remember what I was looking for now. Must not have been too important."

Jackie catalogued this strange behavior in the mental file she was keeping on her mother's health.

"I'm heading into Charleston to pick up a new car," Jackie said. "I thought you might like to go along with me. I'll treat you to lunch at Sermet's, and we can do a little shopping."

"That sounds nice, honey, but I really want to finish this today."

"You have plenty of time to decorate the tree before Christmas, Mom. Come with me, please. It's been a while since we've spent any time together, just the two of us."

"Oh, all right." Lovie closed the lid on the box of ornaments and unplugged the tree lights. "How can I say no to Sermet's?"

Lovie brushed her teeth, fussed with her hair, painted a strange color of orange lipstick on her lips, and grabbed her bag. Twenty minutes later they were on their way.

"What's this about a new car?" her mother asked once they were on the highway heading toward Charleston. "I don't see anything wrong with this one." She ran her hand across the dashboard.

"Are you kidding me? I've been busing boys around in this truck for eleven years, since Cooper and Sean were in kindergarten."

Lovie sniffed. "Where did that fishy smell come from?"

"Lovely, isn't it? I have twins to thank for the horrendous odor."

"Do tell," her mother said.

"Well . . . one day a couple of summers ago, I picked the boys up at the marina after a day out in the Gulf Stream with Captain Mack. Mack had given them a bucket full of fish to take home and clean for dinner. When I swerved to miss a turtle crawling across the road, the bucket spilled over, and all the fish juice leaked onto the carpet on the floorboard. Naturally, the boys never told me about the spill."

"Did they even try to clean it up?"

"Nope, the little rascals. They eventually confessed, several days later, when the fish juice started to smell really bad. But it was too late by then."

"Did you try steam cleaning the carpet?"

"Carlotta and I tried everything."

"I'm surprised Bill let you drive it, smelling like this."

Jackie smiled. "He's buying a new car for me today. That's all that matters."

"What kind of car are you getting?"

"A Cadillac Escalade."

Earl McAdams, the Cadillac dealer she'd spoken to a dozen times on the phone the previous day, was waiting for Jackie in the showroom. She guessed him to be about her age, although his beer gut and ruddy complexion made him look ten years older.

"I have your car all cleaned up and ready for you. If you give me your keys, we can take your new ride for a spin while my boys work up an estimate on your Suburban."

Jackie handed him her keys. "I don't need a test drive."

Earl looked wounded. "Seriously?"

"Anything is an improvement over what I've been driving. But I would like for you to show me how everything works."

"That would be my pleasure." He held the door open for Jackie and her mother.

They walked together to the side lot, where a silver Escalade glistened in the sun.

"She's a beaut, ain't she?" Earl said.

Jackie ran her hand across the hood. "Yes, she is."

"This one's fully loaded, like you said you wanted. But if you don't like the color, I have several others in my inventory." He pointed to a row of Escalades in a variety of colors.

"I like the silver."

Earl's blue eyes twinkled when he smiled. He was pleasant enough to look at. If she weren't so intimidated by his beer belly, Jackie might have asked him for a date. She was done with handsome men. She wanted a real man, someone who respected her, someone who treated her like she was the center of his universe.

Jackie realized the *someone* she'd just described fit the old Bill, the man he was when they got married.

She slid in the driver's seat, and Earl climbed in beside her with Lovie in the back. He began with the air-conditioning system, then worked his way over every inch of the car. Jackie listened intently but understood only half of what he said. She planned to spend the next few nights curled up in bed with the manual.

Jackie was all set to drive away in her gleaming new SUV when the sales manager approached her with an itemized sales receipt. Their offer to buy her Suburban was considerably less than what Earl had approximated over the phone, while the price of the new Escalade was way more than she'd anticipated from her online research.

"I was hoping to get more from my Suburban," Jackie said.

"Well . . . there's the matter of the odor," the sales manager said.

Jackie shrugged. "There is that."

She did a quick mental assessment of her financial situation. Bill had made no changes in the way they managed their money since he moved out. Yesterday, in anticipation of her purchase, Jackie had transferred all but $1,000 from their joint savings account into her private checking account, but that amount would not cover the cost of the car at these numbers.

She'd never been much of a negotiator, but she'd watched Bill haggle with salespeople many times.

"I'm sorry, gentlemen, for wasting your time." She handed the sales form back to the sales manager. "But this amount is way more than I anticipated."

She took her mother by the elbow and led her over to where the Suburban was parked outside of the service department. It took all the guts she could muster not to look back to see if the salesmen were following. They caught up with her as she was helping Lovie into the passenger side.

"Why don't you ladies come inside where's it's nice and cool," Earl said. "If you can give us a moment, we'd like to revisit our numbers, to see if there is any wiggle room."

Jackie tucked her mother in before closing the passenger door. "I don't know," she said as she walked around the front of the car to the driver's side. "You're asking an awful lot of money."

"Listen, Mrs. Hart." Earl leaned on the driver's door, preventing her from opening it. "If you'll give us a chance, we'd like to make the sale. I promise you, we will give you our rock-bottom price. If that doesn't work for you, we can both walk away satisfied that we at least tried."

Jackie imagined herself driving out of the lot in her new shiny silver Escalade, then she pictured the look on Bill's face when he realized their savings account was empty.

"I guess it won't hurt to give you a few more minutes, since our lunch reservations aren't for another hour."

Forty-five minutes later, they were driving out of the lot in her new Escalade. Jackie felt exhilarated. Not only because of the plush interior of the SUV, or for leaving the nasty Suburban behind, but also for the pride she'd experienced at having closed the deal. She'd played hardball. And she'd won.

Lovie sniffed. "I love the smell of leather. You're a lucky girl, Jacqueline. Be sure to thank your husband properly when he comes home tonight."

The pang of guilt she suffered lasted only a few seconds—the time it took to summon the image of Bill driving around in his convertible with his mistress.

She gripped the wooden steering wheel. "I feel like I'm driving on top of a cloud."

They arrived at the restaurant right on time for their reservation. The hostess escorted them to their table, and the waitress appeared immediately with two glasses of water. With her dark auburn hair and hourglass figure, the woman exuded sex appeal.

Good thing Bill isn't around to meet her, Jackie thought.

"Do you wanna hear the specials?" the waitress asked, smacking gum.

Both Lovie and Jackie ordered the same thing they always order, the grilled salmon salad. After the waitress brought their iced tea, Lovie excused herself to go to the ladies' room. Jackie kept an eye on her mother as she walked through the restaurant. She was watching for her return when Bill called.

"That was a low blow, Jack, way below the belt."

"Bill, it's so nice to hear from you."

"This is not a social call. What the hell were you thinking, stroking a check for the full price of an automobile without asking me?"

"News certainly travels fast."

"Yeah, well, I went to the ATM to make a withdrawal and discovered our balance is less than a thousand dollars."

"Since when is a thousand dollars nothing?"

"That's peanuts compared to what we used to have in that account."

"Gosh, Bill. I'm sorry. Were you planning to use the money to buy your mistress an expensive trinket?"

"We're talking about a Cadillac, Jacqueline, an automobile. You can't just go off and buy something like that without talking to me first."

"You moved out, remember? When was I supposed to talk to you?" Jackie stood up, glanced around the restaurant for her mom, then sat back down when she didn't see her. "Anyway, this is all your fault. If you hadn't given me your fancy little convertible to drive while you were in the mountains, I'd never known what I was missing. Did you realize there were close to two hundred fifty thousand miles on the Suburban? I've been driving your sons around in that truck for more than eleven years."

"There is nothing wrong with that truck. I just drove it to the mountains and back without any problems."

"I guess you get used to the fish smell after a while. Except, of course, when it's a hundred degrees outside and the Suburban has been parked for hours in the full sun in an asphalt parking lot."

"All right." Bill sighed. "So maybe you do need a new car, but an Escalade is way more than I can afford right now. Please tell me you didn't trade the Suburban in. It's a perfect car for the boys to drive when they get their license."

"I wouldn't give that car to my dog to drive."

"I take that as a yes, you traded the car."

"Yes, I traded the Suburban. There wouldn't have been enough money in the account if I hadn't."

"Damn it, Jack. Keep the car if it means that much to you. But we need to come up with an agreement regarding our finances during the separation. I've just contacted my lawyer. I suggest you do the same."

"I'm one step ahead of you. I called her last week."

"Her? I don't know of any female divorce attorneys in Prospect."

"She's not from Prospect. She lives in Charleston. I've hired Barbara Rutledge to represent me."

"You mean Barbara the Barracuda?"

Jackie pictured Bill pushing his leather chair back from his desk, his face beaming red—a fat, juicy summer tomato perched atop his favorite blue-striped, button-down shirt and white doctor's coat.

"One and the same," she said. "We've already spoken several times on the phone. We are meeting for the first time in person next week."

"Shit, Jack. Why'd you go and hire her? You know I'll be generous with you. I just bought you a new car, for crying out loud?"

"A woman has to protect her interests." Jackie suddenly remembered her mother, who had not returned from the ladies' room. "Listen, Bill. I've gotta run. I'm having lunch with Mom at Sermet's. Thanks again for the car." She blew a loud kiss into the phone and hung up.

When she went to check on Lovie, Jackie discovered the ladies' room was empty. The restaurant was only so big. Lovie couldn't have left the building without Jackie seeing her. She sought out their waitress, who was delivering an order to another table. "Have you seen my mother? She went to the restroom and never came back."

"By any chance is she . . ." The waitress tapped her head.

"Early stages perhaps, but she hasn't been diagnosed yet."

"Let me put my tray down, and I'll help you find her. Can you remind me of what she looks like? I get so many customers, I can't keep them all straight."

"Short dark hair," Jackie said, leaving out the graying roots part. "She is wearing a red T-shirt and white jeans. I've checked everywhere. She must have left the restaurant."

"Why don't you go look for her out on the street, and I'll keep an eye on your table in case she returns."

Once outside, Jackie spotted Lovie one block over, standing in front of a store window and staring at the handbags and shoes on display. She approached her.

"Oh, Jacqueline. There you are," Lovie said as if she'd been waiting for Jackie to join her. "Isn't that yellow handbag pretty?"

Jackie gave the yellow bag a quick glance. "Lovely, but you can't just wander off like that without telling someone."

"I'm sorry, honey. I didn't mean to worry you."

"Come on back inside, Mom. Our lunch will be out soon. We can shop after we eat." When Jackie tugged at her mother's wrist, a metal object fell from her hand and clattered to the sidewalk.

"My key! Where'd it go?" Lovie paced back and forth, searching for the metal key that was on the ground right in front of her.

"Stop! Before you step on it." Jackie held her mother's arm with one hand while bending down to pick up the key with the other. She held the metal key out in her palm. "What does it go to?"

Lovie snatched the key away from her. "I don't know."

"What do you mean you don't know? Where'd you get it?"

"I've always had it. I used to wear it around my neck, but now I keep it in my bedside table drawer."

"Can I see it for a second?" When Lovie reluctantly released it, Jackie held the key up for inspection. "It's so rusty, like someone left it out in the rain for a decade. It's not the kind of key that fits a post-office box or a safe-deposit box."

"We never had a safe-deposit box. Your father didn't believe in keeping his money in a bank."

"I remember that about him," Jackie said, smiling. "Maybe it fits the drawers on one of your chests, or the secretary you inherited from Grandmother."

Lovie shook her head again. "I've tried them all."

"You'll figure it out eventually." She gave the key back to her mother. "Put it in your pocket for now, before you lose it."

Lovie stuffed the key in her pants pocket. "Has our food come yet? I'm starving."

Their salads were waiting for them when they returned.

Once they were seated, Jackie held her hand out across the table. "Let me see your cell phone, Mom."

Lovie dug an ancient flip phone out of her bag and placed it in her palm.

"Good Lord. This thing is ten years old." Jackie flipped the phone open and saw that it wasn't even turned on. She pressed the green button and waited while the phone powered on. "We need to get you a new one." *Preferably one with GPS tracking in case you wander off again*, she thought.

"Why? I hardly ever use it."

"Well, one day you're gonna need to use it, and it won't work," Jackie said, sliding the phone back across the table.

They finished their lunch and headed down King Street. Against her mother's protests, Jackie took her to Dottie's Boutique and insisted she try on several dresses. Dottie's had something for everyone, from fashionable to frumpy, from age thirty on up.

"But I don't need a dress. Where am I going to wear it?"

Her mother had always worn skirts and blouses, but Jackie could never remember her owning a dress.

"To church, maybe. Or a luncheon or cocktail party."

"Or a funeral," her mom said.

"That, too. Every woman needs to have a dress in her closet that she can count on for any occasion. I want to buy you something nice."

Finally, they settled on a suit, although Jackie wasn't sure whether her mother really liked it or just wanted Jackie off her back.

"The suit flatters your coloring, Mom." Jackie stood behind her mother at the mirror in the dressing room, admiring the way the coral tweed suit complimented her slim figure. "Speaking of which,"—she fluffed Lovie's hair—"when was the last time you had your hair cut and colored?"

Lovie's hand automatically went to her hair. "Why? Does it look that bad?"

"No, but—"

"The girl who usually does my hair moved to Savannah. I haven't had time to find anyone else. Who do you use?"

"Depends on my mood. Sometimes I get Carroll at the Hair Station to give me a quick trim. But if I have a special event, I come to Charleston for the works."

Jackie glanced at her watch. It was not yet two o'clock. And their last appointment of the day—the real reason for bringing her mother to Charleston—wasn't until four. "If we hurry, we still have time."

The Market Salon and Spa didn't normally accept walk-ins, but because Jackie was a frequent guest, they gladly accommodated her mother. One of the newer stylists, Brenda, a woman barely out of her teens with tatted-up arms, had just received a cancellation. Jackie grabbed a stack of magazines and made herself comfortable in the chair across from the stylist's station. She wasn't about to let her mother out of her sight again. An hour and a half later, when Brenda finished coloring, cutting, and blow-drying her hair, Lovie looked ten years younger.

Back in the car, Lovie admired herself in the sun-visor mirror. "What do you think, Jacqueline?"

"I think it looks lovely."

Her mother was so preoccupied with looking at her new hairdo, she hardly noticed when they drove down the driveway of the Hermitage Retirement Community.

FIFTEEN

SAMANTHA

S am had just gotten home from work and was transferring a load of laundry from the washer to the drier when Lovie appeared at the back door, knocking and waving frantically to get her attention. Sam tossed the rest of the clothes in the drier and set the controls before opening the door for her mother. "Mom, your hair looks great."

Lovie grumbled something Sam couldn't understand as she brushed past her.

Sam closed the door behind her mother. "What's wrong? You seem upset."

"I am upset." Lovie spun around to face Sam. "I spent the whole day in Charleston with Jackie. She's on a mission to put me in my grave."

"What are you talking about?"

Lovie climbed up onto a bar stool and buried her face in her hands. "Jackie insisted on buying me a new suit, then took me to her beautician to have my hair done. I've never owned a dress in my life, and I refuse to be buried in one when I die," Lovie said, close to tears.

Sam sat down beside her mother at the island. "I'm sure you

misunderstood the situation." She handed Lovie a napkin. "Jackie probably just wanted to pamper you a little. There's nothing wrong with a daughter doing something special for her mother every now and then."

"Jackie is on a spending spree, all right. She paid cash for a new Cadillac today without even taking it out for a test spin."

That got Sam's attention. What husband buys his wife a new car when he's planning to divorce her? Was Bill using the Cadillac as a payoff to keep Jackie from dragging him through a nasty divorce? Of course, there was always the possibility they weren't getting a divorce, that the car was a peace offering—his way of apologizing for being unfaithful.

She needed time to digest that information. "Let's forget about the car for now. You need to tell me everything that happened today so I can understand Jackie's intentions."

"Fine." Lovie sat back in her chair. "Your sister's intentions are clear. She is trying to get rid of me. She scheduled an interview for me at a retirement home—the Hermitage, I believe the place is called—so y'all will have somewhere to plant me if I don't die of natural causes in the next ninety days."

"Wait, what? Jackie took you to a retirement community?"

"Isn't that what I just said?"

Sam eyed last night's empty bottle of wine beside the refrigerator. She got up from the island, grabbed a full bottle from the case, and poured two glasses, sliding one across the counter to her mother.

"First of all, Mom, there is no y'all about it." Sam took a sip of wine, then set her glass down. "Jackie acted alone in all this."

"But you knew about it, didn't you?"

"Jackie mentioned the idea at lunch the other day, but Faith and I made it perfectly clear we weren't interested in looking for a retirement home. At least not right now. In Jackie's defense, she's trying to think ahead. And she makes a good point. These places have long waiting lists. When the time comes, if the time comes, she wants you to have options. I'm sure the place you visited is a lot nicer than anything we have in Prospect."

Lovie's shoulders relaxed. "I guess you're right about that."

Sam's cell phone rang, and she reached across the island for it. "This is Jackie, Mom. Sip on your wine for a minute while I talk to her." Sam took the phone back to her bedroom for privacy and said, "You've certainly stirred up a hornet's nest, Jackie."

"What do you mean?"

"Mom is here, all worked up into a tizzy. I thought we agreed to wait on the whole retirement-home thing."

"After the day I spent with her, I'm more convinced than ever that now is the right time. This place is nice, Sam, and they have an impressive Alzheimer's unit. Trust me, I think she needs it."

Sam listened while Jackie told her about Lovie disappearing from the restaurant. "When I found her on the street, she was staring at a handbag display in a store window, in a near-cata-tonic state. And she's carrying around this old rusty key. She can't remember what it belongs to."

"Must be the same key she had the night of your party, when we found her rooting around in your attic."

"What're you talking about, Sam? What was Mom doing in my attic?"

"Looking for the missing lock for her rusty key. I guess I forgot to tell you." A thought occurred to Sam. "If you're so worried about Mom getting lost, why'd you leave her at home alone when you got back from Charleston?"

"Because I needed to call you, and Mom wanted to get rid of me so she could finish decorating her Christmas tree."

"Her Christmas tree?" Sam lowered herself to the bed. "But it's only June."

"Tell me about it. Can she stay with you for a while? Someone needs to keep an eye on her."

"That's not fair, Jackie. I just had her over the weekend. It's your turn to let her stay with you. I'm dealing with an angry teenage boy in a wheelchair, but you're all alone with your sons off at camp."

"It makes more sense for Mom to stay with you since y'all work together." Jackie took a long pause before continuing. "I guess we could take turns. But only if we have to. I have a lot going on right now. With Carlotta leaving and all."

Never mind your marital problems, Sam wanted to say, but she held her tongue. Although she didn't understand it, Sam respected her sister for not feeling comfortable discussing her personal problems with her family. And letting their mom stay with her would put Jackie in the awkward position of having to explain Bill's absence. If he was, in fact, absent.

"Look, if I know Mom, she's going to pitch a fit about staying with either one of us. Let's give it a few days. I'll keep a close eye on her at work. She seems fine as long as she stays in her routine. Her days off are the problem, when she has too much time on her hands."

"I can help out on those days, Sam. I'll pick her up after church this Sunday and take her cell-phone shopping. Have you seen her phone? It's outdated by ten years."

"So what? She hardly ever uses it."

"Maybe not, but she needs a phone with GPS in case she gets lost again."

Sam knew parents who used GPS devices to track their errant teenagers. Why not use it to keep tabs on an Alzheimer patient? "Fine, take her to buy a new phone, but no more talk of retirement homes." Sam paused. "By the way, did you really pay cash for a new Cadillac?"

"I don't see how that's any of your business," Jackie said, and hung up without saying goodbye.

Sam returned to the kitchen to find her mother pacing the floors.

Lovie wasted no time in pouncing on Sam. "I know you're

keeping something from me. Do I have cancer, Sam? Am I dying?"

"That's ridiculous, Mom. You heard everything the doctor said. You're the picture of health."

"Then why did you leave the room to talk to Jackie?"

Sam reached for her mother's hand. "I promise you, Mom. We have nothing but your best interests at heart."

"I don't believe you. I wouldn't be surprised if the two of you were plotting to poison me." Lovie snatched her bag off the island and went flying out the door.

Sam drained the rest of her wine and reached for her mother's untouched glass. She lacked the energy to go after Lovie, deciding instead to call her in a few minutes to make certain she got home. Lately, Sam had felt she was losing her grip on everything she controlled—business, house, family. She would have to set priorities, with her troubled son her primary concern.

⁂

Jamie once again refused to eat dinner that night and pushed his plate away.

Sam knew she needed to tread carefully, or her son would go to bed hungry for the third night in a row.

"You need to eat, Jamie, to keep up your strength."

His eyes zeroed in on the year-at-a-glance calendar on the wall beside the phone. Back last fall, when Jamie had received confirmation of his baseball scholarship, Sam had circled July 17 with a red marker—the day he would report to Columbia to begin working out with the university's strength and conditioning coaches. If not for the accident, he would've been five weeks away from seeing his dream come true.

"Really, Mom. What do I need to keep my strength up for, physical therapy?"

"Yes, Jamie. For your recovery. With a lot of hard work and

determination, Moses can have you walking by the end of the summer. You could try out for the team as a walk-on."

"I gave up on that dream a long time ago." Tears filled his eyes, and he wiped them away with the back of his hand.

"Your dreams are still a part of you, honey. They're just trapped in your heart by your grief."

"What about Corey's dreams, Mom? We had plans. He and I were gonna work construction this summer so we'd have the money to buy an Xbox and a flat-screen television and all this cool stuff for our dorm room."

"I know you miss him, Jamie. We all do. But Corey would've wanted you to move on with your life."

"Everyone always says that about dead people, but no one knows it for sure."

"In Corey's case, *I* know it's true. I practically raised him. I know how kind-hearted he was and how much he loved you."

Jamie couldn't argue with that.

"You have it in you to walk again. Moses thinks—"

He slammed both palms on the counter. "I don't give a damn what Moses thinks. When are you gonna get it through your head? I've been sentenced to this chair for life."

"Oh really? And who sentenced you?" When he didn't answer, she said, "You sentence yourself, Jamie. You and I both know it. But it doesn't have to be that way."

"God, Mom." He raked his fingers through his greasy hair. "Will you just stop already with the you-can-walk-again bullshit? I've been trying for months. My legs don't work."

Sam sat back on her stool. She wasn't getting anywhere by coddling him. Time for a little tough love and reverse psychology. "Okay then, if you are so convinced you're never going to walk again, it's time you learn to live with your disability."

"I thought that's what I was doing."

She spread her arms wide. "You call this living? You refuse to see your friends. You sit in front of that television all day. And you've completely let your hygiene go."

"And just how do you expect me to go places? Despite what you think, pushing my wheelchair around town isn't an option."

"There are cars equipped for disabled drivers," Sam said. "I can't afford it right now, but if you put in some hours at the market, we could save for it together. For now, I'm happy to take you anywhere you need to go."

He glared at her, his eyes black with anger. "You're always at the market."

"Your friends would come see you if you'd let them."

"I don't need their pity. What do I have in common with them anymore, anyway?"

"College, for starters. You can go shopping for your dorm rooms together."

"I haven't decided if I'm even going to college."

"You have to get an education, Jamie."

"Carolina was my dream, Mom. How can I go there and not play baseball? How can I go there without Corey?"

"Maybe you can defer your admission for a semester, until you are feeling more like yourself. In the meantime, for your own good, I'm going to limit your screen time. And you need to start doing your chores again."

"Great." Jamie rolled his eyes. "I'm sure the neighbors will get a kick out of watching the cripple push the lawnmower."

"And I'm going to insist you keep your appointment with Dr. Baker tomorrow. You need someone to help you work through your problems."

"Forget it, Mom. I told you, I don't need a shrink. I'm dealing with my situation on my own."

SIXTEEN

JACQUELINE

Jackie ran the Russian Red lipstick across her lips, blotted them with a tissue, then snapped her compact shut and slid it into her evening bag. She hoped to make a bold statement with the obscene amount of bare skin she was showing in her low-cut black-and-white cocktail dress.

But first she had to summon the nerve to enter the party.

She removed the invitation from her visor and studied it for the umpteenth time that day. The old Jackie would have listened to her gut instincts, put her new SUV in reverse, and driven home as quickly as possible. But the new Jackie, the woman emerging from the shell of her former self, the woman whose primary motivation was self-preservation, was determined to save as much face as possible among Prospect's elite.

Bill never missed the Heart Benefit, the one social event he didn't mind paying $300 a head to attend. As the primo cardiologist in the area, the benefit gave him an opportunity to play center stage, to talk to the attendees about advances in the field of medicine, and answer questions regarding heart safety—a hot topic among middle-aged, health-conscious patrons.

Jackie had sent their money in a month ago and promptly received confirmation of their reservation. She'd have to sit next to him during dinner, but she could make nice for two hours if it meant accomplishing her goals. Presenting a united front would go a long way toward dispelling any rumors circulating about their current marital problems. Donna Bennett and Donna Berry be damned.

She entered the side entrance of the country club and eased into the crowd before anyone realized she had arrived alone. She accepted a glass of wine from a passing waiter and wandered to the edge of the terrace overlooking the golf course. A gentle breeze ruffled her hair. The organizers could rest easy. Mother Nature had granted them a perfect evening for a seated dinner under the stars.

Eileen Hanson, one of the event organizers and mother of Cooper's closest friend, joined her.

"I haven't heard a word from that scoundrel son of mine." Her son, Jason, was away at camp in Vermont. "I have no doubt that Cooper is better about writing to his parents."

"Actually, I haven't heard a word from either of my boys since they left. I imagine they'll get around to writing eventually, when —" Jackie stopped in midsentence when she spotted her husband strolling toward the terrace with a woman on his arm.

Eileen gave her a pat. "Don't worry. I made certain you are seated at a different table on opposite sides of the terrace from them."

"Thanks," Jackie mumbled.

Eileen filled the awkward silence with chitchat about planning the party, but Jackie didn't hear a word. She was fixated on the woman who had taken her place in her husband's life.

The other woman, this Daisy person, was everything Jackie was not—curvy, flashy, and loud. The woman's hot-pink dress stuck to her body like Cling Wrap, the cheap fabric accentuating her hourglass figure, her enhanced bust, and her shapely hips. With three-inch heels and straps winding up her leg, her silver platforms were the wrong choice for the dress. She'd teased her yellow hair into an updo with thick ringlets plastered to the sides of her face. She wore fake eyelashes, pink lipstick to match her dress, and a thick coat of foundation that gave her a waxed mannequin look.

From across the terrace, Jackie heard the woman laying it on thick in a lusty voice to Bill's golf partner. "Shame on you for keeping my Billy away from me on Saturday. Maybe you'll let me tag along sometime."

Jackie spirits lifted when Steve's lip turned up as though he'd just eaten a raw lemon. A real man's man, Steve's idea of fun did not include taking a woman along on a golf outing.

Eileen leaned close to Jackie. "He has some nerve bringing her here, if you ask me."

A sarcastic remark perched on the tip of Jackie's tongue and begged for release, but instead she responded, "I'm glad he found someone who makes him happy. Although, I must say I'm surprised he moved on so quickly, considering how distraught he was when I told him I wanted a divorce."

"I must say, your separation came as a surprise to all of us. Nobody realized you were having problems."

A white-gloved waiter appeared with dinner bell in hand, saving Jackie from having to explain. "If you could point me to my table . . ."

"Certainly. You are over by the fountain with the Jacobs and the Hunts." Eileen pointed across the terrace. "See where Keith and Lisa are standing?"

Jackie nodded and maneuvered through the crowd as quickly as possible, praying she wouldn't run into Bill.

She'd never met two of the couples at their table, but she considered the Jacobs and the Hunts her close friends. The event chairs had arranged the place cards in an alternating male/female configuration, which helped disguise the fact that she was the only one at the table without a spouse. She was seated between Keith Jacobs and Andrew Hunt. As she approached, both men jumped up to help her with her chair.

Once she was seated, Keith turned to Jackie. "Just so you know, we all think Bill is crazy for leaving you, especially for that tacky broad he's with."

Jackie wondered if Keith was speaking on behalf of the group in declaring his allegiance to her. The conversation around the table didn't stop, but Jackie knew all ears perked up in anticipation of her response.

"Who says Bill left *me*?" Jackie asked, a wicked smile playing along her lips.

Keith nearly choked on his cocktail. "You mean, you were the one having an affair?"

"A woman doesn't need to have a man waiting in the wings when she knows things are not right in her marriage."

"Thatta girl." He held his drink out to toast her.

She launched into a discussion with the men on either side of her about the independent, modern woman. They agreed that women of the new millennium were equally as accomplished as men. And they confessed that they were turned on by a woman in power. Whether they meant what they said or whether they were just trying to flatter her, Jackie loved being the center of their undivided attention. She responded by flirting shamelessly. On the happenstance that Bill was watching, she flashed her most dazzling smile, batted her eyelashes at regular intervals, and tossed her hair over her shoulder like a teenage tease when she laughed at their jokes.

They had finished their tomato-and-basil salads, and the wait staff was serving a seared Mahi Mahi with mango salsa when Jackie said, "So you say these encouraging things about modern women being sexy, yet both of your wives are traditional stay-at-home soccer moms." Jackie spoke in a low voice, words meant only for her dinner partners.

Keith and Andrew cast quick glances across the table at their wives. Their looks were met with steely glares. Lisa and Isabelle had been eavesdropping all along.

Lisa set her fork down on her dinner plate. "So, Jackie, I have a hard time believing your husband moved out of your house, started dating this woman, and moved in with her, all within two weeks' time."

Isabelle added, "The rumor around town is that he'd been planning to leave you for months but was waiting until after your birthday party."

"Retract the fangs, girls," Keith said. "We're all friends here."

Tears pressed at the back of Jackie's eyes. She wasn't sure what hurt more—that Isabelle and Lisa could be so cruel or that her husband had jumped from their marital bed of twenty years and straight into the bed of a bimbo.

For the rest of the main course, Jackie picked at her fish, not trusting herself to speak. She forced herself to think about all the things she would buy with the money she extracted from her lying, cheating, no-good husband—the black mink swing coat she'd been thinking about since last winter, the facelift she'd been contemplating for several years.

When the waiter brought thick, creamy slices of key lime pie, Jackie excused herself for the ladies' room. But once inside the clubhouse, she flew past the restrooms and out the side door to the empty parking lot. She broke the speed limit in a rush to get home and assess the damage of her failed plan while drowning her sorrows in a bottle of chilled Pinot Grigio.

How dare Bill show up at such a public event with another woman so soon after leaving her? He could've at least given her a heads-up that he was taking Daisy to the benefit. Instead of repairing the damage to her reputation, she'd made things worse by getting caught in a lie about the particulars of her separation.

She'd made herself out to be an independent woman of power, but she'd come across as a pathetic, desperate used-up ex-wife. And all the while her husband had been sitting across the terrace from her, smiling and laughing with his tramp.

She'd have the last laugh when she sued the bastard for everything he was worth.

SEVENTEEN

FAITH

The second Saturday of business at the market was more profitable than the first. All day long, vacationers came and went in a steady stream. A few were just checking things out, but most loaded up on seafood for their week at the beach. Word had spread throughout the Carolinas—Captain Sweeney's was back and better than ever.

Hungry and tired after the long day, Faith and Bitsy arrived home a little before seven to find all makes and models of motor-cycles parked haphazardly in the driveway in front of their trailer. Faith was in no mood for company.

"I don't like it when Daddy's friends are here," Bitsy said.

Faith helped her daughter out of her car seat, then went around to the passenger side for the pizza they'd picked up from Sardis and the Disney movie she'd rented from Redbox. "Don't worry, honey. They won't be staying." All she wanted to do was stuff herself with sausage pizza, take a hot bath, and crawl into bed.

Curtis and company were assembled around the rickety flea market table in their makeshift dining room, a thick cloud of cigarette smoke looming over them. An awkward silence fell over the group when they caught sight of her, an uninvited female in their man cave.

Buck, one of Curtis's nicer friends, stood up to greet her when she entered. "I'm sorry, Faith. Curtis didn't think you'd be home until late."

Faith glared at her husband. "I don't know where he got that impression. I come home from work at the same time every day."

The men needed no further encouragement than the irritation in Faith's voice to get the hell out of her house. They all scrambled at once, stubbing out cigarettes, sweeping plastic poker chips into baseball caps, and gathering their belongings— helmets, leather coats, and leftover booze. They headed in a single file toward the door with Curtis bringing up the rear and staring her down as he passed by her. The pulsating vein in his temple was only the beginning of the rage that would follow. He would eventually come home, and when he did, she would pay.

Once Bitsy was situated in front of her movie with a large slice of pizza, Faith turned her attention to her husband's mess. She opened all the windows and doors and turned on the overhead fans to air out the smoke. She collected all the empty beer and spit cans, then filled a bucket with water and scrubbed the stickiness off the table and linoleum floor.

An hour and a half later, Bitsy had zonked out in front of her movie and Faith was taking her first bite of pizza when Curtis returned.

"How dare you dis me in front of my friends like that?" he shouted, more angry than drunk.

"Shh! Can't you see Bitsy's asleep?" Pulling the blanket tighter around their daughter, Faith got up and took her plate to the kitchen. When she returned, Curtis was still standing beside the sofa where she'd left him. She no longer cared if she made him mad. "I shouldn't have to come home to a smoke-filled house full of drunk men when I've been working hard all day."

With one swift motion, Curtis grabbed a fistful of her hair

and yanked, twisting and turning his hand, until she cried out in pain.

Aroused by the commotion, Bitsy raced to her mother's side. "Don't hurt my mama, you meanie!"

Curtis pointed at Bitsy's room. "If you know what's good for you, little girl, you'll go get in your bed."

Bitsy stomped her foot. "No!"

He let go of Faith's hair and lunged toward his daughter. But she was too quick. She darted behind her mother, grabbing hold of her legs and burying her face in the crook of her knees. Faith pried her daughter's tiny fingers off her leg. "Let me handle this, honey. Run along to your room and climb in your bed. I'll be there in a minute."

As soon as Bitsy's bedroom door clicked shut, Curtis grabbed Faith by the arm and dragged her to their bedroom. Slamming the door behind him, he spun her around and punched her in the nose. Her knees buckled beneath her, and she dropped to the floor like a commercial-size sack of flour. Curtis went after her, kicking her in the torso, the head, and the legs with his pointy-toed boots. When she attempted to get up, he dropped on top of her, straddling her and pinning her arms to the floor with his knees. He wrapped his hands tight around her throat, choking her. When she gasped for breath, he loosened his grip suddenly and rolled off her. "What the hell am I thinking? No way am I going to prison because of you."

Faith twisted onto her belly and wormed her way to the bathroom, leaving behind her a trail of blood from her broken nose. She locked the bathroom door and collapsed on the floor, the cool tile soothing her wounds. The room began to spin as she slipped into unconsciousness.

She woke up later, an hour, maybe longer. She stripped off her bloodied clothes and climbed into the shower, the sound of the running water drowning out her sobs. She stood beneath the spray, letting the hot water massage her aching body. The water pooled at the bottom of the tub, a river of red as it washed the caked blood from her face. She gingerly slipped on her robe, the thin cotton heavy against her bruised skin. She peeked into her bedroom first, relieved to see her husband passed out on the floor where she'd left him, then her daughter's room to make certain Bitsy was sound asleep. Tiptoeing to the kitchen, she opened the cabinet where Curtis kept his booze and pulled down a half-empty bottle of Old Crow. She took three long gulps, wincing in pain as the bourbon burned her throat. She searched the drawer beside the stove for her one sharp knife. She grabbed a bag of frozen peas from the freezer for her nose, and using the cushions and blanket from the sofa, she set up camp in front of her daughter's closed door. She slipped the knife beneath the cushion, out of sight from Curtis but with easy access should she need it.

Faith lay stock-still on her makeshift bed on the floor, assessing the damage. Her whole body ached from where he'd kicked her. She felt certain he'd broken her nose, and probably a rib or two as well.

Comforted by the sound of loud snoring coming from her bedroom, Faith eventually dozed off. When she opened her eyes again, bright light was streaming through the threadbare curtains on the windows.

She slid the knife out from under the cushion, and using the doorjamb behind her for support, she inched her way to her feet. One slow step at a time, she made her way to her bedroom, prepared to drive the knife into her husband's cold heart.

EIGHTEEN

SAMANTHA

Sam opened her eyes and immediately shut them again, wincing at the intense throbbing in her head, the result of too much wine the night before. She cracked one lid and read a blurry 10:30 on the clock beside her bed. She couldn't remember the last time she'd slept so late.

Her to-do list took hostage of her brain, and she mentally sorted through her duties as she organized her day. She would clean inside before tackling the yard, saving the bill paying and grocery shopping for the afternoon.

But first she needed some coffee.

She popped two Advil, slipped on her robe, and stumbled to the kitchen. She set her Keurig to brew the largest-size mug, then went to the refrigerator for bacon. As she watched the bacon sizzle in her cast-iron skillet, she thought back to Sundays before the accident.

With the rare exception of a day at the beach, Jamie and Sam typically ate a big breakfast, attended the early service at church, and then embarked on their chores. Early on, Jamie had claimed the yard as his territory—mowing and blowing and trimming— leaving the indoor duties for Sam. In the afternoons, she went to the grocery store while he finished his homework. When the weather cooperated, they cooked dinner on the grill. If it was rainy or cold, they made chili or spaghetti or lasagna. They occasionally invited her mother for dinner, but Sam preferred her quiet time with her son before the chaos of the week began.

Sam glanced at her bulletin board, where she'd pinned Jamie's new list of chores. She'd incorporated some of his old household responsibilities—tasks he could easily accomplish, like doing the laundry—with a list of new duties she hoped he would take an interest in, like planning the week's meals. The list had been up for two days, and he'd yet to complete a single job.

She flipped the bacon, let it cook for a few minutes on the other side, then forked it out of the pan onto a paper towel. Jamie wheeled in and, without so much as a grunt, went to the refrigerator and poured himself a glass of orange juice.

"Would you like pancakes or eggs with your bacon?" Sam asked.

"I'm not hungry."

When is the last time he ate? she wondered. Certainly not the last three nights. Judging from the contents of her refrigerator and pantry, he ate very little, if anything, during the day while she was at work.

In the overhead light, his skin appeared gray. His eyes looked sunken and bruised, and he'd lost even more weight, progressing from gaunt to emaciated. In the past few days, he'd abandoned his Xbox and spent long hours in bed, staring up at the ceiling with his headphones blasting his eardrums toward premature deafness. To make matters worse, Moses had pulled Sam aside again, after Jamie's therapy session on Friday, to warn her of his increasing lack of motivation and despondency.

Frustrated and worried and strung out from her hangover, Sam did what she'd promised herself she wouldn't do. She lost her cool. She lifted the cast-iron pan and banged it down on the stove. "Not eating is no longer an option."

Jamie started to wheel away, but she caught up with him, grabbing the handles of his chair so he couldn't move.

"That's not fair, Mom."

She spun his chair around to face her. "You want to talk about not fair? I'll tell you what's not fair. What's not fair is me having to watch you starve yourself to death. You are wasting away, and there's nothing I can do about it." A sob caught in her throat and tears spilled from her eyes. She staggered over to the nearest bar stool and lay her head down on the counter, where she wept for a good five minutes. When she finally raised her head and wiped her nose on the sleeve of her robe, she was surprised to see Jamie sitting quietly beside her in his chair.

"I guess I'll have the pancakes."

Sam forced a smile. "Is it asking too much for you to talk to me while I make them?"

"Yes." He turned and wheeled across the room. "Call me when they're ready."

She drew in an unsteady breath. Remember, Sam. Baby steps. At least he agreed to eat.

But agreeing to eat was not the same as actually eating. Despite her efforts to fix Jamie a nice breakfast, he barely touched his pancakes.

"We have a lot to do today, Jamie, if we want to get all our chores done. What say we splurge and cook a steak for dinner?"

He shrugged.

She got up from the island and set her plate in the sink. "I'll get started on the laundry, if you'll take care of the dishes."

Mother and son had a long-standing house rule—the person who cooks does not do the dishes. But when Sam returned ten minutes later, the dirty plates and pans were still in the sink.

∾

Later on that afternoon, Sam was carrying a load of

groceries in from the car when she received a call from her mother's next-door neighbor. Glenda had the reputation for being a busybody, but the genuine concern in her voice caught Sam's attention.

"Sam, dear, I'm worried about your mother. She's been out back for over an hour, wandering from one deck to another, rummaging through everybody's stuff."

Sam dumped her grocery bags on the island. "What do you mean, she's rummaging through people's things?"

"She's lifting up planters and looking under doormats. When I asked her if I could help find whatever it was she'd lost, she seemed confused."

Where the hell is Jackie? Hadn't she promised to take their mother shopping for a new cell phone today?

"I'll be right there," Sam said.

She knocked on her son's bedroom door. "Jamie, I need to run to Lovie's. Please come put these groceries away for me."

He mumbled something unintelligible.

"*Now*, Jamie. I bought some things that need to go in the freezer."

Glenda was waiting for Sam in front of her mother's townhouse. "Thank goodness you're here. The front door is locked. She's around back."

Sam fell in step beside Glenda as they rounded the corner toward the creek side of the complex.

"I tried to get her to come inside for a glass of iced tea. Lord knows it's hot enough. And she seems so agitated. I've never seen anything like it, rooting around in everyone's private space the way she's doing." Glenda grabbed Sam's arm, pulling her to a halt. "Tell me, is it Al's hammer?" she asked in a hushed voice, tapping her head with her index finger.

"Al's who?" Sam asked.

"Alzheimer's. Does your mother have Alzheimer's disease?"

"Not that I'm aware of." Sam started walking again, quickening her step, making it difficult for an out-of-shape Glenda to keep up.

Each townhouse unit had a separate deck attached, all of which varied in size. Some held only a couple of chairs and a potted plant, while others, like her mother's, accommodated a grill, an eating area, and a garden of sorts—herbs, as was the case for Lovie. Sam found her mother trying to cram that same old rusty key in the lock on her glass door.

Sam turned to Glenda. "I appreciate your help, but I'll take it from here."

She waited for the nosy neighbor to leave before she tiptoed up beside her mother, careful not to scare her. "What're you doing, Mom? Did you get locked out?"

"Oh, hi, Sammie." Lovie glanced up at her daughter, then went back to work on the lock. "I'm trying to figure out what this key belongs to."

"But the key that fits this door doesn't look anything like the one in your hand."

Lovie's eyes narrowed in confusion, her brow beaded in sweat.

"Your house keys are on the same ring with your car keys and the keys for the market. Do you have them with you?"

Lovie reached in her pocket and removed a set of keys, dangling them in front of Sam.

"Then let's go inside and get a cold drink. Maybe I can help you figure out the mystery behind the key."

When they were settled in the sunroom with tall glasses of iced tea, Sam held her hand out and asked to see the key, promising to give it right back. Lovie reluctantly complied.

Without straying from her mother's direct line of sight, Sam wandered around the townhouse, trying the key in any lock that looked like a possible fit—keepsake boxes, the drawers on her secretary, the corner hutch in the dining room. When nothing worked, she returned to the sunroom and dropped to the chair beside her mother.

"You're wasting your time," Lovie said. "I've tried every lock in this house. The key fits something outside."

"How do you know that, if you can't remember what it goes to?"

"I have a strong feeling, is all."

Sam inspected the key carefully. "It's plenty rusty, like it belongs to something outside, but I can't imagine what type of outdoor structure it might fit."

"Maybe a shed door?"

"I don't think so, Mom. It's too small for that. How long have you had the thing?"

"Your father would know what it fits, if only he were alive."

"Wait, what, you've had this key that long? How come I've never seen you with it?"

"Because I usually keep it in the top drawer of my bedside table."

Sam returned the key to her mother. "Then why are you suddenly so desperate to figure out what it fits?"

Lovie sat back in her chair. "I don't know how to explain it. Just knowing I had the key if ever I needed it has always given me comfort. Now is the right time. I feel it in my bones, the way my arthritis acts up when it's going to rain."

"Like woman's intuition?"

"Well . . . more like a mother's intuition."

"If we put our heads together, maybe we can solve the mystery." Sam stood up. "In the meantime, why don't you come home with me for dinner? I bought two New York strips on special at the Harris Teeter, and I can't eat a whole one by myself."

"You don't have to ask me twice. I haven't eaten a steak in ages." Lovie dug a thin silver chain out of her pocket, slipped the key on the chain, and fastened it around her neck.

On the drive over, Sam filled her mother in on Jamie's increasing bad attitude and continued weight loss. Lovie stared out of the window for most of the way, fingering the key around her neck, showing no sign that she was listening.

A melted container of butter-pecan ice cream greeted them in a puddle of goo on the kitchen island. And Jamie was nowhere to be found. He didn't respond to her texts, and her calls went straight to voice mail. Sam was ready to call the police, when the sound of a car horn—two quick beeps followed by an impatient blast—got her attention. She raced to the window and saw Jamie pumping his chair across the road in front of a jacked-up pickup truck.

Sam dashed out the door and across the front lawn. "What's wrong with you?" she yelled at the driver. "Can't you see he's in a wheelchair?"

"That's what the sidewalk's for, lady!" the angry driver shouted through his open window.

Sam maneuvered her son's chair up and over the curb. Once on the sidewalk, she kneeled beside him. Perspiration covered his face, and his hair was damp with sweat. "What were you thinking, honey? You could've been killed."

NINETEEN

SAMANTHA

All thoughts of taking a mental health day vanished when Faith called in sick with another migraine headache on Monday morning. After Jamie's run-in with the angry truck driver the night before, Sam had polished off a bottle of wine by herself. Despite her throbbing headache, she dragged herself to work.

"It's just as well Faith didn't come in today," Sam said to her mother later that morning. After another stellar Saturday at Sweeney's, business had come to a screeching halt.

Donna Bennett's write-up in the *Prospect Weekly* had damaged their reputation with the locals. The townies peered through the window as they drove by, hoping to catch a glimpse of the too-uptown-for-small-town renovations, but few bothered to come in. Seeing an empty showroom did little to gain their confidence. Sweeney's couldn't survive on Saturday sales alone. If business from the locals didn't improve, they would be filing for bankruptcy by Christmas.

Sam found the stack of fliers Faith had made on the desk in the back office. Printed on plain white paper, the seaweed-green logo appeared in bold across the top with the week's homemade lunch specials listed below—a variety of items packaged in easy to-go containers, everything from Caesar salads to cucumber gazpacho to fresh tuna salad.

Sam left her mother alone to run the market, but with strict instructions to call Roberto out from the kitchen if a rush of customers came in.

Lovie waved her on. "Don't worry about us. We'll be fine."

Sam stopped by the marina store first and left a stack of fliers with the clerk, hoping their premade sandwiches would attract the charter-fishing crowd who might need a boxed lunch. Her next stops included the hospital office building and two construction companies where she knew some of the workers. On her way into the police department, she ran into Eli, the handsome young police officer who had befriended Jamie at physical therapy two weeks ago.

He held the door open for her on his way out. "You're Jamie's mother, right? I met you at the rehab center. I'm Eli Marshall."

"Good memory. I'm Sam. Sam Sweeney."

"Your boy's a nice kid. How's he doing?"

"He's hanging in there."

Eli took a step inside and let the door close behind them. "Is there a chance he'll walk again? I'm sorry. I don't mean to pry. It's just—"

"Not at all. I appreciate your interest in my son." Trust did not come easy for Sam, but she sensed this handsome police officer with the pale-gray eyes genuinely cared about Jamie's well-being. "His back has healed, and the doctors are convinced he will walk again, but Jamie seems to think he's stuck in that chair forever."

"If there's anything I can do . . ."

"Thanks, but the only person who can do anything about any of it is Jamie. I only hope he figures it out while he still has choices."

Eli eyed the fliers in her hand. "If you're advertising food, you've come to the right place."

Sam handed him a flier. "My family operates the seafood market on the corner of Main and Creekside. We're promoting our new line of take-out lunches. You'll see from the menu here, we have a variety of items. Sweeney's would be a nice break for you from McDonald's."

"Hey now. I take offense to that." He stroked his tight abs. "If you're insinuating I should be on a diet . . ."

Sam swatted him with her rolled up stack of fliers. "Don't be ridiculous."

He scanned the menu items. "What, no sushi?"

"I've never eaten sushi, if you can believe that."

"Never eaten sushi? That's a crying shame. It's my favorite."

"I'll have to try it sometime." She held her stack of fliers out to him. "Can I give these to you to distribute?"

He pointed at the heavyset officer at the front desk. "Actually, Bud Carter is the take-out expert around here. He'll be sure to spread the word."

"Thank you, Sergeant." She saluted him before heading over to meet Bud Carter.

When all fliers were distributed, Sam stopped by the post office and found their mailbox crammed with bills and junk mail. She dumped the catalogs and advertisements in the trash can, and then stood at the counter in the lobby sorting through the bills. She opened the entire stack, one after another, surprised to find every bill stamped *Past Due*.

A wave of nausea hit Sam's empty stomach like a tsunami.

During the past three years, she'd worked hard juggling their finances in order to save for the renovations. When they began construction back in April, the money they needed was in the bank. As with most construction projects, they'd gone over budget in certain areas, but not enough to strap them for cash.

Faith had surely known about the overdue bills. Why had she never mentioned them?

Sam stuffed the bills in her bag. She was headed toward the parking lot when her calendar alarm chimed, reminding her of Jamie's appointment with Moses. A confrontation with Faith would have to wait.

She noticed Jamie's blinds were still drawn as she rounded the back corner of the house. Panic rose in her chest. Her apprehension had been on heightened alert since the incident with the angry driver in the jacked-up pickup truck. Opening Jamie's bedroom door, she found him sound asleep with his mouth wide open and his body perfectly still. She ran her fingers across his cheek, relieved to feel the warmth of his skin.

She snapped open the blinds, allowing the bright midday sun to flood in. "Get up and get dressed, Jamie. Or you'll be late for your appointment with Moses."

Jamie rolled onto his side, facing the wall. "I'm not going to PT today."

"I don't have time for this today, son. I have a crisis at work I need to deal with."

"Then go deal with your crisis and leave me alone." He pulled the blanket over his head.

Sam whipped the covers back. "Get up out of that bed, brush your teeth, and let's go. You can't cancel on Moses at the last minute. He has a long list of patients waiting for the opportunity to see him."

He glared at her, his dark eyes cold and hard. "What part of *I'm not going* don't you understand?"

Sam lowered herself to the edge of the bed. "Jamie, I know you are going through a rough time." She rubbed his back through the blanket. "But I refuse to allow you to live a dead-end life."

He jerked the blanket off his head. "Dead-end life. That's good, Mom. At least you are finally acknowledging the truth."

"Maybe that was a poor choice of words, but—"

He scooted his body over, nudging her off his bed. "Please. Just go away and leave me alone."

Fresh out of words of encouragement, Sam turned and left the room. She couldn't make him go to physical therapy any more than she could make him walk again. Jamie had always been an easy kid, kind and happy and considerate of others. His behavior now surpassed teenage surliness. It was dangerously volatile, and she had absolutely no control over him.

Alone in her Jeep in the driveway, Sam punched the steering wheel and kicked the dashboard, bawling hysterically. When her well ran dry, she pulled out a packet of tissues and wiped her face before backing out of her driveway.

She could not afford to fall apart. Not when so many people relied on her. Sure, she was overwhelmed having to cope with so many different crises at once, but she was tough. She could handle it. She would deal with her problems one at a time.

She took a left onto Main, then another onto Creekside. She pulled into the parking lot at the market, but she left the engine running while she made out her list on the back of one of the past due notices.

• Call Moses.
• Examine the account books at the market.
• Confront Faith.
• Find a way to get through to Jamie.

Sam punched Moses's number into her cell phone. After apologizing for her son's no-show and offering to pay for the missed session, she said, "Jamie is slipping further and further away from me, Moses, and I can't seem to reach him no matter what I say or do."

"Have you been to see Dr. Baker?" Moses asked.

"No. Jamie refuses to go." Sam felt a lump in her throat. "Moses, I'm scared. After last night . . ."

"What happened last night?"

Sam told him about the incident with the truck driver. "I want to believe that it was an accident, that he simply didn't see the truck coming, but I have this sick feeling in my gut that Jamie had every intention of hurting himself."

Moses sighed. "Listen, Sam, my afternoon is full, but I will call you this evening. If I finish earlier enough, maybe I can stop by and see Jamie on my way home from work."

Sam spent the rest of the afternoon at the market, studying the records in their financial management software on the office computer. When she discovered several checks unaccounted for, she checked their online bank account and found that all the missing checks were made out to Faith, payable in the amount of several hundred dollars each.

It was past seven o'clock by the time she had finished printing the documents she needed as evidence to confront Faith. When she stopped by the house to check on Jamie, she was disturbed to find him still lying in bed.

She snatched the iPod out of his hand and yanked the earbuds from his ears. "I've had a hard day, Jamie, and it's about to get even more difficult. I have to run out to Faith's. I need you to get dinner started. We are having tacos. Please unthaw the hamburger meat and cut up some vegetables. I will be back in an hour, hopefully less." She shoved the iPod in her pocket and left before he had a chance to argue.

Faith's truck was in the driveway, but no one answered the door when she knocked. Sam went around to the back of the house, peeking in windows and banging on doors. She was turning her Jeep around in the driveway when she saw movement in the front window, a pair of brown eyes peering between two slats in the blinds. She jumped out of the car and raced up the front steps.

She banged on the door. "Open the door, Faith. We need to talk."

The door creaked open two inches, and a tiny face, wet with tears, appeared through the crack.

Sam bent down, eye level with her niece. "What's the matter, Bits? Does your mom have another one of her headaches?"

Bitsy shook her head and stuck her thumb in her mouth, something Sam had not seen her do in years.

"Can I come inside?" she asked in a soft voice.

Bitsy opened the door wider and stepped aside to let Sam in.

"Is your mom in bed?"

"Yes," Bitsy mumbled around the thumb.

"Can you take me to her?"

Sam made her way through the darkened room to her sister's bedside. Peering down at her face, she saw that Faith's lip was busted, her eyes were black, and her nose was swollen and crusted with blood.

"Oh my God, Faith. What the hell happened to you?"

Tears pooled in Faith's eyes and trickled down her cheeks. Bitsy climbed in bed and curled up next to her mother.

Sam nodded at Bitsy. "Did he hurt—"

"No." Faith grimaced, bringing her fingers to her busted lip. "At least not this time."

"Where is he, the rotten bastard?" Sam asked with fists clenched. "I'll kill him with my bare hands."

"He's gone." Faith glanced at the alarm clock beside her. "I haven't seen him since he did this to me, late Saturday night."

"Why didn't you call me? Or Mom?"

Faith shrugged.

"Why the hell are you even still here?" Sam felt her patience slipping. "Are you waiting for him to come back and finish the job?"

Faith smoothed her daughter's hair back and kissed her forehead. "There's something I need to tell you, Sam. I did something I'm not proud—"

Sam held a hand up to silence her. "I already know about the money." Gently, so as not to hurt Faith, she sat down on the edge of the bed. "Why didn't you come to me? You know I would've loaned you money if you'd needed it."

"Pride, I guess. We got behind on our payments, and the bank was threatening to kick us out of the trailer. At the time, it seemed simple enough to borrow a little from the market. We paid it back immediately that time, and Curtis and I agreed we'd never do it again, but . . ."

"But what?" Sam ran her finger down her sister's bruised cheek. "It's okay. You can tell me. I won't get mad."

"Curtis got greedy. He started drinking heavily and gambling more than usual and—"

"Now he's out of control and taking his frustration out on you. You're coming home with me." Sam jumped to her feet, but Faith grabbed her wrist and pulled her back down.

"I can't, Sam. That would only put you and Jamie in danger."

"What about your safety, Faith? Have you looked in the mirror? You can't protect your daughter any more than you can protect yourself."

Faith drew her daughter's small body closer to her. "I know, but—"

"No buts." Sam grabbed Bitsy's bare foot and shook it playfully. "How would you like to come and stay with me for a while?"

Bitsy removed her thumb from her mouth and smiled.

Sam held her arms out for Bitsy. "Let's you and I go pack your stuff, then we'll come back and help your mother."

"I can manage my things." Faith struggled to sit up. "But we should probably hurry. Curtis could come home at any minute."

TWENTY

FAITH

Despite the pain in her ribs, Faith managed to drag her beat-up rolling suitcase down from the top shelf of the closet. She stuffed it full of shorts, shirts, underwear, and pajamas. When the bag was bulging, she retrieved a handful of paper grocery bags from the kitchen pantry and filled them with the few valuables she owned—her string of pearls and her antique clock and Bitsy's baby book. She would never come back here. She'd rather live on the streets than in the home she'd shared with a monster.

She removed cash from her wallet and sealed it in an envelope she found in her kitchen drawer. She wrote Curtis's name on the envelope and left it on his pillow, with no other note. Sixty dollars would keep him liquored up for a couple of days, which should give her enough time to come up with a plan. She wouldn't impose on Sam for long. The last thing she wanted was for her family to get caught in the cross fire.

Faith was loading her things in her truck when Sam and Bitsy appeared, their arms laden with Bitsy's bags.

"What're you doing?" Sam said. "You can't drive in your condition."

158

"I need my truck, Sammie. I can't leave it here."

"Then we'll come back and get it later, when you are not in so much pain."

"No way. When Curtis discovers I've left him, he'll destroy my truck just for the fun of it. I can't take that chance. This bucket of rust is all I got that's worth anything."

"You've got Bitsy. And me. And Jamie and Mama."

"And enough junk to fill a few grocery bags." Faith slammed the truck door and went around to the other side.

"You've got your share in Sweeney's," Sam said over the bed of the truck.

"Which I plan on signing over to you as payment for the money I owe you. Unless you'd rather have cash, then I'll gladly sell the truck, or work for free for the next ten years. Whatever it is, Sam, it'll never be enough to show you how sorry I am for what I did." Faith buried her face in her hands and began to sob.

Her sister rushed to her side and took her in her arms. "I'm not worried about the money, Faith. And I don't want you to worry, either. You need to concentrate on getting well and staying safe."

"I embezzled funds, Sam. That's against the law. I could go to jail."

"That's not going to happen. We'll figure out a way to put the money back." Holding her at arm's distance, Sam brushed Faith's hair out of her face. "Our biggest concern right now is getting out of here before Curtis comes home."

"I'm not going anywhere without the truck."

"Fine." Sam lifted Bitsy into her car seat. "But only on three conditions. Follow me, drive slowly, and stay close."

Faith's eyes stayed glued on Sam's bumper as they drove toward the main road. When they turned right, toward town, she breathed her first sigh of relief. And she relaxed a little more with each mile she put between her and the double-wide in the woods. She faced many obstacles ahead of her, but knowing she'd taken the first step gave her confidence. For the first time in years, she felt free.

She stole a glance in the rearview mirror. Faith hated to see Bitsy sucking her thumb, but she was resigned to let the bad habit slide. At least for now. After what she'd been through, her daughter needed comfort wherever she could find it.

"Are you okay, honey?" Faith asked.

Bitsy met her mother's eyes in the rearview mirror. She nodded, then stared out the window, searching perhaps for the single headlight of her father's motorcycle in the oncoming traffic.

If only she'd approached Sam earlier for help, she could've spared Bitsy both the physical pain she'd suffered at her father's hand and the mental anguish she'd experienced from witnessing his cruelty to her mother. Faith hoped her daughter's memories of this time would eventually fade away.

The drive through the center of Prospect was quiet, typical of a Monday night there, but as they approached Sam's street, traffic on either side of Main slowed to a halt. Angry drivers blasted horns and flashed bright lights. Faith rolled her window down and hung her head out, craning her neck to catch a glimpse of the commotion. She saw Sam jump out of her Jeep and signal to the oncoming traffic to stop.

"What's Aunt Sam doing?" Bitsy asked.

"I'm not sure. Maybe there was an accident and she's going to see if anybody needs help."

"Why are all those cars honking their horns?"

"I don't know, honey. I can't see much in the dark." Faith stuck her head a little farther out the window. "It looks like a homeless man in a wheelchair is blocking traffic." Blue lights appeared, illuminating the scene enough for her to see that the homeless man with the scraggly hair and beard was her nephew.

Two policemen got out of the patrol car. The tall bald-headed one directed traffic while the shorter one bent down to speak to Jamie.

Faith's mind raced. What was he doing in the middle of the road in his wheelchair? Was he confused and disoriented? Jamie had never been one to drink too much or do drugs. But he hadn't been himself since the accident.

The policeman wheeled Jamie between the waiting cars as he headed toward Sam's Jeep. Sam appeared in Faith's headlights, her face contorted in devastation.

"Look, Mama, there's Jamie!" Bitsy shouted. "Is that policeman taking him to jail?"

"No, honey. He's helping him get in the car."

"But why?"

"I don't know, sweetheart. Maybe Jamie tried to go too far in his wheelchair and got tired."

Once the wheelchair was stowed away on the back of the Jeep, the policemen spoke briefly to Sam before returning to his patrol car. A single siren sounded, and the cruiser spun out in front of Sam, offering her a lead. Faith followed the small caravan the short distance to her sister's house. The cruiser parked on the curb out front, and Sam pulled in the driveway with Faith behind her.

After helping Jamie back in his wheelchair, the shorter policeman wheeled him down the sidewalk and around the back of the house, with Sam walking alongside and holding her son's hand.

Bitsy struggled to get out of her car seat. "Let's sit here for a minute, honey, and give them a chance to get Jamie settled inside." Faith turned to face her daughter, stroking her bare leg to comfort her.

She ran a mental checklist of her options. She could go to her mom's house. Or to Jackie's. Or she could drive the hell out of town and never look back, although she wouldn't get far considering she'd left all her cash for Curtis. But she knew she couldn't stay here when Sam was already dealing with problems of her own. Jamie needed, and deserved, his mother's undivided attention. Unwanted company in the house would only complicate the situation. She had no idea when, or if, Curtis would ever come home, but when he discovered she wasn't there, he would drive straight to Sam's house looking for her. If he saw the patrol car out front, he would assume Faith had called the police on him. Which, in his current frame of mind, might cause him to go postal.

Faith opened her door. She would go inside to tell her sister she was leaving. She'd have to take Bitsy to her mom's house for the night, but in the morning she'd figure something else out.

Faith helped Bitsy out of the car, and the two entered the house through the kitchen door. They crept through the small dining room and stood in the doorway to the sitting room. The scene in front of her broke Faith's heart. Sam knelt beside Jamie with her arms wrapped around him while he sobbed hysterically. "Why can't you just let me die? Don't you get it? I don't want to live anymore like this."

Sam kissed the top of his head. "We're going to get you help, son," she said in a soft voice. "But I will never, ever give up on you. Do you hear me?"

Faith was backing out of the sitting room, pushing Bitsy toward the kitchen, when Jamie caught sight of them. He stopped sobbing. "Why'd you have to go and drag them into my problems?" he asked his mother.

Faith locked eyes with her sister. "I'm gonna take Bitsy over to Mama's. You've got your hands full without having to worry about us."

"Oh no, you're not. You would scare Mom into an early grave if you showed up at her house like that."

Jamie's eyes narrowed as they zeroed in on her. "What happened to your face?"

All eyes in the room fell on Faith at once.

"Did Curtis—"

Faith held her finger to her lips, and pointed at her daughter.

Seeing Bitsy for the first time, Jamie turned his attention to his cousin. "Are you okay?"

She stuck her thumb in her mouth and cowered behind her mother.

"Aw, Bits. Did I scare you?" He spread his arms for her. "Come here."

She peeked at him from behind her mother's legs.

"Please." He opened his arms even wider.

She crawled onto his lap and snuggled up to his chest. Stroking her hair, Jamie whispered something only Bitsy could hear and got a smile in response.

The short officer approached Faith. "Evening, ma'am. I'm Officer Marshall, and my partner over there is Officer Swanson. But please call me Eli, and he's Brad."

Brad waved at her from across the room.

"Evening," Faith said.

Eli studied her face. "Do you want to tell me how this happened?"

Faith shielded her face with her hand. "It was a silly accident. I wasn't watching where I was going, and I ran smack into the doorjamb."

The officer lifted her chin and turned her head one way then another. "Must have been reinforced with steel. Did you report this doorjamb to the police?"

Faith shook her head.

"Have you seen a doctor?"

"No. But I'm fine, really."

"You don't look fine to me. I'm certainly no doctor, but I'd be willing to bet your nose is broken. Even if you don't want to press charges, you need to document the assault so we have it on file. It puts us one step ahead of the process if something like this happens again."

Sam was suddenly at Faith's side. "He's right, you know. You should let Eli take your report."

"Unfortunately, it's a little more complicated in your sister's case," Eli said to Sam, then turned back to Faith. "We are happy to take your statement, but it won't do much good unless we have a doctor's account of your injuries to substantiate your claim."

Faith turned to her sister. "Really, Sam. I don't want to be any trouble. Why don't I go to Jackie's?"

"I doubt you'll find much sympathy there. Anyway, I agree with Eli. I think your nose is broken. You're going to have to deal with it sooner or later."

Faith saw the deep worry lines in her sister's forehead and decided not to argue with her. "All right, fine. But can't it wait until tomorrow? It's been a long day."

"Honestly, no. I think it's important you get seen tonight." Eli locked eyes with his partner. "Why don't you run her over to the ER while I finish up here with Jamie?"

"What about my daughter?" Faith asked.

Officer Marshall glanced over at Bitsy, who was still curled up in Jamie's lap. "Doesn't look like she's going anywhere, anytime soon."

Faith prepared herself for a long wait in the emergency room but was surprised when a soft-spoken nurse called her name right away.

"One of the rare benefits of having a police escort," Brad said when he recognized her surprise.

Faith appreciated Officer Swanson's efficient manner and corny sense of humor. She tried to imagine him with hair, a sandy crew cut to match his eyebrows.

As they passed through the double doors leading to the examining rooms, Faith spotted Captain Mack, sporting a bandage from elbow to wrist on his left arm and heading in their direction from the opposite end of the hall.

"What happened to your arm?" Faith asked.

"My rookie mate gaffed me. The worst part is, we lost the fish." He noticed her face. "The bigger question is, what the hell happened to you?"

Faith beamed red. "It's a long story."

"Yeah. One that ends with me beating the shit out of that scrawny husband of yours." Mack gently examined her bruises. "Good thing your father isn't alive to see this."

"The police are handling the situation, Uncle Mack," she said, gesturing toward Officer Swanson. "No need for you to get involved."

"This little lady is my goddaughter, Officer. Her father was my closest friend."

"I understand." Swanson tipped his hat to Mack. "We'll take good care of her."

The nurse coughed, reminding them she was waiting.

Mack engulfed Faith in a one-arm bear hug. She buried her face in his chest, inhaling the scent of sweat mixed with fish that reminded her so much of her father.

"You call me if things get out of hand," he whispered. "I know people who can help."

A nervous giggle escaped Faith's lips. Mack would never hurt a fly, but he had a reputation of hanging out with some pretty rough characters.

"Please don't tell Mama. She has enough to worry about already."

Mack furrowed his brows. "You're not still living with him, are you?"

Faith shook her head. "I moved out today. I'm staying with Sam. At least for the moment."

"All right. I'll keep your secret safe this once. But there better not be a next time."

"There won't be. I promise," she said, making a promise she hoped she could keep.

He gave a little bow. "Well then, my lady. I'll be off." He popped his red Inlet View Marina cap back on his head and disappeared down the hallway.

Officer Swanson parked himself at the nurses' station and proceeded to chat up the ladies while Nurse Erica completed the preliminary part of Faith's examination. Faith appreciated the nurse's gentle touch in taking her vitals and her nonjudgmental manner when questioning her and photographing her bruises. It took a special kind of person to be a nurse, a person whose silent presence helped a patient relax.

When Faith returned from X-ray, Swanson was ready with pen and paper to take her statement. While they waited for the doctor to come in, Faith told the officer about Curtis's inability to hold a job and the money problems they'd had because of it. She told him about the unauthorized withdrawals she'd made from Sweeney's. And she told him about the drinking and gambling and abuse.

"I guess you could say you walked into your own trap," Officer Swanson said.

"The first time I borrowed money, I had every intention of paying it back as soon as my husband found a job. But when that didn't happen, he threatened me into taking more. I should have told my sister from the beginning."

"We all make mistakes, Mrs. Evans. It's how we make amends for those mistakes that counts."

Faith smiled, ignoring the pain in her busted lip. "I'm lucky to have a sister like Sam."

"And she's lucky to have you, too. You need to lean on each other right now."

"Faith." Dr. Neilson appeared in the doorway. "I didn't expect to see you again so soon. Especially not in this condition."

She smiled, as much as she could with her lip busted. "I

didn't expect to be here, Doctor. Especially not in this condition." She was flattered he remembered her name. He must see hundreds of patients every week. She could only imagine what he thought of her, a helpless battered wife.

He sat down on the edge of the bed with his back to the others. "Don't worry. We'll get you all fixed up, good as new." As he listened to her heart and lungs with his stethoscope, he asked, "How's your sweet mother? She hasn't had any more spells, has she?"

"She's fine. Better than me, or so it seems."

He pressed gently on her rib cage, then flashed a penlight up her nose. "Your nose is broken, but it appears to be minor."

"Does that mean it will heal on its own?"

"In time. Protect it as much as you can for the next couple of weeks. Icing will help the swelling go down. You also have two broken ribs. Both on your right side. Unfortunately, there's not much I can do about them, either. Take ibuprofen or acetaminophen as needed for the pain. And no bending or heavy lifting for at least a week. Will that be a problem for you in your workplace?"

Faith wasn't sure she even still had a job. "No, I have a desk job managing the books for my family's seafood market."

Neilson cocked an eyebrow. "Sweeney's?"

"That's the one, the only seafood market in Prospect."

"I'm a big fan. Although I'm embarrassed to say I haven't been in since you reopened."

"You should stop by sometime. We introduced a whole new line of products you might like."

Dr. Neilson stood. "I'll do that. It'll give me a chance to check up on you and your mother." He fished a business card out of the top pocket of his scrubs and scratched a number on the back. He handed the card to Faith. "My office number is on the front and my cell is on the back. If you need anything at all, do not hesitate to call."

Faith took the card from him. "Thank you, Dr. Neilson."

He leaned down close to her ear. "I thought we agreed you'd call me Mike."

"Okay, Mike," she said softly.

He touched her hand. "A man who loves his wife does not break her nose and fracture two of her ribs," he said in a voice meant only for her. "And I can promise you, if he's beaten you once, he'll do it again. I hope the presence of your police escort over there"—Mike aimed his thumb at Officer Swanson —"means you have left your husband."

"Yes. I'm staying with my sister for the time being."

"Do you have children?"

"Yes, I have a six-year-old daughter."

"Which complicates the situation. For both your sakes, file a police report and get a restraining order. Whatever you do, don't let him come within five miles of you."

Faith's eyes welled. "I understand."

"I'm serious, Faith. You wouldn't believe the number of women who refuse to take my advice. I see them in here time and again, battered and bruised worse than you. Yet the majority of them refuse to leave their husbands."

"Why is that?"

"Lack of money or family support, oftentimes both. Many women feel their only choice is to stay in an abusive relationship. But there are always other choices. If things don't work out at your sister's house, I would be happy to help you find a shelter."

TWENTY-ONE

SAMANTHA

Sam finally got through to Moses on her fifth call. When he pulled up in front of her house five minutes later, she was waiting for him on her porch. She quickly filled him in on the events of the evening.

"I can't handle this, Moses." Sam paced up and down the porch. "My son has given up on his life. He wants to die."

"Come here." Moses pulled her to him and wrapped his big arms around her, whispering words of comfort and rubbing her back until she calmed down.

"Tell me what to do." She pushed away from him, drying her tears with her shirttail. "Obviously I can't keep him safe here."

"Where is Jamie now?" Moses asked.

Sam reached for the doorknob. "Inside, talking to a police officer."

Sam and Moses stood to the side, listening to Jamie answer Eli's questions.

"Who's the little girl?" Moses gestured toward Bitsy, who was fast asleep on Jamie's lap.

"My niece, Bitsy. I rescued her mother, my younger sister, Faith, from her abusive husband this afternoon."

Moses stared at Sam in disbelief. "As if you need any more drama in your life. Where is Faith now?"

"At the hospital, getting a doctor's report of her injuries."

"Are they staying here with you?"

"I couldn't very well turn them away, considering their circumstances."

"Of course not." Moses pursed his lips and rubbed his chin in thought. "In fact, having them here might work to your advantage."

"How so?"

"I can tell by the way he's holding her, Jamie seems very protective over his little cousin."

"He is. His whole demeanor changed tonight when he saw my sister's battered face."

"Focusing on someone else's problems might be what Jamie needs to get his mind off his own."

The idea made sense to Sam. "I hadn't thought about it like that, but you might be right."

"We need to decide how to proceed," Moses said. "I can have Dr. Baker admit him to the hospital tonight."

"To the psych ward?"

"Unfortunately, yes. That's where they will put him on suicide watch."

The alternative was to conduct her own suicide watch. While the idea scared the hell out of her, having her son admitted to the psych ward was even less appealing.

"Do I have another option?"

"He needs to be in therapy, Sam, if not with Dr. Baker then with someone else."

"I've tried, Moses. Jamie flat-out refuses to see anyone."

"And look where that's gotten him. He's too tired tonight to listen, but if you're comfortable waiting until the morning, I can be here first thing. Jamie and I are close enough that I can talk to him straight, about what happened tonight and about getting some help. But I warn you, Sam, if I have any concerns for his safety, I will have no choice but to find someone to commit him."

꒰꒱

Sam showed the officers to the door, then locked the dead bolt and pocketed the key. "God, I need a drink. Care to join me?" she asked Faith.

"Sure, but let me check on Bitsy first. Where is she?"

"Asleep. In the guest room with Jamie. The two of them conked out while he was reading her a bedtime story, and I didn't have the heart to separate them."

Sam was waiting in the den with a bottle of Chardonnay and a plate of cheese and crackers when her sister returned.

Faith gripped the arm of the sofa as she lowered herself to sit.

Sam uncorked the bottle and poured two healthy glasses of wine. "You shouldn't drink this if you're on pain meds."

"The doctor only prescribed Tylenol and Advil." Faith accepted a glass of wine from Sam.

Sam clinked her sister's glass. "Let's hope this wine kills all our pain tonight."

Faith picked at a loose thread on her jean shorts. "Why didn't you tell me things had gotten so bad with Jamie?"

"For the same reason you never told me about Curtis."

"I guess I deserve that." Faith took a small sip of wine, followed by a bigger one. She grimaced in pain as she rearranged herself into a more comfortable sitting position.

"Moses, Jamie's physical therapist, stopped by while you were at the hospital. He's coming back first thing in the morning to talk to Jamie. We might have to hospitalize him, Faith, if we can't get through to him."

"For his own safety. I get that."

"I'm scared to death he'll try to hurt himself again on my

watch. I thought I was doing an okay job of protecting him, but I screwed up big time."

"You're a great mom, Sam. And everybody knows it, especially Jamie. Even if you can't give him the kind of help he needs, you're smart enough to find it for him. It sounds to me like you trust this Moses person?"

"I do, and so does Jamie."

"Then let Moses guide you."

Sam set her wine glass on the coffee table and rubbed her bloodshot eyes with her balled fists. "Suicide is major, Faith. How did I miss the signs?"

"Because you were too busy worrying about the rest of your family—namely, your pitiful, helpless little sister. I think Bitsy and I should stay with Jackie for a while. The last thing you need is a madman threatening your family. I'd never forgive myself if Curtis hurt you or Jamie in any way."

Sam picked her glass up and sipped on her wine as she contemplated how much she should tell Faith about their sister's situation. On the one hand, she respected Jackie's privacy, but on the other, Faith was as loyal as a lapdog. Knowing she wasn't the only one with problems in her marriage might give Faith the strength she needed to stand up to Curtis. What were families for, if not confiding in one another and offering support in times of need?

"Trust me, you don't want to go to Jackie's. She's dealing with her own marital crisis du jour."

Faith's face changed from shock to bewilderment to disappointment as she processed this information. "Why am I always the last one to know everything?" she asked, her lip trembling.

"Oh, honey. It's not like that at all." Sam rubbed her sister's arm. "Jackie hasn't confided in me. She doesn't even know that I know."

"Then how—"

"Bill and I had a little run-in, one that didn't place him in the most favorable light."

Faith looked at Sam over the rim of her wine glass. "Did you catch him in the act?"

"Yep. Pretty much." She gave Faith the abbreviated version of her encounter with Bill outside his mistress's house. "Last I heard from him, he was planning to ask her for a divorce."

"I don't get it. Bill doesn't seem like the type to cheat on his wife."

"I know, right? I was so angry with him at the time, but once I thought about it, I realized how out of character it is for him. I guess you never really know about a person."

An awkward silence filled the room, and Sam wished she could take back her words. Nothing Curtis ever did surprised Sam. He'd been a rotten egg from the beginning, and everyone in her family knew it. Everyone except Faith.

"Why wouldn't Jackie talk to us about her problems, Sam?"

"Same reason you didn't talk to us."

"Ouch. That hurts."

"I'm sorry. That was uncalled for."

"Maybe Jackie is afraid to leave him."

Sam nearly choked on her wine. "Jackie's the most fearless woman I know. If anything, she's in denial, too proud to admit her life is less than perfect."

"I think you're wrong about them," Faith said, a determined look on her face. "They love each other too much to let an affair ruin their marriage. My guess is, they'll work things out."

Sam threw a wadded-up cocktail napkin at her sister. "You are a hopeless romantic."

Faith grabbed the napkin and tossed it on the coffee table. "What have you told Mom about my situation?"

"Nothing. It's up to you to decide how much you tell her about Curtis, but as far as I'm concerned, the situation with the money stays between us." Sam reached for the bottle of wine and poured herself another glass. "I don't think you want Mom to see you looking like that, any more than I want her to know what happened with Jamie tonight. I'm not trying to keep anything from her. I just don't want to overwhelm her with too much at once."

"But we'll have to tell her something to explain my absence from work." Faith stared into her empty glass, unwilling to meet her sister's eyes. "That is, if I still have a job."

"Don't be ridiculous. Of course you still have a job. You made a mistake. It's not the end of the world." Sam poured Faith another glass of wine. "In any case, you know I'm helpless when it comes to accounting."

"Sammie, about the money—"

Sam held her hand up. "Don't worry about the money."

"But with business so slow . . ."

"We'll figure something out. You and I both have more important things to worry about right now."

TWENTY-TWO

FAITH

Faith woke before sunrise the following morning. She allowed herself a few extra minutes in bed to enjoy the coziness of the soft comforter and the warmth of her daughter's small body lying next to her. For the first time in a long time, she felt safe.

Last night, she'd begged Sam to let her sleep on the couch so as not to disturb Jamie from his peaceful sleep in the guest-bedroom bed, but Sam had refused, insisting that Faith's body needed rest in order to heal. Sam wanted Jamie in his own room so she could watch over him during the night, and Faith would've done the same thing in her sister's shoes.

She owed Sam a debt of gratitude she'd never be able to repay. Not just for rescuing her from Curtis. Any sister would move heaven and earth to get her sibling away from an abusive spouse. But Sam had chosen to forgive her for the money she'd stolen from the market.

Faith glanced at the digital clock on the table beside the bed. Six thirty. Moses was coming over to talk to Jamie at eight thirty, which left her a small but workable window of opportunity.

Officer Swanson had given her detailed instructions on where to find the forms and how to file them.

Time for Faith to take control of her life.

Despite her sore muscles and aching ribs, Faith forced herself to get out of bed. She slipped a sundress over her head and tiptoed down the hall to the desktop computer in the sitting room. She downloaded and printed the forms. Thirty minutes later, when she had finished filling out all the information, she returned to the guest bedroom for her bag.

She nudged Bitsy. "Mama's gonna run out for a while. I won't be long."

Bitsy nodded, but she didn't open her eyes.

"Aunt Sam's here if you need her. You sleep as long as you like."

Her daughter responded by burying herself deeper under the covers.

Faith snuck out the front door and around the back of the house to her truck. She stroked the dashboard like a beloved pet as she turned the key in the ignition. "Don't you quit on me now, Rusty, ole girl." The engine fired on the first try, and Faith hit the highway, fighting to keep her eyes open as she drove the forty-five minutes to Charleston. She located the courthouse, filed her forms with the family-court clerk, and was headed back home in less than thirty minutes.

When she entered the kitchen, she heard hushed voices coming from the sitting room—her nephew's, her sister's, and a deep, pleasant voice she assumed belonged to Moses. She brewed herself a cup of coffee and went about making breakfast.

Faith was piling pancakes onto a serving platter when Sam strolled in.

"How'd it go?" Faith asked.

"Okay, I guess. I will continue to hope for a miracle, but after last night, I'm grateful for baby steps." She dropped to the bar stool. "For the first time in a long time, Jamie opened up. Not much, but enough to consider it a start."

Faith brewed her sister a cup of coffee. "Are they going to hospitalize him?"

"Not yet. Jamie convinced Moses to give him more time." Sam blew on her coffee, then took a tentative sip. "Don't get me wrong. I firmly believe that putting my son back in the hospital would be the worst thing for him, but as long as he's under my roof, the burden of keeping him safe falls on me."

"Where is Jamie now?"

"In the shower." Sam clasped her hands together and lifted her eyes to the sky. "Which is an answer to one of my prayers in itself."

Faith pulled a bar stool close to her sister. "I'm here, Sammie. You can share the burden with me."

Sam let out a deep sigh of relief. "I know. Just having you here helps. And thank you for making breakfast. You didn't have to go to so much trouble."

Faith had set four places at the island with plates, napkins, silverware, and orange juice, then set a platter mounded with pancakes, sausage, and strawberries in the center.

Sam grabbed a fork and speared a sausage link. "Why are you up so early? After yesterday, I expected you to sleep in."

"I'll have you know, I've already been to Charleston and back," Faith said, a smirk playing along her lips.

Sam stopped, the sausage link poised in front of her lips. "I thought we agreed you wouldn't go out alone."

"I went to the courthouse to file for an order of protection." When a confused look crossed Sam's face, she added, "You know, a restraining order."

Sam set the sausage down on her plate and offered her sister a fist bump. "I'm proud of you for taking control." She pointed her finger at Faith. "But don't even think about leaving this house unchaperoned again."

"Where do you expect me to find a chaperone?"

"I'll chaperone you, Aunt Faith." Jamie wheeled up beside his mother. "That's about the only job I can manage in this chair."

Sam's jaw dropped. "You shaved." She ran her hand down her son's smooth cheek.

He batted his mother's hand away. "It was starting to itch."

"You look handsome, Jamie," Faith said. "More like your old self." She pushed the platter of food toward her nephew, and he filled his plate with pancakes.

Sam's eyes met Faith's. "Baby steps," Sam mouthed.

"Where's Bits?" Jamie asked. "Isn't she going to eat?"

"I assume she's still asleep." Faith glanced at her watch. "But it's almost ten o'clock. I'll go wake her up."

Panic gripped Faith's chest when she discovered the bed in the guest room empty. She searched in the closet and in the corner behind the rocking chair. When she lifted the bed skirt, a pair of green eyes stared back at her. She reached in and dragged her daughter out from beneath the bed. She wrapped her arms around Bitsy's trembling body and rocked her back and forth while the child wept. "Hush now, baby. You need to calm down and tell me what's wrong so I can make it all better."

"I heard a man's voice, and I thought it was Daddy."

"No, sweetheart. That was Jamie's friend Moses. He came by earlier to see him."

"But you left me here all alone."

"No, honey." Faith kissed her daughter's sweaty head. "I would never leave you alone. Aunt Sam and Jamie were here with you the whole time."

Bitsy stared up at her mother, her long lashes heavy with tears. "But where'd you go?"

"I had a very important errand to run. I filed some papers so the police can make Daddy stop hurting us."

"Really?" Lip quivering, Bitsy inhaled an unsteady breath. "Do you think it will work?"

"I hope so, but for the time being, I'm going to stick to you like a piece of chewing gum on the bottom of your shoe."

Bitsy giggled.

"Let's go get some pancakes." Ignoring the pain in her ribs, Faith swept Bitsy up and carried her to the kitchen.

Jamie noticed his cousin's tears right away. "What's wrong, Bits?"

"I heard a man's voice, and I thought it was Daddy coming to take me away," she said, clinging tighter to her mother's waist.

"We're not gonna let that happen." He pointed to the empty seat beside him. "Come here, and sit down next to me."

Faith set her daughter on the bar stool while Jamie lifted two pancakes onto Bitsy's plate. He cut one of the pancakes in half and arranged the two pieces on top of the whole one in the shape of a Mickey Mouse face.

"I have to go to the potty before I eat." Bitsy hopped down and scurried off.

Jamie wheeled off after her, returning less than a minute later with a metal lockbox on his lap. He reached for his mother's keys on the hook by the back door. One by one, he flipped through all of the keys on the ring.

"Where is it?" he asked his mother.

"I'm not telling you." She held her hand out to him. "Give me the box."

He placed his arm protectively over the box. "No."

"So what's in the box?" Faith asked.

"My gun." He darted a glance at Faith, then stared back at his mother. "Give me the key, Mom. It's my gun."

"It's the pistol Daddy gave him," Sam explained to Faith. "Under the circumstances, I'm not comfortable with it being in his possession."

No mother in her right mind would put a gun in the hands of a suicidal teenager, Faith thought.

She placed a hand on her nephew's shoulder. "I agree with

your mother, Jamie. Seeing that gun might frighten Bitsy more than she already is."

"But what if Curtis shows up? Somebody has to protect you," he said to Faith.

Faith leaned down next to Jamie's chair. "I appreciate your concern, Jamie. Really I do. But I have think about Bitsy. And I think it's in her best interest for me to let the police handle the situation."

"But . . ." Jamie started, and then backed down.

"We have to trust Faith to handle her crisis in her own way, son. There's plenty we can do to help that doesn't involve using a gun." Sam held her hand out for the box. "I'll put it back in its safe place. For now."

Faith drove Jamie to his two o'clock appointment with Moses. They were pulling in the driveway on the way home, when Bitsy asked, "Jamie, will you teach me how to play Xbox?"

He turned around to face her in the backseat. "I'm not sure I have any games you can play."

Bitsy pouted her lower lip. "Please."

"Oh no. Not the lower-lip treatment."

She stuck her lip out even farther.

"You can suck the lip back in." He poked at her lip with his finger, making it flap up and down. "I'm sure we can find something you can play. Maybe *Angry Birds*."

Once the kids were settled in front of the television, Faith went out back to her sister's garage, a freestanding wooden building at the end of the driveway. She wiped the dirt off the window and peeked inside. The garage was a complete mess, packed with tools and recreational items in all shapes and sizes. With a little organizing, there might be just enough room for her truck.

Ignoring the pain in her head and her ribs, Faith carefully lifted the heavy garage door. She started by pushing out the big items—things with wheels like the lawnmower and wheelbarrow and Jamie's bicycle—and lining them up in the driveway, making enough room to move around inside. She stored the duck decoys, hunting gear, and gardening supplies on the shelves along the sidewalls. She filled a large plastic tub with baseball bats, lacrosse sticks, and fishing rods, then a smaller one with balls of every type. She was organizing the gardening tools on the workbench in the back of the shed when Jamie and Bitsy came out to check on her.

"What're you doing, Mama?" Bitsy asked.

Faith brushed a lock of hair out of Bitsy's face and tucked it behind her ear. "I wanted to do something nice for Aunt Sam for letting us stay with her, so I decided to clean out her garage."

"Can I help?"

Faith surveyed the now semiorderly mess. "I'm not quite ready, but in a little while, you can help me push all the big stuff back inside the garage."

"Okay. Just let me know when you're ready." Bitsy grabbed a hula hoop from the corner and took it out into the yard.

Jamie wheeled up beside Faith. "I'm not sure it's a good idea for you to be out here alone."

"I'm not alone anymore, now that you're here."

"You know what I mean, Aunt Faith. With Curtis on the loose and all."

Faith watched her daughter, barefoot in the grass, having fun as she struggled to make the hula hoop stay on her hips. "If I let Curtis control my life, wouldn't that be just as bad as letting him beat me?"

Jamie spun his chair around in a circle as he inspected the clean garage. "Funny, there's just enough room in here for your truck."

"Busted." Faith popped her hands up. "So maybe I am letting Curtis control my life a little bit."

"If that bastard tries to come on my property, he won't live to see the next sunrise." Jamie beat his palm with his fist.

Faith had witnessed Jamie's off-and-on anger all day. He'd spent the morning watching a *SpongeBob* marathon with Bitsy, laughing as if he were six years old again and it was his favorite show. But then he got frustrated when they couldn't get his wheelchair in the truck, and annoyed when Faith refused to drop him off at therapy and come back for him later. She understood how his feelings might be confused after everything he'd been through. She only hoped the compassionate, less volatile side of Jamie held true in the end.

"Curtis is a very dangerous man, Jamie. You've seen what he did to my face. I'd never forgive myself if something happened to you because of me, especially if you were protecting me. Promise me you won't try to be a hero."

"Don't worry. I can take care of myself." He rolled over to the bucket of balls, picked out a basketball, and shot it at the hoop over the garage door. The ball bounced off the rim, hit the backboard, and fell through the net.

Faith caught the rebound and tossed it back to Jamie. "I'm impressed. You still have all your upper body strength. Rumor has it, you might walk again."

He shot the ball and made it a second time. "My mom's the one who started the rumor. And here she comes." He motioned toward his mother's Jeep turning in the driveway. "Please don't get her started on that."

Sam hopped out of the Jeep and grabbed a rectangular cardboard box from the backseat. "What's all this? Isn't it a little late for spring cleaning?"

"It's a surprise for you with an ulterior motive for me," Faith said.

"Whatever your motive is, it's fine by me. I haven't seen the floor of this garage in years."

"What's in the box?" Faith asked.

Sam set the box in Jamie's lap. "Burgers and steaks and ribs. A meat distributor came by today offering samples. What do y'all think about adding a butcher at Sweeney's?"

"That's the dumbest idea I've ever heard." Jamie handed the box back to his mom and wheeled off.

"What's so dumb about it?" she called after him.

"Because having meat would take the attention away from the seafood," he responded as he maneuvered his way into the house.

Sam turned to Faith. "What do you think?"

Faith had no opinion one way or another about adding a butcher. She was simply relieved to know she still had a voice in the decisions. "Well, I think the idea is interesting. And we certainly have the space to add a butcher counter. But I can also see what Jamie is saying. We don't want to diversify too much, or we'll lose our main focus."

"True. And we've already added the wine section and the prepared foods." Sam set the box down in the wheelbarrow. "I guess we need to start turning a profit before we make any more changes."

"But that doesn't mean we can't sample the goods." Faith opened the lid on the box and rummaged through the contents. She held up a large rack of baby back ribs.

Bitsy rolled her hula hoop over to them. "Are we having ribs for dinner?"

"Not unless we cook them in the oven." Sam pointed at the dark clouds moving in from the west. "Looks like a storm's coming." As if on cue, a bolt of lightning was followed by a not-so-distant rumble of thunder.

Faith moved her truck into the garage, and then the three of them parked everything else around it.

"I think we better get inside." Sam lowered the garage door and sprinted across the grass to the back door as the first sprinkles began to fall.

The thunderstorm passed quickly, but the rain set in for the night. At Sam's suggestion, they built a fire in the fireplace and cooked hotdogs and marshmallows on coat hangers. Jamie helped Bitsy build a blanket tent under the dining room table, and the four of them crawled inside to eat campsite-style.

Faith appreciated her sister's efforts. Sam claimed it was for Bitsy's sake, but her impromptu campout lightened everyone's mood. Faith recognized the faraway look in Sam's eyes as a sign of exhaustion. She had no doubt Sam would spend another night on the floor beside her son's bed, holding vigil. Devoted mother and sister and daughter, Sam had always been all things to everyone in their family. But they had never all been in crisis at the same time. And Faith could tell their situation was taking its toll on her sister. Try as she might, Sam would never find answers to any of their problems in a bottle of wine.

TWENTY-THREE

JACQUELINE

Anxious to begin the process that would end her marriage, Jackie arrived thirty minutes early for her first appointment with her attorney. She'd spoken to Barbara Rutledge several times on the phone, but this would be their first face-to-face meeting.

With a sunshine-yellow facade and electric-blue front door, the office building for the law practice of Browning, Rutledge, and Rankin was the biggest and brightest of all the townhouses on Rainbow Row. The receptionist, a young woman dressed in a black pencil skirt and white starched blouse, greeted Jackie from behind a tiny desk in the foyer and ushered her to the adjoining waiting room. Jackie refused her offer of coffee and made herself at home on the leather sofa with the current issue of *Garden & Gun* magazine. Aside from the constant ringing of the telephone, the office was quiet. The waiting room was handsomely appointed in a masculine way with rich coffee-colored walls and oriental rugs. After twenty minutes and three back issues of *Garden & Gun*, she heard voices coming down the stairs. A handsome couple appeared in the foyer—Barbara Rutledge, whom

Jackie recognized right away from her photographs in the newspaper, and a man who was undoubtedly a client.

Jackie judged the client to be in his mid to late fifties and newly divorced, as evidenced by the absence of a wedding ring and his presence in a divorce attorney's office. With dark hair graying at the temple . . .

Jackie caught herself. What was she thinking? She'd vowed never to fall for a good-looking man again, regardless of how nicely his taut body filled out his impeccably tailored suit.

Barbara Rutledge opened the front door for her client and followed him outside.

Jackie thumbed through the rest of the magazine. She was beginning to wonder if her attorney had forgotten about their appointment and taken the handsome man out for a late lunch, when Barbara suddenly reappeared.

"I'm Barbara Rutledge." She extended her hand to her new client. "It's nice to finally meet you in person."

"Believe me, Ms. Rutledge, the pleasure is all mine."

"Please. Let's dispense with the formalities. I'm Barbara, known to my clients as Barbara the Barracuda, which is a nickname I'm proud of and work hard to maintain. Shall I call you Jackie?"

"Or Jacqueline. Anything but Jack."

Barbara smiled. "Because that's what your husband calls you."

"How very perceptive of you."

"Shall we go upstairs to my office?" Barbara motioned toward the stairwell.

Jackie gathered her things and followed Barbara's shapely figure up the steep flight of stairs. Wearing a summer khaki pantsuit, pale-blue silk blouse, and nude Manolo Blahnik pumps, Barbara set a striking example of a classic Southern professional woman.

The attorney's office was a more feminine version of the waiting room downstairs with soft cream walls and Oushak rugs in neutral shades. Her Queen Anne mahogany desk sat in front of a bank of windows that overlooked East Bay Street below. Bookcases covered one wall, while a pair of large contemporary paintings offered splashes of color on another.

With legal pad in hand, Barbara joined Jackie on the sofa. "This first meeting is mostly about you and me getting to know one another. I typically start by asking my clients about their expectations—the obvious being, what do you hope to get out of your divorce?"

"Full custody of my sons and every penny I can possibly extract out of my husband."

A smile appeared across Barbara's rosy-pink lips. "Then you've come to the right place." She consulted her legal pad. "You mentioned on the phone that your husband has been having an affair. Is there any evidence of that?"

"Plenty. The happy couple is certainly not trying to hide anything. We've been separated for less than two weeks, and they're already living together. He's strutting his new trophy around town. He even had the nerve to show up at a benefit with her on his arm the other night."

"Did anyone take pictures at the event that we might use as evidence?"

"My husband's mistress or girlfriend—or whatever you want to call her—has plenty of pictures plastered all over her Facebook page. And not just from the event. There are photographs of them taken at restaurants and parties. There's even a selfie of them lying on the beach together with that woman wearing the most inappropriate little pink bikini."

Barbara arched her perfectly shaped eyebrow. "Really?"

"See for yourself." Jackie pointed at Barbara's computer. "Her name is Daisy Calhoun."

"I'll check that out later." Barbara scribbled a few notes on her legal pad. "Tell me about your boys." She settled back on the sofa and crossed her legs. "How are they handling the separation?"

"We haven't told them yet. They're away at camp."

Barbara looked up from her note taking, an expression of surprise on her face. "I've been through a divorce myself, Jackie. As a parent, I strongly suggest you tell them about the separation as soon as possible. The last thing you want is for them to hear about the breakup from their friends. And considering the many means of communication available these days . . . . You just told me yourself that their father's picture is all over his mistress's Facebook page."

"They are not allowed to have their cell phones at camp."

"The twins are what . . ."—Barbara consulted her legal pad —"sixteen. They're junior counselors then?"

"That's correct."

"Which means they are privy to more than the campers. If they get their hands on a computer . . ."

"I hadn't thought of that."

"Hot news like this spreads as fast as the speed of the Internet. Kids these days know everything, almost before stuff even happens."

Jackie knew Barbara was right. But she couldn't think of a delicate way to break this kind of news to her boys, aside from making the seven-hour drive to camp. Writing a letter seemed too impersonal and would deprive her of the chance to answer their questions, console, and reassure them.

For the next forty-five minutes, Jackie answered detailed questions about her lifestyle—about their home and monthly expenses and how much they'd saved for the twins' college tuition; about the size of Bill's practice and Jackie's career as a decorator, or lack thereof, since she'd recently resigned. When Barbara asked which parent the twins turned to for advice, Jackie answered truthfully—their father. After they'd discussed Jackie's immediate family at length, Barbara moved on to questions about her extended family, searching for skeletons in the closet. By the time Jackie left the attorney's office a few minutes before two, her emotional tank was empty. Lacking the energy to drive home, she grabbed a ham and swiss on rye from a nearby deli and drove down to Battery Park.

She made her way to the same park bench under the sprawling oak tree. As she took the first bite of her sandwich, her attention gravitated to the scene unfolding at the stately gray home across the street. Pink helium balloons were tied off on the iron stair railings, decorations for what Jackie assumed was Lilly's birthday party. Dressed in ballet attire—pink leotards, white tights, black slippers—a group of about twenty little girls chased one another around the porch. Lilly ran behind them, desperately shouting to get their attention. When the girls continued to ignore her, she burst into tears and ran inside, returning a minute later with her mother in tow.

"I'm not sure what to do," Jackie heard the mother say to her daughter. "Irina is not answering her cell phone. She either forgot about the party or she got tied up in traffic."

"But, Mommy, how are we supposed to have a ballet party without Irina? Can you teach us?"

Lilly's mother patted her daughter's head. "No, honey. You know I have two left feet. Your friends will have to settle for Musical Chairs."

Lilly stomped her slipper-clad foot. "No!"

Jackie stuffed the second half of her sandwich in her bag and wandered across the street. "Excuse me," she called out to Lilly and her mother. "I don't mean to pry, but I was eating my lunch on the park bench across the street, and I couldn't help but over-hear. I'm certainly not a dance instructor, but I know a few moves I could share with the girls."

Mother and daughter exchanged a look of concern about the strange lady intruding on their party.

"I'm Jacqueline Hart." She continued up the sidewalk. "I live in Prospect, but I had a meeting in town and was just enjoying a little picnic before heading back home."

"Kate Morgan." The mom extended her hand. "And this is my daughter, Lilly."

Lilly tugged at Jackie's hand. "Oh, please. Can you help us?"

"I don't know . . ." Kate hesitated. "You certainly don't look like a pedophile, but you can't be too careful these days."

"You'd be doing me a favor, actually. I have twin sixteen-year-old boys. I've always wanted to know what it was like to have a birthday party for little girls."

One of the little girls slipped and fell and started to cry. "Well . . . since I am obviously desperate, I would be grateful," Kate said. "At least for a few minutes while I tend to the wounded and try one more time to get the dance instructor on the phone."

"Okay then." Jackie took a deep breath. "Here goes." She approached the group, capturing their attention with three loud claps, a technique she'd learned from raising boys. "Girls, are you ready to dance your hearts out?"

The girls spun around in circles and bounced on their toes in response.

Jackie spotted a Wi-Fi speaker on a table in the corner of the porch. "Lilly, can you hook us up with some music?"

Lilly picked up her iPod from the table and thumbed through her playlist. "Hip-hop, country, or pop?"

"Hmm. How about something that will motivate us to be creative?"

"I know." Lilly danced a little two-step. "How about *The Lion King*?"

"*The Lion King* is perfect. Why don't we go down to the garden. Can you bring your speaker with you?"

The girls lined up behind Jackie in single file and followed her down the steps and around the side of the house. The garden extended the depth of the house. Aside from a small flower bed that bordered the perimeter, the rest of the garden was grass, plenty of room for the girls to express themselves.

"I want everyone to gather around me in a circle and close your eyes." When all eyes were closed, Jackie said, "Now I want you to picture an animal, a leopard or a lion perhaps, roaming the plains in Africa. Lilly is going to turn on the music, and when I tell you to open your eyes, I want you to pretend to be that animal."

One little girl raised her hand, her eyes shut tight.

"Yes, sweetheart. Do you have a question?"

"This sounds like fun and all, but it's not exactly dancing."

"That all depends on your interpretation of the animal's movements. Do you know what I mean?"

Eyes still closed, the little girl shook her head.

"Well . . . you can imagine that you're a cheetah and run as fast as you can with long strides, or you can pretend to be a graceful gazelle leaping and bounding across the open plains. Does that make sense?"

The child's face lit up. "Yes."

"Okay, music please, Lilly."

Lilly turned on the music, and the girls bounded across the grass in all directions. After a few minutes, they gathered together and followed one another around the yard, laughing and singing as they leaped. Every now and then, Jackie shouted the name of a different animal, and they adjusted their moves accordingly. Giraffes gave them some difficulty, but they had the most fun imitating elephants and monkeys.

Twenty minutes later, the girls were taking a break, when Kate came down to the garden. "It's official. Irina is MIA," she said under her breath to Jackie. "And this isn't the first time she's pulled such a stunt."

"Do all these girls take ballet from her?"

"Yes. She's the dance instructor at Finley Hall. My husband is on their board of directors. He won't be very happy when he hears about this."

"I don't imagine he will."

"I can't thank you enough for helping out, Jackie. You were really good with them."

"This was fun for me. Definitely a change of pace from my boys."

"I have a son myself. No doubt boys march to a different beat."

Jackie snickered. "Yes they do. My boys like to hunt and fish and play football. Most days, I feel like an alien in my own house. You are lucky to have a daughter on your team."

Lilly appeared, once again tugging on Jackie's hand. "Will you teach us something else? Please, Miss Jackie."

She glanced at Kate, who nodded her consent. Jackie leaned down and whispered in Lilly's ear. "What about a little line dancing?"

Lilly's eyes grew wide. "Is that okay, Mommy?"

Kate spread her arms wide. "It's your birthday."

Lilly frowned. "But I don't have any country music."

"Do you have any Taylor Swift?" Jackie asked.

Lilly bobbed her head with enthusiasm.

Jackie clapped her hands. "Then what are we waiting for?" She shepherded the girls back up to the porch and divided them into three lines. For the next thirty minutes, they stepped and shuffled and strutted until they were covered in sweat and ready for cake.

"I'm pretty sure Finley Hall will be looking for a new dance instructor. Is there any chance you might be interested?" Kate asked Jackie as they were cutting the last slice of cake.

"Me?" Jackie asked, licking the icing from her fingers. "I'm flattered, but dancing has never been anything more to me than a hobby. Anyway, I'm too old to be a dance instructor."

"You underestimate yourself. I watched you line dance. You're agile and light on your feet, and you're not sweating nearly as much as the girls."

Jackie laughed out loud. "You just can't see the perspiration stains on this white blouse."

"Well, you definitely have a special way with the girls." Kate handed Jackie a slice of cake. "I'm probably premature in saying anything, but if you give me your number, I'll certainly give you a call if something opens up."

Kate removed her cell phone from her back pocket and entered the numbers as Jackie called them out to her.

Jackie finished her cake, said goodbye to the girls, and set off in the opposite direction of her car, not quite ready to face her empty house. She wandered aimlessly, thinking about the interesting twist the day had brought. She'd forgotten how much she enjoyed losing herself in dance, in letting the music invade her mind and control her body. She'd forgotten about a lot of things that were once important to her. She'd connected with those little girls in a way she'd never connected with the twins' friends. What did she know about baiting a hook or football penalties? Bill had always been the one to take them on Boy Scout hikes and overnight hunting trips. She'd answered Barbara Rutledge's question honestly—the boys had always turned to their father first for everything, not just for advice. Sure, she'd been meticulous in planning their extracurricular activities. Because, the busier they were, the more free time she had for work. And all for what? She had nothing to show for the sixteen years she'd spent with Motte Interiors. No client base. No portfolio of magazine articles showcasing her talents. No reference, since she and Mimi had parted on such shaky terms. She'd have to find another job. And soon. Otherwise, she'd lose her mind to boredom.

She had circled back and was four blocks away from her car when Jackie spotted a sign advertising a guest cottage for rent. The main house was similar to Kate's, narrow in the front but long and deep with a small side yard. She peeked through the iron gate, hoping for a better view.

"Would you like to have a look?" a squeaky voice from the porch above called down.

Shielding her eyes from the afternoon sun, Jackie stared up at the elderly woman. "I don't have much need for a guest cottage at the moment, as charming as this one appears."

The woman came down from the porch, moving with surprising agility for someone her age. "The natural light is wonderful, the perfect space for an artist." She opened the iron gate and waited for Jackie to walk through. "Do you paint?"

Jackie surprised herself by saying, "No, I'm a dancer."

"With hardwood floors, this cottage would make for a wonderful dance studio. Of course, you'd have to move all the furniture out, which you might want to do, anyway, if you have your own things. Furnished or unfurnished. I aim to please."

Jackie stopped in the middle of the gravel path. "I'm sure it's lovely, but really, I don't have any need for a cottage."

The woman looped her arm through Jackie's. "Let me show it to you anyway. Word of mouth is the best advertising. You never know when you'll come across someone looking for a place just like this."

Jackie allowed herself to be dragged toward the cottage. She was never one to turn down a house tour, especially one of an antebellum home, even if this was the guest cottage out back.

"I'm Clara, by the way. Clara Graves." The old woman unlocked the side door of the cottage.

"And I'm Jacqueline Hart. Very nice to meet you."

They entered a small eat-in kitchen. "Kitchen's a little outdated," Clara said, "but all the appliances are in good working order."

Outdated? Try vintage late '60s with lime-green Formica countertops and a lemon-yellow linoleum floor. At least it appeared to be clean.

She followed Clara through a short paneled hallway into the living room. Jackie gasped. With big picture windows stretching across the front and french doors leading to a private terrace on the back, the room offered the most amazing natural light of any room Jackie had ever seen. "It's stunning. Why would you ever want to rent this out? Surely you must have family or friends who need a place to stay when they come to visit."

"Both my daughter and son live on the West Coast. They don't come this way very often, but when they do, there's plenty of room for them to stay in the main house. Come on, let me show you the rest."

The tour upstairs revealed only two bedrooms and one shared bath. The sunlight filled the bedrooms from dormer windows on both sides of the house. Jackie imagined setting up the smaller of the two as a dance studio and using the main room downstairs as a combination living/work room.

Was she really considering going into business for herself?

"My husband recently passed away after a long illness," Clara said. "I've been cooped up here for so long, taking care of him. Not that I minded, you understand. I loved my dear old Howard, God rest his soul."

"I'm sorry for your loss."

Clara blinked away her tears. "I've been taking care of other people for most of my life: first my children, then my husband. I decided it was time for me to pamper myself a little before I die."

Thinking about how quickly time goes by, Jackie couldn't help but imagine herself in Clara's shoes.

"Do you have big plans? To pamper yourself, I mean?"

Clara spread her arms wide. "I'm planning to travel the world. I have several trips planned for this fall—a three-week vacation in Europe with some friends in September followed by an extended trip to California to visit my children for the holidays. My hope is to find someone to rent the cottage before I leave, to help look after things in the main house while I'm gone." A mischievous twinkle appeared in her eyes. "So . . . are you interested?"

Jackie laughed at the absurdity of the whole thing. But at the same time, she was intrigued by the idea of having her own little hideaway.

"I'm tempted, Mrs. Graves." She let out a deep breath. "I live in Prospect, and I've recently separated from my husband. My boys are still in high school, but they are basically self-sufficient. Seeing your charming cottage has made me realize how much I need a fresh start."

Jackie waited while Clara turned out the lights and locked the side door. "It's not about the rent money, Jacqueline, if that makes a difference to you. We can work out a price that fits your budget. The most important thing is for me to find a nice person, such as yourself, that I can trust to take care of things in my absence."

She handed Jackie an old-fashioned calling card, embossed with only her name, address, and phone number. "If you think you might be interested, I'd be happy to hold it awhile for you."

Jackie searched her bag for a pen and a scrap of paper. She jotted down her cell-phone number. "I need a couple of weeks to think about it, at least until my boys get back from camp and I have a chance to talk to them." She handed the number to Clara. "I couldn't ask you to hold it for me, but I'd appreciate it if you would call me before you rent it to someone else."

TWENTY-FOUR

FAITH

After Tuesday night's rain, the clouds lingered well into the afternoon on Wednesday, casting a somber mood over the household. Faith suggested going to the movies or bowling, which probably wasn't a good choice considering Jamie's condition. When the sun finally came out around three o'clock, she tried to convince them to go fishing down at the pier, but neither child could be persuaded off the couch, away from their game box.

Determined not to spend another day cooped up in her sister's house with a sulky teenager and traumatized child, Faith packed a picnic and loaded the kids in the car for a trip to the beach on Thursday.

Faith had begun to feel more like her old self. The bruising and swelling on her face was almost gone, and the soreness around her broken ribs had lessened. She even managed to get Jamie's chair into the bed of the truck, although she hadn't considered how difficult it might be to maneuver the wheels through the thick sand at the beach.

Once Jamie was settled, with Bitsy playing in the sand at his feet, Faith made several trips to the car for their supplies—towels and chairs, picnic basket and a cooler, plus the assortment of buckets and shovels Bitsy had discovered yesterday in Sam's garage.

For the rest of the morning, Bitsy played at the water's edge while Faith flipped through the current issue of *People* magazine. Out of the corner of her eye, she kept tabs on Jamie, who was staring at the ocean in deep thought. When he ran the back of his hand over his eyes, as if to wipe away tears, she put down the magazine and debated whether to say the things she'd been wanting to say to him for days.

She wrapped her hand around Jamie's. "If there's something on your mind you want to talk about . . ."

He glanced down at their hands, then up at her. "No offense, Aunt Faith, but I'm tired of talking." He pulled his hand away. "It doesn't do any good."

"Depends on who's doing the talking and who's doing the listening."

He studied her face, as though trying to decide whether he could trust her, then returned his attention to the crashing waves.

"According to your mom, your last MRI showed that your spinal cord has healed. The doctors think something's holding you back from walking again. Do you want to talk about what that something is?"

His shoulders drooped, and he hung his head. "It's not that easy."

"Nothing in life worth having ever is. These things take time. And you're a gifted athlete. You of all people should understand how hard physical work can pay off."

"This is different. My mind wants to believe I can do it, but the rest of my body won't cooperate."

"What about your heart?" she asked.

"What does my heart have to do with anything?"

"You have to trust in your heart that you can accomplish your goals, then let the rest of your body do the work."

Tears welled in his eyes.

She reached for his hand again. This time he did not pull away. "That's the problem, isn't it? Your heart won't give your body permission to move on?"

"Pretty much," he said, biting his lower lip.

"Let it go, Jamie. There's no one here but you and me." Faith glanced over at her daughter, who was dancing in the edge of the surf.

Faith scooted her chair closer and rubbed his head, cooing soft words of encouragement for a good ten minutes, while he cried. Finally, he reached for a beach towel and wiped his eyes.

"Feel better?" Faith asked.

"I guess."

"The only way to get it out of your system is to give in to your grief." She placed her hand in the middle of his chest and felt the distant thumping of his heart. "Corey's death was not your fault. You have to stop punishing yourself." She placed her hand on his chest. "Deep down inside, you know how much he loved you. He would want you to go on living your life. He would want you to walk again."

He rested his head on the back of his chair. "I just can't stop thinking about all the things Corey's missing out on. All because of me."

"Answer me this. What if Corey had been driving the Gator and you were the one who'd been killed? Would you want him to bury himself in guilt?"

"No, of course not." He was silent for a minute. "I know what you're saying is true, and I've tried to put myself in Corey's shoes, many times. But it doesn't help."

"I know it's hard."

Jamie sniffled and wiped his nose with the towel. "You have no idea what I'm going through. "

"Ha." She sat back in her chair. "Have you looked at my face lately?"

"You're not going back to him are you, Aunt Faith?"

"Not if I can help it."

He jerked his head toward her. "That doesn't sound very convincing."

"Like you said, it's not that easy. I'm scared to death that, when the time comes, I won't have the strength to stand up to him." She reached for the cooler and dragged it closer to her. "How about if we make a deal?"

"What's that?" he asked.

She handed him a pimento cheese sandwich. "I'll help you find the courage to walk again, if you help me find the courage to stand up to Curtis."

He unwrapped the sandwich and took a bite. "Throw in a bag of barbecue chips and a Dr. Pepper, and you have a deal."

She pinched his stuffed cheek. "I'm glad you shaved. You shouldn't hide your handsome face behind all that scruffy beard." She sat back, studying him. "I give a mean haircut, you know."

TWENTY-FIVE

SAMANTHA

Sam's mood brightened when she arrived home from work and saw her son looking better than she'd seen him look in months. Healthy, with a trace of sun on his cheeks, and handsome, with his dark curls cut back over his ears. She was even more pleased to find Jamie and Bitsy preparing dinner in the kitchen. Bitsy mixed spices for a dry rub for the ribs while Jamie grated the secret ingredients he used in his famous macaroni-and-cheese recipe.

She found Faith at the computer in the den, doing research on battered women.

"Discover anything interesting?" Sam asked, reading the computer screen over her sister's shoulder.

Faith pointed at one of the bulleted facts on the website she was browsing. "Did you know that in domestic violence situations, seventy-five percent of calls to police for intervention happen after the victims separate from their abusers?"

"Knowing that statistic will only make you worry more."

"I guess you're right." Faith clicked the mouse and exited the Internet browser.

"So . . . how'd you do it?" Sam asked.

Faith pushed back from the desk. "How'd I do what?"

"How'd you talk Jamie into letting you cut his hair?"

Faith smiled. "That was easy. He was ready to get rid of all that hair."

Sam felt a distinct twinge of jealousy. Should it bother her that her sister could convince Jamie to cut his hair when she'd been harassing him about it for months? Faith and Jamie had always had a special bond. She knew she should be happy that her son had found someone to confide in. She only wished that *that someone* was her.

Jamie started the grill, and the grown-ups talked on the back deck while Bitsy played on the tire swing that hung from the big maple tree in the yard. The evening was pleasant, hot and humid but not unbearable. For a brief moment in time, they were an average family enjoying a cookout—all thoughts of abusive husbands, wheelchairs, and failing family businesses forgotten.

Sam and Faith were taking turns painting barbecue sauce on the ribs when they heard the loud rumble of a motorcycle engine in the driveway. Before they had a chance to react, Curtis appeared, dressed in a leather jacket and pants, with a bandana wrapped do-rag-style around his head.

"Looks like I'm just in time for grub." He strolled toward the deck as though he'd been invited to dinner.

At the sound of her father's voice, Bitsy sprinted across the yard, took the deck steps two at a time, and dove behind her mother's legs.

Curtis held his hands out to her. "Aww, Bitsy. Don't be like that. Aren't you gonna give your daddy a hug?"

With the child clinging to her leg like a koala attached to a tree, Faith managed to get Bitsy over to the back door. She pried her daughter off her leg and pushed her forward. "Go inside, sweetheart, and turn on the television."

"You can't keep me from seeing my own child, Faith. I got

rights." Curtis made a move toward the back door, but Faith blocked his path.

"You gave up your rights when you broke my nose."

He glared at her, his lip curled up in disgust. "Look at you, all confident now that you got your family to protect you. Did you tell your sister about the money you stole from her?"

Jamie locked eyes with his mother, but she ignored his questioning stare. "As a matter of fact she did, Curtis," Sam said. "But I blame you for that, not Faith. It's your fault for not being able to hold down a job."

Curtis took a step closer to Faith, examining her face. "Looks like your nose is healing up nicely. Too bad I'm gonna have to break it again."

Jamie wheeled his chair over to Curtis. "Get off my property," he said, pointing the grill fork at his uncle.

"What're you gonna do, you little punk, stab me with your kitchen fork?"

"You're damn right." Jamie jabbed at the air with his fork. "I'm not a punk, and I'm certainly not afraid of you."

Curtis laughed, the crazed cackle of a deranged man. "You should be."

Jamie held Curtis at bay with his grill fork in one hand while tossing Sam his cell phone with the other. "Call the police, Mom."

Sam dialed 911. When the woman in dispatch answered, she blurted, "Send the police to 210 Dogwood Lane right away. My name is Sam Sweeney and my brother-in-law is here threatening my family. My sister has a restraining order out against him."

"Restraining order?" Curtis said. "I don't know nothing about no restraining order."

"Is he armed?" the dispatcher asked Sam.

"Not that I can see."

"The police are on the way. Do you want to stay on the phone with me until they get there?"

"Yes, I do." She hoped that keeping the dispatcher on the line would prevent Curtis from doing something stupid. Sam held the phone away from her ear. "The police are on the way. You might want to leave while you still have a chance." Ten seconds later, they heard sirens. "Too late now."

Curtis's right hand disappeared behind his back. He was reaching for something tucked inside his waistband when Officers Marshall and Swanson rounded the corner of the house.

Eli drew his weapon. "Freeze! Drop the gun on the ground and put your hands in the air."

Gun? Sam's heart pounded in her chest. They'd been flirting with death without even realizing it.

Curtis tossed his revolver in the grass and raised his hands.

Eli forced Curtis against the side of Sam's Jeep and frisked him while Swanson secured the weapon.

"You can't arrest me," Curtis cried when Eli slapped the handcuffs on him.

"Oh no?" Eli whipped his prisoner around to face him. "Watch me."

"On what grounds?"

"Carrying a concealed weapon, for starters," Eli said.

"With intent to cause bodily harm," Officer Swanson added.

Sam chimed in, "And he's violating Faith's protection order."

"I already told you," Curtis said. "I don't know nothing about no restraining order."

Sam shot her sister a quick glance. "I thought you took care of this."

"I did. I filed the papers on Tuesday morning."

"Did the judge sign the order?" Eli asked.

"No, I filed them with the clerk of court. He told me they would notify me of the court date. I just assumed . . ."

Swanson shook his head in frustration. "The judge should have granted a temporary order of protection."

"We can deal with that in the morning. In the meantime,

your husband here"—Eli jerked on Curtis's handcuffs—"will be spending the night in jail."

"Don't hold your breath." Curtis spit a large wad of chewing tobacco at his captor's feet. "I'll be out of jail by the time you finish your shift."

"Get him out of here." Eli handed his prisoner over to his partner, who hustled him down the driveway to the patrol car.

Eli surveyed the faces of his captive audience. "Who wants to tell me what happened?"

Sam recapped the incident with Faith and Jamie filling in the parts she missed.

"Is there any way he can get out of jail tonight?" Faith asked.

"Not tonight. But I doubt we'll be able to keep him over the weekend—that is, if he can post bail." Eli gripped Jamie's shoulder. "You did a brave thing tonight, buddy. You kept your cool during a dangerous situation. Not everyone your age could've handled the pressure so well."

Jamie shrugged. "All I could think about was keeping Bitsy safe." He spun his chair around. "Speaking of Bitsy, maybe I should go inside and check on her. I'm sure she's scared."

Faith waited for Jamie to make his way down the sidewalk and up the ramp before she spoke. "The other night, while we were at the hospital, Dr. Neilson mentioned something about helping me find a shelter. I thought maybe I'd take him up on the offer."

"That's ridiculous, Faith. I'm not letting you go to a shelter." Sam put her arm around her sister's shoulders. "You are staying here with Jamie and me. We're your family."

"And I love you, which is why I need to leave. Curtis has gone batshit crazy. He had every intention of shooting someone with that gun. And that someone could've been Jamie." Faith choked back a sob. "I don't know what I'll do if he takes Bitsy away from me."

Sam gripped her sister's shoulder. "That's not going to

happen. At least not while you're here. I can't protect you if you leave."

"It might not be a bad thing for you to explore your options," Eli said to Sam. "Your sister is right. By letting her stay here, you are placing your own life and your son's in danger. Everything turned out all right tonight, but you never know what might happen next time."

"You're assuming there will be a next time," Sam said.

"We have no choice but to prepare for a next time," Eli said. "We will do the best we can to protect you, but we can't be here all the time. You have to consider Jamie. I don't need to tell you that being in a wheelchair places him at a disadvantage."

"I'm well aware of the challenges of Jamie's condition. You'll just have to do the best you can, because nobody is going anywhere," Sam said, her jaw set.

"Okay then," Eli said. "We'll play it your way. Once Curtis is released from jail, I'll make certain a patrol car drives by your house at least every hour,"—then turning to Faith—"and I'll see what I can do about getting you on the judge's docket as soon as possible so we can get that temporary protection order in place."

"I appreciate all your help, Eli," Faith said.

"It's my job." Eli handed Sam his business card with his cell number scribbled on the back. "Call me anytime, day or night."

She slipped the card in her back pocket. "Thanks. I feel better having a direct line to Prospect's finest," she said with a smile.

Faith and Sam watched the squad car pull away from the curb with Curtis glaring at them through the back window.

"What do we do about his bike?" Sam motioned toward Curtis's motorcycle parked behind her Jeep.

"Move it to the curb for now. The bike will be our way of knowing he's out of jail." Faith kicked up the kickstand and walked the Harley down the driveway to the street.

Sam waited for Faith to return, and the two of them walked

arm in arm back to the deck. Sam went in the kitchen and returned with a bottle of wine and two glasses.

"None for me, thanks," Faith said. "I need to keep my wits about me."

"That leaves more for me," Sam said, filling her glass to the rim. "After what happened here tonight, I might polish off the whole bottle."

"I'm worried about you, Sam. You've been drinking an awful lot lately."

Sam raised her glass to her sister and took a big gulp. "I'll quit once your husband is locked up for good." She didn't need anyone telling her how to handle her stress. She'd never been much of a drinker before, and she had little doubt that she could quit whenever she wanted to.

She set her glass down and opened the lid on the grill. "Looks like our dinner is charred." She used the fork Jamie had threatened Curtis with to poke at the blackened meat.

Faith took the fork away from Sam and closed the grill lid. "Listen to me, Sammie. Bitsy and I can't stay here any longer."

"I thought we already settled this."

"No." Faith pointed the fork at Sam. "You settled it. Not me. You made your mind up, like you always do, without giving me my say."

Sam pulled a chair up to the table and sat down. "Fine. Have your say."

"Will you at least admit that tonight was a game changer?" Faith asked as she sat down next to Sam.

"Fine. Tonight was a game changer. We just need to be better prepared for next time."

"And how do you propose we do that?"

"For starters, we can teach Bitsy how to dial 911 and what to say to the operator in the event of an emergency. We can handle this, Faith. Together, as a family. You don't need to go live in a shelter with strangers."

Faith pounded the table with her fist. "You're not listening to me, Sam. Jamie's safety is in jeopardy. Did you see the way he went after Curtis with that fork? I love Jamie. But he's a wild card with all that anger he's holding on to. Who knows what would've happened if the police hadn't shown up when they did."

"Come on, Faith. We could sit here all night talking about the what-ifs, but the bottom line is, we are all safe. We just need to be more careful in the future."

Faith stared her down. "Will you at least talk to Jamie about it?"

"Talk to me about what?" Jamie asked from the doorway.

"About dinner." Sam pointed her wine glass at the grill. "Your ribs are charred."

"I'll go get the box of meat," he said, and pumped his chair back inside the kitchen.

"Please talk to him." Faith pushed back from the table. "If he has any concerns for his own safety, or for yours, we will find somewhere to go." She went to the door. "In the meantime, I'm going to check on Bitsy, to see if I can convince her to come back outside."

Faith held the door open for Jamie while he wheeled his way onto the deck. He set the box on the table and began rummaging through it. "We have pork tenderloin or hamburgers," he said, a tenderloin in one hand and a package of individually wrapped hamburger patties in the other.

"The tenderloin would be better with your mac and cheese. Besides, I don't have any hamburger rolls."

Jamie speared the charred ribs off the grill, set them on a metal cooking sheet on the table, and scraped the grates with a wire brush. "Did Aunt Faith really steal money from the market?"

Sam inhaled a deep breath. "I don't consider it stealing when you take something that already belongs to you. I do wish she'd talked to me first, though."

Using his teeth, Jamie tore open the tenderloin package and laid the meat out on the grill. "How'd you find out about it?"

"I found some past-due notices."

His head shot up. "Was it a lot of money?"

"By itself, no. The money she borrowed was not enough to hurt us. But considering how business has been off lately, I'm not sure we can absorb the loss."

Jamie closed the grill lid and joined her at the table. "I guess I've been too wrapped up in my own problems to ask about Sweeney's. I didn't realize business has been so bad. Is there anything I can do to help?"

Market business was once a nightly topic of discussion for them, especially during the summers when they worked together six days a week. She had never encouraged Jamie when he spoke of one day taking over the business. She wanted him to seek a career of his own first, then if things didn't work out, she would invite him to join her at Sweeney's. Assuming Sweeney's was still in business.

"You can start by praying for some positive publicity." She winked at him. "Seriously, though, Jamie. Faith asked me to talk to you. She is concerned for our safety. She has it in her mind to move to a shelter, but if she goes anywhere, it'll be to Jackie's."

"No, Mom, you can't let them leave. Bitsy is already terrified. Making her move would only scare her more."

"You were brave to go after Curtis tonight, but as strong as you are, you are still in a wheelchair. I'm not willing to put your life in danger."

"That coward hasn't got anything on me, in or out of a wheelchair."

To see her son's cocky attitude return lifted Sam's spirits, but it was that same cocky attitude she worried about. "Don't be flippant, son. We are talking about a potentially dangerous situation. Curtis had a gun on him tonight. If we hadn't called the police when we did, he might've used it."

ASHLEY FARLEY

He picked the grill fork up and waved it at her. "I promise I'll never attack Curtis with a grill fork again." He grinned his bad-boy grin, the one that made her hair turn gray. "Next time I'll use my pistol."

❧

Complaining of a headache, Faith went to bed right after dinner. Sam took her glass of wine out to the front porch to watch the pink sky fade away. She was settling in on the swing when a silver pickup truck pulled up to the curb. She almost didn't recognize Eli, dressed in street clothes—a pair of khaki pants and a black polo shirt that showed off his tan and made his gray eyes look smoky.

He approached the house. "Nice night for porch sitting."

"It is, as long as Curtis stays locked up in a cell."

"He's eating gruel and stale bread as we speak." He motioned at the empty seat next to her. "May I join you?"

"Of course." She slid over to make more room. "Can I offer you some wine?"

"No, thanks. I'm driving."

"Of course you are. How about some iced tea, then?"

Eli waved her off. "I'm fine, really."

Jamie appeared on the porch. "Is anything wrong? I heard your truck pull up and thought maybe . . ."

"Relax, Jamie. Everything is fine. Curtis is locked up, safely behind bars."

"Then why are you here?" Jamie asked.

"Actually, I was on my way home, and it occurred to me that you might like to go fishing with me in the morning."

"Who, me?" Jamie asked.

"Yes, you. I'm going with my friend Robert. He's a nice guy. You'd like him. We are leaving around ten, but we won't be gone long because Robert has to be at work at three."

Jamie's face darkened. "Thanks for the offer, but my chair would only get in the way on a boat."

"Who said we're taking the chair with us?"

Jamie scrunched his face in confusion. "I don't understand."

"Listen." Eli leaned forward, eye level with Jamie. "Robert has an old forty-five-foot sportfish. We can leave the wheelchair on the dock and plant you in the fighting chair in the cockpit. If you need to go inside the cabin for anything, I can help you get around. We aren't going out far, maybe three miles, to see if anything is biting. If you are uncomfortable, we'll bring you right back in."

"And you're sure your friend is okay with having a cripple on board?" Jamie asked.

A smile tugged at Eli's lips. "He said he's fine with it as long as you have the upper-body strength to reel in the fish."

A beam of hope crossed Jamie's face. He turned to Sam. "What do you think, Mom? Should I go?"

"I don't see why not."

"Then I better go get my stuff together. You don't mind if I take my own rod, do you?"

Eli gave him a thumbs-up. "You can take anything you want, buddy. I'll swing by to pick you up about quarter 'til ten."

Jamie spun his chair around and headed for the door.

"Wow," Sam said once Jamie disappeared inside. "I haven't seen him that happy since his grandfather gave him his good-luck rod. Are you sure about this?"

"Absolutely." He placed his hand over his heart. "I'm a sucker for a good kid with a damaged soul."

Sam sipped her wine, thinking about the boy she loved so much, who was currently lost to her. "He really is a good kid."

"He'll come back to you, Sam. Just wait and see."

"I just hope I recognize him when he does. I'm afraid his innocence perished in the accident and that this bitterness is here to stay."

"Fear is your worst enemy. Jamie is counting on you to have faith in him, in his full recovery. If you're afraid, he will sense your fear and react to it."

Sam wondered what had happened to Eli in the past to make him speak with such strong conviction. She knew little, next to nothing really, about the handsome officer with the mysterious gray eyes.

"Do you often make after-hours house calls, Officer?"

"Only when I'm worried about one of my victims."

"So I'm a victim now?"

"Bad choice of words. You don't exactly fit the victim mold." He shifted in his seat to face her, placing his arm across the back of the swing. "You seemed shaken earlier. I wanted to make sure you're okay."

Tears sprung to her eyes as the events of the evening came crashing down on her. "The whole thing was surreal. If you hadn't arrived when you did . . ." Sam's voice caught in her throat, and she couldn't continue.

Eli rubbed her shoulders until she'd composed herself.

"Tell me something, Eli. How do I protect my family from a lunatic with a loaded handgun?"

"You stay as far away from him as possible. You see him coming, you run."

"Which would be great advice, except my son can't run."

"No one's forgotten that, Sam. Least of all me. Maybe I'm oversimplifying the situation, but you know what I mean." Ticking off points finger by finger, he said, "Keep your doors and windows locked at all times. Be aware of your surroundings when you are out in public. Keep a charged cell phone with you at all times. And, by all means, call 911 at the first sign of trouble."

Their eyes met, and Sam experienced a strange sensation in her gut, simultaneously tingly and jittery, nervous and exciting. She couldn't remember the last time she felt butterflies in her belly.

As if sparked by the emotions crackling inside of her, fireworks appeared in the sky above the trees in the direction of the water, a sign that the Fourth of July holiday was approaching.

When the fireworks display subsided, Eli said, "You have a lot on your shoulders, Sam. Who do you lean on for support?"

Sam shrugged. "Nobody."

"What about Jamie's father?"

"He's never been a part of Jamie's life."

Eli looked surprised. "By choice?"

"His choice, not mine." Sam looked away and stared across the porch into the night. "We'd been dating for two years when I got pregnant. Naturally, I . . ." Her voice trailed off.

"Naturally, you assumed the two of you would marry and live happily ever after."

"He left town after I told him I was pregnant. He never even said goodbye."

"Have you heard from him since?"

"Nope. Not a word."

"That's unfortunate. What about his family, Jamie's paternal grandparents? Do they live nearby?" Eli added, "If I'm prying . . ."

Allen's betrayal had caused her so much pain that she had closed the door long ago on that part of her life.

"You're fine. It happened so long ago. Allen never talked much about his family. He's a boat captain, a vagrant who'd lived in a dozen different places before he came here. Jamie has all the family he needs, right here in Prospect. My father loved him like a son, and my mother worships the ground he walks on."

"You mentioned your father in the past tense."

"My dad passed away several years ago. He was a great big man, large in size and spirit." Sam held her arms out in front of her to illustrate her father's girth. "If Dad were alive today, he would know just what to say and do to help Jamie and Faith."

"I doubt he could do any better than you're doing," Eli said in a soft voice, almost a whisper.

"What exactly am I doing, Eli, other than making a bigger mess of things?"

"You're doing the best you can. No one can ask for anything more than that."

"The problem is, my best is not working. My son is grieving the loss of his best friend, and I can't reach him no matter how hard I try. I don't want to give up, but he's making it hard."

"Never ever give up, Sam. As long as you don't give up on Jamie, he won't give up on himself."

They sat in silence for a while, watching the fireworks off in the distance. When Eli got up to leave, Sam walked with him to his truck.

He leaned back against the truck's hood. "I hate to bring up a sore subject. But have you warned your mother to be on the lookout for Curtis? You mentioned that she lives here in town."

"Born and raised. In fact, she started Captain Sweeney's Seafood in the parking lot of the Inlet View Marina more than fifty years ago."

Eli's gray eyes widened. "That's an interesting bit of local history I didn't know."

"My mom's been having health issues lately. Faith and I agreed not to add to her stress by worrying her about Curtis."

"I understand your concerns, but you need to consider her safety."

Sam understood the stakes had changed tonight. "I guess you're right. We should probably tell my sister Jackie as well."

"I don't remember you mentioning another sister."

"I'm not as close to Jackie as I am to Faith. But she also lives in Prospect, at Moss Creek Farm, a big property on the water just outside of town." When his face registered recognition, she asked, "You know the place?"

"I've never been there, but I've driven by it many times on

patrol. Has Faith considered staying with her? I'm sure a home that size has plenty of security."

"Jackie is dealing with her own set of problems. But you're right, we need to at least make her aware of the situation with Curtis."

With the boys off at camp, alone in her big house, Jackie was an unsuspecting target for the likes of a deranged brother-in-law. One of her heirloom sterling candlesticks would support his boozing habit for a month.

TWENTY-SIX

JACQUELINE

An invitation for dinner with her family came as a surprise to Jackie. Other than major holidays, their Sunday dinners had become a thing of the past after their father died and their mother moved from her creekside cottage next door to a town-house. Jackie suspected her sister of having a hidden agenda. She assumed Sam had heard the rumors circulating around town and wanted confirmation that Bill had, in fact, left her for another woman.

She considered declining the invitation, but she couldn't put off the dreaded discussion forever. Sooner or later she would have to tell her family about her impending divorce.

"What time?" Jackie asked.

"Around six thirty. Can you pick up Mom on your way?"

"Is that really necessary?" Jackie snapped. "Mom has her own car, you know."

"That's hypocritical coming from you. Aren't you the one who insisted Faith drive Mom to your party the night of your birthday?"

"That's different."

"Why, because you're the one who's being inconvenienced

took a tentative bite. Her eyes grew wide. "I'm not a big fan of mackerel but that tastes surprisingly good." She added a big blob of mackerel to her cracker and popped the whole thing into her mouth.

"Have you heard anything from Cooper and Sean?" Jamie asked.

"I've had one letter from them." She held up her index finger. "Not one letter from each of them. One letter from both. Sounds like they're having a good time, enjoying the privileges of being junior counselors."

"When are they coming home?" Jamie asked.

"I'm going to pick them up on Saturday." She heaped mackerel spread on another cracker before turning her attention to her niece. "What're you working on over here?" She kissed the top of Bitsy's head. "Did you make that cornbread all by yourself?"

Bitsy chewed on her bottom lip. "Aunt Sam brought it home from Sweeney's. Roberto made it."

"I didn't realize he could bake," Jackie said.

"Oh yes," Lovie said. "He came equipped with a treasure trove of secret recipes."

"Well it smells delicious." She turned to Sam. "What can I do to help?"

Sam handed Jackie a stack of placemats and a fistful of silverware and sent her outside to the deck to set the table. Relieved to have a moment alone, she took her time carrying out her designated task. She was glad her sister decided to eat outside. Why waste a nice evening crammed around a tiny table in a stuffy dining room?

When she finished setting the table, she poured six glasses of iced tea while the others loaded up the table with food. Sam offered an appropriate blessing for Father's Day, thanking the Lord for giving them such a wonderful father in Oscar. They all dug in, as though they hadn't seen a proper meal in weeks. Jackie drank a half glass of each of the wines with her dinner and placed her vote for the Pinot Grigio. "But don't let me be the judge," she said. "I'm biased. I've always been partial to Pinot over Chardonnay or Sauvignon Blanc."

After clearing the table and rinsing the dishes, Bitsy and Jamie took their desserts to the sitting room to give the adults a chance to talk.

Sam handed Jackie a huge slice of key lime pie.

Jackie pushed the plate away. "I only want a sliver."

Sam slid the plate back across the table. "You won't say that when you taste it."

Jackie took a small bite and savored the rich, creamy filling in the graham cracker crust. "Oh my God. Is this one of Roberto's secret recipes, too?"

Lovie beamed. "The pies are a new product for us, made by a local woman. Key lime is the most popular, but peach is my favorite."

"I like the chocolate chess the best." Faith set her fork down and wiped her mouth. "Mama, Jacqueline. There's something I need to tell you."

Faith cast Sam a tentative glance, and Sam signaled for her to continue.

"Curtis and I have split up. Bitsy and I have moved out of the trailer, and we're living here with Sam. At least for the time being."

Relieved not to be the one on center stage, Jackie let this tidbit of news sink in. "I tried to warn you, Faith," she said. "You never should have married that redneck."

When Sam glared at her, Jackie glared back. "Well, it's true, isn't it?"

"You can't just give up like that, honey," Lovie said. "Every marriage has its ups and downs. You and Curtis will just have to try a little harder. For Bitsy's sake."

Jackie's heart sank. If her mother was so opposed to Faith leaving a deadbeat like Curtis, there was no telling how she'd react when Jackie told her she planned to divorce Bill, a cardiologist and outstanding member of society.

Jackie pointed her fork at Faith's face. "For Pete's sake, Mom. Don't you see the bruises?"

Lovie got up and went around to the other side of the table. She took her youngest daughter's face between her hands and studied the yellow bruises that stood out against Faith's pale skin in the late-day sun. "Are you saying Curtis did this to you?"

Faith hung her head. "He's not the same person I married, Mama."

"Looks to me like Curtis is exactly the same person you married," Jackie said. "Where is he, by the way? Why is his bike out front?"

"Curtis is in jail," Sam said.

"In jail?" Lovie lowered herself into Bitsy's vacated chair next to Faith. "What on earth?"

"The police arrested him when he came over here Thursday night with a loaded pistol." Faith went on to describe all the events involving Curtis during the past week.

"He hasn't done anything to hurt Bitsy, has he?" Lovie asked.

"I can't say for sure," Faith admitted. "They were alone together a lot while I was at work. She's terrified of him. I know that much."

Lovie reached for Faith's hand. "We will get through this together, as a family."

"How long can they keep him in jail?" Jackie asked.

Sam said, "According to Eli, my contact at the police station, Curtis was unable to make bail when he appeared before the magistrate on Friday."

"I imagine one of his loser friends will bail him out eventually," Faith said.

"You and Bitsy could stay with me. I have an alarm system designed to protect Fort Knox."

Faith smiled at her sister. "Thanks, Jackie. I appreciate it, really I do, but Bitsy feels safe here with Sam and Jamie. That's not to say I won't take you up on it at some point in the future."

"Well, if you change your mind . . ." Jackie was secretly relieved her sister had declined her invitation. She couldn't very well have Faith as a houseguest without explaining Bill's absence. Considering the confusion their mother had experienced earlier, and now Faith's confession, Jackie thought Lovie had faced enough drama for one night. She'd wait for another time to tell her family about her own plans for divorce.

"Eli promised to contact us when they release Curtis," Sam said.

"We'll know anyway when his bike disappears," Faith said.

"But when that happens, the two of you need to be on the lookout for him"—Sam looked at her mother, then her older sister—"in case he decides to come after one of you."

"I seriously doubt he's that desperate," Jackie said.

"He's unemployed and broke, and that makes him desperate," Sam said. "Throw in gambling and alcohol addictions, add an anger-management problem, and he becomes dangerous. Maybe I'm being a little overdramatic, but I think it's important for all of us to be on alert."

Jackie had her own problems to worry about without having to concern herself with her delinquent brother-in-law. She'd offered for Faith to stay out at the farm. What more could she do?

She got up and began clearing the table. She was placing the last dessert plate in the dishwasher when Sam sought her out in the kitchen.

"I didn't get a chance to ask you how Mom was when you picked her up."

Jackie, glancing around to make certain they were alone, leaned back against the counter. "When I got to her townhouse, I found Mom sitting in her car with the car running. She had no clue where she was supposed to be going."

Sam poured the last of the Pinot Grigio into her glass. "Tell me everything."

Jackie described her mother's latest episode of confusion in detail, including the mystery behind the rusty key. "I've never seen that key before in my life, but Mom seems convinced the key fits something at my house."

"That's strange. Why would she think that?"

"Who knows? Maybe the key does fit something at the farm. She lived next door in the cottage for all those years. I'll take a look around the property tomorrow and see what I can find."

"I guess it can't hurt. I must say I'm curious." Sam paused, thinking. "I know you are dealing with your own issues right now, but . . ."

Irritation crawled across Jackie's skin at Sam's subtle-yet-undeniable proclamation. She knew about Bill's affair and was providing Jackie with the opportunity to come clean about their problems. But Jackie refused to be bullied into a confession. She would tell them on her own terms.

"But what, Sam?" Jackie said, her jaw set firmly.

"Can you at least help out with Mom on her days off? With Faith staying here and Jamie in a wheelchair, my hands are full."

"I can't this week. I have an important meeting in Charleston on Wednesday, and I'm picking the boys up from camp on Saturday."

"That's perfect. I'm sure the boys will love spending some time with their grandmother on Sunday."

Jackie imagined the dreaded drive home from the mountains with the twins. After learning of their parents' divorce, she doubted that Cooper and Sean would be in the mood for entertaining their grandmother.

"I'll try, Sam. But I can't promise anything. As you mentioned earlier, I have my own problems just now."

TWENTY-SEVEN

SAMANTHA

S am heard from Eli late Monday afternoon when he called to
tell her Curtis had been released, but she didn't see him
again until he showed up at Sweeney's late Wednesday morning
with a woman in tow who needed no introduction—Janie Jasper,
known throughout coastal South Carolina as the authority on all
things Lowcountry. As reporter for the weekly magazine
Lowcountry Living, Janie received invitations to the best parties
and offered the best tables in the trendiest restaurants in and
around the Charleston area. In a drop-dead-gorgeous Angelina
Jolie kind of way, she appeared even more glamorous in person,
with shiny mahogany shoulder-length hair, amber-colored eyes,
and a toned body that made her simple white sheath look
elegant.

What are they even doing here? Sam wondered, once the shock
of having a celebrity on the premises wore off.

Unsure of how to approach them, she opted to keep things
professional. "Let me know if I can help you with anything."

"Thanks." Eli gave Sam a perfunctory nod. "We're just
looking around."

She experienced a pang of jealousy when Janie grabbed Eli's

anything romantic. She didn't have time for romance, anyway, not with all the chaos controlling her life.

"My trust does not come cheap, but you've earned it, Eli. And I thank you for that."

He leaned down and planted a soft kiss on her cheek. "You are welcome," he whispered. "You said you were dying to try sushi, right?"

♞

Eli, Sam, and Jamie talked about Janie's article all the way to Charleston. They speculated on when the next issue of *Lowcountry Living* would hit the stands and how soon before they might see an increase in business. Sam warned Jamie not to be overly optimistic, even though she couldn't suppress her own feelings of hope.

Su-shay was located on East Bay Street just down from Magnolias. While small, the restaurant was appropriately uptown for big town. The walls were painted a high-gloss orange, and the tables were dark, modern wood. A nature-inspired water fountain dripped streams of water down the banquette wall on one side of the restaurant while workers prepared food in an open area, the sushi bar, on the other.

"I'm not sure we have time to wait," Sam said when she saw the mob of hungry-looking customers gathered around the hostess stand.

"We have a reservation." Sam looked surprised, and Eli said, "I know the owner. I texted him we were coming."

A shorter version of Eli made his way through the crowd toward them. "Hey, bro." He engulfed Eli in a bear hug. "Next time give me a little notice."

"You know me. I operate by the seat of my pants. Sam, Jamie, this is my brother, Kyle."

Kyle's dazzling smile and bright blue eyes mesmerized Sam.

She offered her hand to him, but pulled it back in shock when she felt metal fingers grip hers. She stared down at his forearms, which were fitted with state-of-the-art prosthetic devices. "Oh, sorry." Sam blushed. "I didn't realize."

"No worries." He balled his metal fingers up tight, offering Jamie a fist bump. "Nice to meet you, dude."

"Can you believe Sam and Jamie have never eaten sushi?" Eli said.

Kyle slapped his metal palm to his forehead. "Never eaten sushi? That's a crime. We'll have to remedy that right away." He started toward the back, motioning for them to follow.

Eli helped Jamie maneuver his chair through the crowded restaurant to the last table along the banquette. Eli and Sam slid onto the upholstered bench against the wall, and Jamie wheeled up opposite them.

When Kyle pulled up a chair next to Jamie, Eli said, "Glad you can join us, man."

"It's not every day my brother blesses me with his presence."

An Asian woman with flawless skin and shiny black hair approached the table. "Since when do we take lunch breaks?" the woman said to Kyle, her arms crossed.

"Blame it on me for showing up unannounced during the middle of your lunch crowd." Eli stood, and leaned across the table to kiss her cheek. "Shay, I'd like you to meet my friends, Sam and Jamie Sweeney. Shay is a candidate for sainthood for marrying my brother."

Sam snapped her fingers. "I get it now. Shay, as in Su-shay."

Eli patted Sam on the head. "She's a fast learner."

Kyle winked at his wife. "Sweetheart, can you believe Sam and Jamie have never eaten sushi?"

"You've come to the right place. One sampler coming up." She executed a dainty bow.

When Shay left the table, Jamie turned to Kyle. "What happened to your arms?"

"Jamie!" Sam said. "Don't be rude."

"I'll make a deal with you," Kyle said. "I'll tell my story if you tell me yours."

"Deal," Jamie said, and they shook on it. "But you go first."

"Okay, fine." Kyle settled back in his chair. "I was on my last week of duty in Afghanistan when a defective explosive device detonated in my hands."

"You mean one of our own weapons?" Jamie asked, his eyes wide.

"Yep. My recovery was brutal. For a long time, all I wanted to do was die."

"I know how that feels," Jamie said.

Shay approached the table with two large bottles of sparkling water. "Shay was my nurse. She saved my life, didn't you, honey?"

She set the water on the table. "He was a real bastard in the beginning."

Kyle grabbed his wife's hand and kissed it. "She makes me pay for it now. Every single day."

"How did the two of you get into the restaurant business?" Sam asked.

"I grew up working the food industry," Shay said. "My parents own a sushi shack back in Seattle, where I'm from."

"Don't let the name fool you. This Sushi Shack"—Kyle used air quotes—"is a three-story palace packed with people all year long."

When a server delivered two platters of sushi to the table, Shay pointed to each piece while Kyle listed the ingredients and then described the accompanying sauces. Next, he gave a quick tutorial on how to hold the chopsticks, using his metal fingers and amazing everyone with his adept demonstration.

"Your turn, Jamie," Kyle said once Shay had returned to the kitchen and their plates were full of sushi. "How'd you end up in the chair?"

"An ATV accident. I was driving, and my best friend was

killed," Jamie said, maintaining composure despite his quivering lip.

"Sorry, dude. I know how that feels. I lost a lot of buddies in Afghanistan. After a while, I stopped making friends, because I couldn't deal with the pain of losing them."

Everyone dug into the sushi to avoid the awkward silence. They tasted and sampled, each one talking about which rolls they like the best.

Kyle dipped a California roll in the soy sauce. "What's your prognosis, Jamie, if you don't mind me asking?"

Jamie cast a nervous glance at his mother. "According to my doctors, I should be walking by now."

Chopsticks poised in midair, Kyle asked, "What are you waiting for?"

Jamie shrugged. "It's not that easy."

"Ha. Nothing ever is." Kyle placed a metal hand on Jamie's shoulder. "Seriously, bro. I lay in that hospital bed for months wishing I had died in the accident, wondering how in the hell I would make it through life without my hands. But Shay and Eli helped me see how selfish I was being."

Jamie narrowed his eyes. "Selfish?"

"Yes. Selfish. God had spared my life, and I owed it to all my friends who died in Afghanistan to make the best of it. I may not have any hands, but I'm alive. I have a beautiful bride, and one day I hope God will bless us with children. And I can cook, the one thing I love to do above all else."

"I like to cook, too," Jamie admitted. He popped a tuna roll in his mouth. "Now that I think about it, I've eaten sushi before. Not with all this fancy stuff, but raw tuna straight out of the ocean."

Kyle pointed his chopsticks at Jamie. "Now you're talking."

Jamie took a slice of sushi between his fingers and studied the contents up close. "How do you get all these little pieces to stay in there like that?"

Kyle set his chopsticks down, pushed his chair back from the table, and reached for the handles on Jamie's wheelchair. "Come with me, and I'll show you how it's done."

As soon as they left, Sam turned to Eli. "Thank you."

"For what?" he asked.

"For bringing us here. For giving Jamie the opportunity to see that people can live full lives with physical challenges. For introducing me to your adorable brother and his beautiful wife. For teaching me how to eat sushi."

Eli shook his head. "I can't take credit for teaching you about sushi."

Sam considered his response. "Okay, so I'll give Kyle credit for teaching us to eat sushi. But thank you, Eli, for taking Jamie fishing the other day and for keeping an eye on Curtis and for arranging the interview with Janie."

Eli held his hands up to silence her. "I get the picture. And you're welcome. You can take me out to dinner on Saturday night to pay me back."

Sam smiled. "As long as you're okay with McDonald's, which is about all I can afford at the moment."

"Throw in a chocolate sundae and you've got a deal." When his eyes met hers and she thought he might kiss her right there in the middle of the crowded restaurant, Kyle and Jamie reappeared.

Eli reached for his wallet, but Kyle refused. "It's on the house, bro. I enjoyed the company. Just don't be such a stranger."

They said their goodbyes, then hustled out to the car and across town to pick up the wine. They were headed back toward the Ashley River Bridge when Sam spotted her sister hurrying from the main building of Finley Hall to her SUV parked out front.

Sam slapped the dashboard. "Pull over."

Eli whipped his truck across two lanes to the curb.

Sam rolled down the window. "What on earth are you doing at Finley Hall?"

"I can't talk now," Jackie said, flustered. "Cooper's been in an accident."

Sam hopped out of the truck. "What kind of accident?"

"He slipped while hiking this morning. They medevacked him to Charlotte Memorial. He has a fractured skull and a broken arm, but I don't know the details." She pointed her key at her car door, but couldn't get it to unlock. "I've got to get to him, Sam."

Sam took hold of her sister's shoulders. "Look at me, Jacqueline. You can't go anywhere until you calm down. Take some deep breaths. Do you know how to get to Charlotte from here?"

"Yes. You take I-26 to I-77. My GPS will get me there."

Sam's brain kicked into crisis mode. "Okay, but since you don't know how long you'll be there, why don't I pick up some of your things and bring them to you at the hospital?"

Visibly relieved, Jackie removed her house key from her key ring and handed it to Sam. "Here's my key. I'm so glad I saw you. I'll text you my alarm code when I stop at the first stop light."

"Don't worry, Aunt Jackie," Jamie called from the car. "Cooper's gonna be fine. He has a really hard head."

Jackie managed a smile for her nephew. "He does have a hard head, doesn't he?" Then, turning to Sam, she said, "I need to get on the road now."

"Has anyone called Bill?" Sam asked.

"Not unless someone from camp called him."

Sam hugged her sister tight. "Cooper will make it through this, Jackie. But he will need the strength of both his parents to do so."

TWENTY-EIGHT

JACQUELINE

As soon as Jackie hit I-26 heading toward Columbia, she called the hospital in Charlotte to tell them she was on her way. The nurse assured her they were doing everything possible for Cooper and cautioned her to drive safely.

She placed a second call to Bill, who answered his cell right away.

"Cooper has been in an accident," she said, her tone curt. "He's at Charlotte Memorial. According to the camp director, he fell during a rock climb earlier today. He has a fractured skull and several broken bones in his left arm. That's all I know. I'm on my way there now."

There was silence on the other end, and Jackie imagined Bill massaging his eyebrow in worry. "Where's Sean?" he asked.

"He's in the emergency room with Cooper. But I haven't spoken to him yet. I don't even know if he has his cell phone, but I will try to call him when I hang up with you."

"I can be on the road in thirty minutes," he said. "I just need to run to the house and throw a few things in a bag."

Irritation crawled across her skin. "By house, I assume you mean the place where you now live with your lover."

"Now is not the time, Jack."

"There's no need for you to come, Bill. I can handle this alone. In my book, when you walk out on your wife, you walk out on your family."

"Don't be ridiculous. Of course I'm coming. When you speak to the doctor, please have him call me on my cell."

"I'll think about it," she said, and hung up.

Jackie knew she was acting like a teenage drama queen who'd recently been dumped by her boyfriend. Bill's expertise as a doctor would be invaluable in this situation, but she hated being in the position of needing anything from him.

Images of the past flashed before her as she drove. The tournament-winning blue marlin the twins caught with their grandfather. The excitement on Cooper's face when he shot his first deer, and the pride on Sean's face when he killed his first buck with a bow and arrow. The touchdowns Cooper had scored and the tackles Sean had made. Each of them had suffered a concussion along the way, but somehow they'd managed to avoid major head trauma. Until now.

It dawned on Jackie that these images were merely snapshots in her mind. She'd held the camera but had no memories associated with her photographs. She had never taken an interest in activities her sons enjoyed. She'd never gone fishing with them. Or hunting or crabbing or mud-hole punching. She'd never gone to their out-of-town football games. Hell, more often than not, she'd missed the first quarter, if not the first half, of their home games. Hunting and fishing and football were pastimes men enjoyed, dirty activities unsuitable for a lady. Yet Sam had done all those things with Jamie, had never missed a single one of his baseball games. Cooper and Sean still had two more years of high school. She'd make it up to them. If she got the chance.

The headmistress at Finley Hall had basically offered her the dance-instructor position. Interim, of course, until they could find someone permanent. Accepting the offer would mean moving to Charleston, which would enable her to rent Mrs. Graves's guest cottage and start building her client base for the interior-design firm she hoped to launch. But the cottage wasn't big enough for the three of them. And she certainly couldn't uproot the twins in their junior year of high school. Moving to Charleston meant leaving Bill alone to raise the boys. No way would she allow that to happen with Daisy Calhoun in his life. She'd all but accepted a job offer and rented a cottage without giving one ounce of consideration to her sons. What kind of mother was she?

A selfish one.

The nurses were wheeling an unconscious Cooper into surgery when she arrived at the hospital. She walked alongside his gurney and kissed his forehead before they whisked him into the operating room.

The doctor, an orthopedic surgeon with a salt-and-pepper beard and an aquiline nose, spoke briefly with Jackie. "Your son suffered a compound fracture to the humerus and extensive damage to the elbow on his left arm. We are going in now to repair the damage to both."

"What about his brain injury?" Jackie asked.

"The CT scan showed a simple linear fracture—the good kind of brain injury, if there is such a thing. Dr. Blackwell, one of our top neurologists, is monitoring your son closely. He will be in to speak with you shortly."

Dr. Grossman directed her to a waiting room, where she found Sean crumpled in a heap in the corner. His eyes were red and swollen from crying. His clothes were torn and bloody, whether from the scratches on his arms and legs or from his brother's injuries.

"Sean?" In a state of shock, it took a minute for her son to assimilate her presence. But when he broke down in sobs, she took him in her arms and held him tight.

When his sobs finally subsided, she pulled away from him. "It's okay now, son. Everything's gonna be all right."

"I couldn't hold on to him," Sean said, his voice hoarse. "He tripped on a rock and fell over the ledge. He was hanging on to a tree limb, but I couldn't reach him. His hands slipped and he fell, right in front of my eyes."

Chills traveled Jackie's spine. "How far did he fall?"

Sean wiped his nose with the back of his hand. "Not that far. But he landed on a huge boulder. He hit his head and tore up his arm. The bone was sticking out of the skin."

Jackie rubbed her son's back. "We're at a trauma hospital, in the best possible hands. All we can do now is pray."

She grasped Sean's hand, and they sat side by side on the sofa in the waiting room, staring out the bank of windows in front of them. Jackie had a hard time letting go of his hand when the nurse called his name.

"You're welcome to come with us," the nurse said. "I'm just taking him down to the ER to get him cleaned up."

Jackie glanced at the double doors that led to the operating room, then back at Sean. She'd never been torn between her boys before. They'd always been a package deal. They'd never needed her; they had always been there to support each other. But now, one without the other, both of them alone. She had no idea how to choose.

"You need to stay here, Mom, to wait for an update," Sean said.

She nodded. "That's probably best."

Bill arrived a few minutes later. Sinking to the sofa beside her, he wrapped his arm around her and told her everything would be okay, as though nothing had changed between them. The warmth of his body reminded Jackie of nights they used to lie in bed, talking until the late hours. Now he spent his nights with Daisy, making plans for his future with her.

"I spoke to the orthopedist on the phone. It sounds like the worst of the damage is to Cooper's arm and not his head, like we originally thought."

"He has a fractured skull, Bill. Any kind of brain injury is serious in my book."

"I won't argue with you there," he said. "Do we have any idea how things are going in surgery?"

"*We?*" Seething with anger, she pushed him away. "How dare you come in here acting as though we're a family again, just because we are in crisis."

"Shh! Lower your voice," he said, glancing around the room. "As far as the boys are concerned, we are still a family. I haven't told them about our separation. Have you?"

"That exciting news is yours to share, not mine."

"Look, Jack, I know you're mad—"

"You don't know the half of it." She lowered her voice to a loud whisper. "You are a bastard for breaking up our family. As far as I'm concerned, you don't deserve to be here."

"For the sake of the boys, we need to put our differences aside."

"Does that mean you're willing to put Daisy Calhoun aside?"

"I can't win with you. Where's Sean?"

"In the emergency room, getting cleaned up." Bill removed his cell phone from his coat pocket and began texting. "For God's sake, Bill. Can't you even be apart from your lover for a minute?"

"Give it a rest, Jack. I'm responding to e-mails from patients."

Jackie moved to the empty chair opposite them, sitting sideways so she could look out the window behind her. While Bill conducted his business, she watched the people in the courtyard below, coming and going through the hospital's side entrance.

Sean returned from the ER a little while later. The nurse had bandaged his scraped-up hands and given him a clean pair of scrubs to wear. "Any word?" he asked, sliding onto the sofa beside his father.

Bill shook his head. "Not yet. We are probably in for a long wait. Tell me how this happened, son. You must have been terrified."

Sean reported a much longer version of the accident to Bill than the one he'd told her earlier. He spoke in such a hushed tone Jackie could only hear bits and pieces of what he said. She could have been in another room, for all the attention they paid her. Meanwhile, his adoration and respect for his father was written all over her son's face.

What will Sean think of his father when he learns he's left them for another woman? she wondered.

The waiting room had cleared by the time Sam arrived with bags of burgers and fries and a carton of milkshakes from Cook-Out. She offered Jackie a foil-wrapped burger.

"Seriously, Sam. How could I possibly think about eating when my son's fighting for his life on the operating table?"

"Because you need to keep up your strength for Cooper."

Jackie waved the burger away, and Sam put it back in the bag.

Without asking them to move over, Sam crowded in next to Sean on the sofa. She used her teeth to open a packet of ketchup, then squirted the condiment over a box of french fries. When she handed Sean a fry, he gobbled it down in one bite.

Jackie's boys had always cozied up to their aunt. Sam had a sixth sense, the mother's intuition Jackie lacked, for knowing what they needed, food or sleep or someone to help them work out a problem at school. And it irritated the hell out of her.

Sam nudged Sean. "How're you holding up?"

"Not so good. I can't get the image of Cooper hanging from that tree branch out of my head. It's all my fault. If only I could've reached him."

"You can't blame yourself," Sam said, rubbing his back. "Accidents sometimes happen, no matter how careful we are."

"Sean has been through enough for one day, Sam," Jackie said with a snarl. "Don't make him relive the accident again."

"He doesn't have to talk about it if he doesn't want to. But sometimes it helps." Sam looked at Sean for confirmation, and he nodded. She fed him french fries while he repeated his story again, remembering details he'd left out the first two times.

Why is Sam even here? No one invited her to come. Jackie had respected her sister's privacy after Jamie's accident. She hadn't rushed food over to the hospital or held Sam's hand while Jamie was in surgery.

The waiting was torture for Jackie as she watched the second hand on the wall clock tick away one agonizing second at a time. It was nearly eight o'clock when an OR nurse appeared. "The surgery went well. Dr. Grossman will be up to talk to you soon."

"How soon is soon?" Jackie asked.

"Another hour, maybe a little longer," the nurse said.

They watched the nurse disappear through the double doors. "I reserved two rooms at the Marriott next door," Sam said to Jackie. "I'm happy to go with you, if you want to freshen up."

Jackie glared at her little sister. "You've just thought of everything now, haven't you?"

"Geez, Mom," Sean said, rolling his eyes. "She's only trying to help."

Bill removed a prescription pill bottle from his coat pocket. "Your mother's under a lot of stress, son. We all are." He unscrewed the lid and shook a few white caplets out in his hand. "Here, take one of these." He held his hand out to her. "It will help take the edge off."

"I don't handle my problems by popping pills." Jackie swatted his hand away, sending the pills to the floor.

"What is wrong with you, Mom?" Sean asked, aghast.

"You wanna know what's wrong with me?" Jackie's face was purple with rage. "I'll tell you what's wrong with me. Your father thinks he can waltz in here and act like nothing's wrong after he's spent the last three weeks in another woman's bed."

A range of emotions paraded across Sean's face—confusion,

shock, and then disbelief. His eyes met his father's, his brows raised in question.

"Let me explain, son."

Sean jumped to his feet. "You mean it's true?"

Bill stood to face him. "Yes, but—"

Sean shoved his father aside and bolted down the hall.

Bill glared at Jackie. "You handled that well," he said and took off after his son.

Jackie stared after them in a daze. She'd blown it. Instead of considering what was best for Sean, she'd let her need for revenge take control.

Jackie grabbed her purse, and with Sam on her heels, she ran toward the bank of elevators in the hall. She arrived as the elevator doors were closing, swooping Bill and Sean away to another part of the hospital.

TWENTY-NINE

SAMANTHA

S am knew better than to stop Jackie from pounding on the elevator door or tell her to be quiet when she screamed, "Let me in," over and over again. They were alone in the hallway, and Jackie needed to get it out of her system.

Finally exhausted, Jackie collapsed against the elevator with her forehead pressed to the steel door.

When Sam placed a comforting hand on her shoulder, Jackie turned around to face her. "Please don't give me a lecture, Sam. I'm not in the mood."

"Come on." Sam grabbed Jackie by the wrist and attempted to pull her into the empty elevator next to them. "You need some fresh air to clear your head."

"I can't leave. I need to be here for Cooper."

Sam nudged her sister inside the compartment and pressed the button, gripping Jackie's arm until the doors closed. "According to the nurse, the doctor won't be up for another hour. Why don't we get your bag out of my car, so you have your things with you tonight?"

They descended three floors and exited onto the second level of the attached parking deck. They walked in silence, the stench of car fumes overwhelming them. When they reached the Jeep, Sam opened the hatch door and removed Jackie's small black suitcase.

"I packed all your toiletries, a couple of nightgowns, and several changes of clothes." She handed the suitcase to Jackie. "I hope I got everything you need."

Jackie extended the handle on her suitcase and began wheeling it back the way they'd come.

Sam clicked her doors locked and rushed after her. "Not so fast, Jackie. We need to talk." She should've had this conversation with her sister weeks ago.

"Not now, Sam. I have to get back to the waiting room. I still haven't spoken with the neurologist."

"This won't take but a minute. The least you can do is hear me out, since I drove from Charleston to Prospect and all the way up here to Charlotte so you could have your toothbrush tonight."

Jackie stopped dead in her tracks. "That's on you, Saint Sammie. I never asked you to play martyr."

As much as the insult hurt, Sam couldn't deny the accusation. True, she'd insinuated herself into the situation without invitation, when her sister so clearly resented her presence. But, whether Jackie realized it or not, she needed Sam to save her from herself. And, solicited or not, Sam would offer her advice, and then she would leave. If her sister chose to self-destruct, then so be it. At least she'd tried.

"You're worse off than I thought. Be careful, big sister, or you'll drive your sons away just like you—" Sam stopped herself.

"Just like I what? Just like I drove my husband into the arms of another woman?"

Sam had already crossed the line. No reason to hold back now. "If the shoe fits . . ."

"Don't you dare talk to me about shoes," Jackie hissed. "Until you've walked a mile in mine."

Sam stared down at her worn-out Sperry Top-Siders, then

over at her sister's Manolo Blahnik wedges. "I'll take your Manolos over my beat-up deck shoes any time. The way I see it, you have everything you've ever wanted—sons who worship you, a husband who adores you, and a big house with a closet full of Tory Burch sandals and Stuart Weitzman boots."

"I've made my share of sacrifices. I gave up a chance to work with the top interior decorator in New York when I married Bill."

"You gave up a job, Jackie, not a career. You've been working at Motte Interiors all these years. You have a resume and a client base. You have choices. Either find a new job, or start your own firm. You're fifty, not eighty. It's not too late for you to start over."

"My career is not the issue here, anyway." Jackie took off again, wheeling her suitcase in and out between the rows of cars.

Sam ran to catch up with her. "I'm well aware of the real issue, Jackie. What I'd like to know is why you never bothered to tell your family that your husband left you for another woman."

Jackie kept on walking. "I wanted to spare myself from having to watch you gloat."

When they reached the elevator, Jackie jabbed her finger at the Up button three times before she finally made contact. The elevator doors opened, and Jackie wheeled her suitcase inside.

"Take it out on me all you want." Sam placed a foot against the door to keep it from closing. "But Sean is vulnerable right now. He is angry and hurt and scared. He needs love and support. If he can't get it from you, he will turn to his father. Don't make him have to choose. He needs both of you. Just as Cooper will during his recovery."

"Are you through? Because I've heard about all the advice I need to hear for one day."

The stubborn set of Jackie's jaw told Sam it was pointless to argue any longer. She doubted Jackie had heard a word she'd said. "It's too late for me to drive back tonight. I'll be at the Marriott if you need me."

"Thanks, but no thanks. Your services are no longer needed," Jackie said, and kicked Sam's foot out of the way of the door.

⁂

Unaccustomed to the pungent taste and slow burn of whiskey, Sam nursed her Dewar's and soda at the bar in the deserted hotel lounge. No wine tonight. Her fight with Jackie dictated a swift blast of numbing agent to her nerves.

Walk in her shoes, my ass. Jackie had no idea what it was like to raise a child alone, with absolutely no one in the world to rely on. No husband to rub your feet after a long day at work or tell you your new haircut looks nice even though you know it doesn't. No father to take your son on Boy Scout hikes or teach him how to shave. So what if Jackie's pride was bruised over Bill's affair with another woman? At least she had someone to support her while their son was on the operating table.

A tap on her shoulder interrupted her thoughts and brought her back to the present. She was alarmed to see Bill looming over her. "Is everything okay? Is Cooper out of surgery?"

"Yes. They finished up a little while ago." Bill rested his hand on the back of the empty bar stool next to her. "Do you mind if I join you?"

"Not at all." She moved her bar stool over to give him more room.

Bill slid onto the seat beside her. "Looks like an off night at the Marriott." He flagged down the bartender, who was glued to the Yankees game at the other end of the bar. "I'll have what she's having."

"Dewar's on the rocks?" the bartender asked Sam, having already forgotten what his lone customer was drinking.

"Dewar's and soda," she said, and the bartender snapped his fingers. "Right."

"I've never known you to belly up to the bar, Sammie."

Several sarcastic remarks came to mind, but she settled for, "It's been a long day." There was no room for animosity in their situation.

"Indeed it has." Bill proved it by guzzling a large mouthful when the bartender handed him his drink.

"Were they able to repair the damage to Cooper's arm?"

"With the aid of several pins and screws, yes. He's still unconscious though, which has the doctors somewhat perplexed. Only two people are allowed to be with him at a time. Jackie and Sean refused to leave his side, and since I'm in no position to argue . . ." He took another swill of his Dewar's. "I'm probably going to head home in the morning. The situation is awkward. Jackie and Sean don't need me adding to their stress."

"I don't think—" Sam stopped herself. When Bill looked expectantly at her, waiting for her to finish, she held her fingers to her lips, pretending to turn the key.

He nudged her. "What were you going to say?"

She shook her head. "Jackie made it clear she wanted me to butt out."

"Come on, Sam. I'm at a loss here, and I could really use your advice. I know what it's like to be the doctor, consulting the terrified family in the waiting room, but being the parent is a whole different ball game. Seeing your son unconscious and hooked up to all those machines makes you feel so . . ."

"Helpless?" she asked.

He let out a deep breath. "You've been through this. You know what to expect."

She paused, considering what to say. "I don't have any great words of wisdom for you, Bill. Except that I don't think you should leave. Whether she realizes it or not, Jackie needs you right now. Obviously she's struggling, as evidenced by her meltdown in the waiting room. And she won't talk to anybody. She has yet to tell any of us—Mom, Faith, or me—about your separation."

"That's strange. Why wouldn't she talk to you?"

"I have no idea. I think she's gone into self-preservation mode. All I know is, she shouldn't have to go through this alone. Like I did."

"Believe it or not, Sam, I know what it's like to be alone."

She raised a questioning eyebrow at him.

"It's true. Some of the loneliest people are the ones trapped in unhappy marriages."

She clinked the ice cubes in her glass as she considered the institution of marriage. She knew women who were single parents, and women like Faith who were trapped in abusive marriages, but she'd never thought about the married couples. In her mind, it was cut and dry. A man and woman stayed married if they were happy together. Otherwise, they filed for divorce.

"I have to admit, I never saw it coming," Sam said. "I always thought you and Jackie were happy."

Bill signaled to the bartender for two more drinks. "You, of all people, should know what an expert your sister is at putting up a good front."

"True."

"We put up a show, mostly for the boys but also for our friends and coworkers. Hell, we even put up a front for ourselves. It's easy to fall into the trap. You tell yourself to give it just one more day, that things will get better, and the next thing you know, twenty years have flown by and nothing has changed."

"So you found love someplace else?" Sam asked.

"Not love. Lust." Bill waited for the bartender to refill their drinks before continuing. "Daisy kept coming on to me. After a while, I couldn't resist her charms. The attention made me feel good about myself."

"Are you going to marry her?"

He took a long time to answer. "Daisy reminded me of what it's like to really connect with another human being, to share the joys in life, to stay up late talking about your hopes and dreams.

the nurse had given her. *The Old Man and the Sea*. Hemingway, of course. Required reading to prepare her boys for their American lit class in the fall—and a perfect choice for the twins who loved the ocean so much. Cooper, the more studious of the two, often read aloud to his brother at night before they went to sleep. He'd probably been hounding Sean to finish his summer reading while at camp.

She thumbed through the book until she found the dog-eared page, and began reading out loud to Cooper, soon finding herself immersed in Hemingway's simple, beautiful words.

As the first rays of sunshine streamed through the blinds, Jackie leaned back in her chair, closed her eyes, and tried to remember a time when she was truly happy. Long ago, before everything went wrong.

Four years out of college, she'd been working for a well-known decorator in Charleston when the splashy New York firm offered her a job. She'd been hesitant to accept. Not because she doubted her talents as a decorator—she received frequent compliments on her impeccable tastes—but because she couldn't imagine herself, a born-and-bred Southerner, fitting in with New York's society. So when Bill asked her to marry him, she opted to play it safe as the wife of a small-town doctor. In the process, she'd left a piece of herself on the table.

She tried to imagine her life if she'd broken up with Bill and moved to New York. She wouldn't be getting divorced or have a group of backstabbing bitches for friends. But she wouldn't have her boys, either. She'd taken them for granted, but as she watched them now, one sleeping peacefully and one in a coma, she realized they were the true loves of her life.

Sean blinked his eyes open, then raised his chair to the sitting position, suddenly awake and alert. "Is he—"

Jackie shook her head. "Nothing has changed since you've been asleep."

"Mom, about last night . . ."

Jackie reached across Cooper's feet for Sean's hand. "You had every right to say those things to me. You helped me put things in perspective. For that, I am grateful. And I'm sorry."

THIRTY-ONE

FAITH

F aith was relieved to see her sister return from Charlotte. As the numbers person, Faith knew all about bank deposits and payroll but understood little about the operation side of the seafood market. Sam had left her without any instructions, and not knowing how long her sister would be gone, Faith had stayed up late making plans for the weekend ahead. Saturdays were always their busiest day, but the Saturday coming up would be one of the busiest.

Most beach properties rented weekly from Saturday to Saturday. With the nation's birthday falling on a Saturday this year, and still over a week away, renters were faced with vacationing either the seven days prior to the holiday or the week following. Those who could afford it, of course, would stay for both. Faith and Sam had no way of knowing whether the same amount of business would be spread out over two weeks or whether the unique situation would allow more people the opportunity to enjoy a Fourth of July at the beach, which meant more money in the till at Sweeney's.

Sam watched over Jamie's shoulder as he sliced into a sushi roll. "How'd you learn to do that so quickly?"

"It's really not that hard, once you experiment a little." He smiled up at his aunt. "Faith and I decided this weekend would be a good time to test the market."

"And I know just the spot to showcase them," Sam said. "In the refrigerator case on the side where we keep the salads."

Faith cast a nervous glance toward Jamie. "We were thinking front and center by the checkout counter might draw the most attention."

"That would probably work. Let's go have a look." Sam draped her arm around Faith's shoulders and guided her to the showroom.

"Hey, boss," Roberto called out to Sam. "Don't forget my cousin's wedding is this weekend."

"I haven't forgotten," Sam said, over her shoulder. "But thanks for reminding me."

"He never mentioned that to me," Faith said. "How can we possibly do without him on a busy weekend like this?"

"Roberto has it all figured out," Sam said. "He's stocking up today and tomorrow, then he plans to come in early on Monday to replenish anything we sell out of over the weekend."

When Lovie caught sight of Sam, she rushed over to her, leaving a customer waiting at the cash register for her credit card receipt. "How is Sean? I've been so worried. Why haven't you called?"

Sam shot Faith a death stare. "Let's give this lady her receipt first, Mom, then I'll tell you about Cooper." Sam tore the white slip of paper from the credit card machine and handed it to the customer.

"Why did you tell her?" Sam mouthed to Faith, over her mother's head, once the customer was gone.

Faith shrugged. She didn't think Sam could've done a better job placating their mother in her current, seemingly constant, state of confusion. When Jamie and Eli returned from Charleston with two cases of wine but no Sam, Lovie had harassed Faith

chairs and smashed the glass in the frames of the family photos scattered about. Using Jamie's baseball bat, he'd shattered the screens on the flat-screen television as well as the desktop computer. And he'd written graffiti on the walls in what appeared to be ketchup and mustard—*bitch* and *slut*, respectively.

"We should take pictures." Eli held out his iPhone to use as a camera. "If you have homeowner's insurance, they will replace your valuables and pay to have the house professionally cleaned."

"What's valuable to me, Eli, are things like Jamie's artwork." Sam pointed to the ruined watercolor above the mantel. "He painted that in art class his freshman year. That's a scene from his favorite spot on the inlet. Those things cannot be replaced."

Faith hung her head in shame. She'd warned her sister this might happen, but that didn't make her feel any less guilty.

Eli removed a small notepad from his top shirt pocket. "We need to determine what valuables are missing. Jewelry. Cash. Things like that."

"I hadn't even thought of that," Sam said, raking her fingers through her short hair. "Let me go check my room." With Faith and Eli on her heels, Sam dashed down the hallway to her bedroom.

"None of my jewelry is worth much, except the diamond studs I bought for myself and the silver bangle Jamie gave me for Christmas two years ago." She opened her jewelry box and poked through the contents. "Which are both gone."

"What about the pearls Daddy gave you?" Faith asked, thinking about her own pearls tucked away under the lining of her suitcase.

Sam poked a little more. "Nope. They're gone, too." She closed her jewelry box and took in the rest of the room, the pile of shredded clothes strewn across her bed and floor. Her eye caught sight of an empty metal box on the floor of her closet. "Oh God, no." She dropped to her hands and knees and dug through the shoes and handbags in her closet. She sat back on her feet, dazed and bewildered. "I can't believe that bastard took Jamie's gun. My father gave Jamie that revolver, Eli. It was the first gun Daddy ever owned. How do you replace a sentimental object like that?"

Eli helped Sam to her feet. "I will get Jamie's gun back for him, Sam, if it's the last thing I do. And when I find Curtis, I'm going to make him pay."

Faith sensed a change in Eli. Despite his obvious feelings for Sam, he'd maintained a professional approach to their case. Until now. Faith could tell by his clenched teeth and the deep grooves in his brow that the situation had become personal.

The house phone rang, startling them all back to reality. Sam reached for the cordless, her eyes zeroing in on the caller ID. "Mom, I'm in the middle of something. Can I . . ." She paused, listening, the color draining from her face. "I'm on my way. Lock your doors and stay in your bedroom. I'll let myself in with my key." She ended the call and tossed the phone on the bed.

The hair on the back of Faith's neck stood to attention. "What happened?"

"Curtis broke into Mom's house. He was waiting for her when she got out of the shower. He held her at gunpoint and demanded she give him all the money in her wallet. I assume the gun was Jamie's, since the police confiscated his."

"He won't get far on five dollars," Faith said.

"She had five *hundred* dollars on her, Faith. Apparently, she was planning to do some early Christmas shopping on Sunday." Sam made for the door. "I've got to get over there."

"I'll drive you." Eli removed his handheld from his belt and barked some orders to his partner. "I'm leaving Swanson in charge while I'm gone," he said to Faith. "He's bringing the kids inside where they'll be safe."

Sam and Eli had barely cleared the front door when Swanson came down the hall with her exhausted sleeping daughter in his arms.

"Let's put her in here." Faith entered the room ahead of the policeman and swept the remnants of clothing from the bed to the floor.

Swanson lay the sleeping child on the bed. When Bitsy rolled over and closed her eyes, Faith pulled the coverlet up over her daughter's small body. When she straightened, she saw the love note from her husband. Using her Pink Possibilities Maybelline lipstick, Curtis had scribbled *Die Bitch* on the mirror above the bureau.

"What do you make of that?" she asked Swanson, her head inclined toward the mirror.

Swanson grew still. "I have to treat that as a death threat."

"That's what I thought," she said, and began sorting through what was left of her wardrobe on the floor.

The time had come for Faith to set in motion the plan she had been formulating for days. She refused to let Curtis take his anger out on Sam. She hoped that removing the cookie from the cookie jar would eliminate his temptation.

While she waited for Sam to return with their mother, Faith packed the clothes that were still wearable and shoved the scraps of ruined garments in a trash bag. She was folding Bitsy's clothes into her suitcase when Jamie appeared in the doorway.

"What's going on?" she asked, kicking the suitcase under the bed where he couldn't see it.

"I just got a text from Sean," he said, grinning from ear to ear. "Cooper has regained consciousness."

THIRTY-TWO

SAMANTHA

S am stepped over the debris on the floor in a hurry to get to the brown paper bag she'd left on the island earlier. She removed the bottle of Wild Turkey from the bag, got a glass from the cabinet, and poured herself two fingers of brown liquid. She kicked it back in one gulp.

"That's not going to help, Sammie," Lovie said.

"Like hell it's not." Sam poured another shot.

Eli searched for a clean spot to set Lovie's overnight bag. "Listen to your mom, Sam. The booze might seem like it's helping now, but when the drinking spirals out of control, and it always does, you'll have another whole set of problems to deal with."

"I'll worry about that when it happens. Right now, this whiskey is making it a hell of a lot easier for me to face this mess." She downed the brown liquid and went to the laundry closet for the broom.

"Mom, guess what!" Jamie arrived on the scene with Faith on his wheels. "Sean just texted me. Cooper woke up."

"Oh, thank heavens." Lovie's hand flew to the rusty key around her neck.

Sam stared at her mother in disbelief. "I just told you that, Mom, remember? Jackie called while we were in the car on the way over here."

Lovie's face turned red. "Oh yes, of course. I remember," she said, although no one in the room believed her.

Sam softened, reminding herself that a deranged lunatic had just robbed her mother at gunpoint. "I didn't mean to snap at you, Mama." She put her arm around her mother's shoulders. "It's been a tough night."

Lovie patted Sam's hand. "I understand. You're under a lot of stress."

Sam locked eyes with her sister across the room. Aside from making a poor choice of husbands, none of this was her fault. "Jackie insists we stay at her house. Why don't you take Mom and Bitsy, and Jamie if he wants to go, on over tonight while I clean up here?"

"No way I'm leaving you here to clean up by yourself." Faith glanced at the clock, hanging askew on the wall. "It's almost nine, anyway. Bitsy is sound asleep, probably out for the night."

"If we all pitch in, we can have this mess cleaned up in no time," Lovie said.

Sam took in the eager faces of her family members. Lovie and Oscar had led by example, teaching Sam and her sisters that hard work is the foundation on which everything in life is built. "I can't offer you any dinner in this mess."

"We'll clean up first and worry about food later," Jamie said.

"Let's get to work, then." Sam handed her mom the broom and returned to the laundry closet for additional supplies.

"My shift ends at nine," Eli said, lining the bottles of Lysol, Windex, and Soft Scrub up on the island as she handed them to him. "I'll run Swanson over to the station, change my clothes, then come back and help."

"Eli, really. You've already done enough." Sam grabbed a

handful of rags and a bucket, and closed the closet doors. "We will have this all cleaned up in a flash."

"And you'll be starved when you finish. How about if I grab some food on the way back?"

Too tired to argue, she said, "On behalf of my cleaning crew, I accept."

Once the policemen were gone, Sam divvied up the chores. She assigned Jamie the job of cleaning the counters in the kitchen and removing the photographs from the broken frames around the house. Faith was responsible for scrubbing the graffiti off the walls while Lovie swept the kitchen floor and vacuumed the sitting room. Sam retreated to her bedroom with the bottle of Wild Turkey, where she tackled the mess in her closet and on the floor.

Eli returned an hour later with a bag of burritos, and they gathered around the now-clean island to eat. While devouring their food, they discussed Cooper's health. According to Jackie, the doctors anticipated a full recovery.

Why can't Jamie be so lucky? Sam thought.

After they finished eating, Eli joined the cleaning brigade by scrubbing the ketchup stains on the sisal rug in the sitting room with a stiff brush and hot, soapy water. Sam sensed him watching her while they worked, keeping tabs on the number of times she refilled her glass. She considered him a friend—he'd certainly earned that title—but they were far from being close enough for him to criticize her for drinking too much.

They'd done all they could do, without a gallon of paint and a steam cleaner, when they decided to call it a night around eleven.

"What's to prevent this from happening again?" Sam asked Eli when she showed him to the door.

He pointed at the police cruiser parked across the street. In the dark, Sam could barely make out a figure in the driver's seat.

"That unit will be here as much as possible throughout the night, but I can't guarantee they won't get another call. We're

Sam passed out in a bourbon coma on the sofa sometime around three, only to be awakened four hours later by the relentless ringing of Faith's alarm clock.

"Turn that damn thing off," Sam hollered, wincing at the pain of her own voice echoing in her head. She reached for the nearly empty bottle of bourbon on the coffee table and shoved it under the sofa, where no one could see it.

When Faith's clock continued to buzz, she yelled, "Come on, Faith, I'm exhausted. Turn it off."

After several more minutes, she rolled off the sofa and stumbled down the hall to the guest room, where she discovered Faith's bed empty and her suitcase gone. Her nightmare from a few nights ago came rushing back to her. In her dream, Faith had been wandering around a dense forest of pine trees at night, dragging her suitcase behind her with Bitsy hanging from her hip. Sensing a presence lurking in the forest, her sister had begun to run. With only the light of the full moon to guide her, Faith ran for what seemed like miles, dodging in and out of the pines, until she came to a dead end at the water's edge. She could either jump in and swim, or turn around and face her assailant.

Sam had woken up in a cold sweat, with Curtis's malicious grin embedded in her memory.

※

Even though she knew she wouldn't find her, Sam searched the house from one end to the other for her sister. Faith had warned Sam that she might go into hiding. While Sam applauded her baby sister for having the courage to make good on her threat, she knew Faith had placed her life, and her daughter's, in even more danger. Being out in the open, without her family to protect her, made Faith and Bitsy easy targets. Curtis was out for revenge. And not just against Faith. He wanted Sam's blood as well. He'd harbored his hatred for her since that Christmas Eve long ago.

Sam found her cell phone, the battery dead, at the bottom of her purse. She plugged the phone into the charger and waited for it to power up. Her phone pinged with incoming e-mails and chimed with one lone text message from Faith: "Thanks for everything. Don't worry about me. I have a plan. I can't continue to put your lives in danger. xoxo Faith."

Sam dialed Eli's number. His voice was husky with sleep when he answered.

"Eli, it's Sam. I'm sorry to call so early, but Faith has disappeared."

"Disappeared? As in kidnapped?"

"I don't think so. She sent me a text message. She and Bitsy have gone on the run, but she didn't say where. At some point, she mentioned a shelter."

"Does Faith have access to a computer?"

"Only mine, which—"

"Curtis destroyed in his rampage yesterday." Eli sighed. "All right." Sam heard the rustling of bed sheets. "Let me get down to the station. I'll stop by the market later and let you know what I find out."

Sam set six strips of bacon in a pan to fry, knowing the aroma would rouse her mother and Jamie out of bed. They both appeared, bed-headed and groggy-eyed, within a few minutes. "We have a problem," she said, and went on to explain Faith's disappearance.

Lovie's eyes grew wide. "But she has nowhere to go."

"I think Faith has in mind to go to a shelter, Mom. Eli is already on the case. With any luck, she won't get far."

Lovie fingered the key around her neck. "Poor little Bitsy, shuffled from here to yonder. She must be scared to death."

"I'm sure Faith is taking good care of her daughter." Sam returned to the stove, forking the cooked bacon onto a paper towel. "In the meantime, we have other important things to worry about—namely, how we are going to manage the busiest weekend of the year with two of our employees gone?"

"Thanks to Roberto, we have enough food to last a week," Jamie said.

"I'm not as worried about prepping the food as I am about having the staff to wait on the customers. I fully expect business to pick up this afternoon, with homeowners eager to arrive ahead of the renters."

Sam's day flew by. In between servicing the crowd that had begun to trickle in early, she processed a shipment of seafood and stocked the wine racks and produce bins. But the constant distractions didn't stop Sam from worrying about Faith. Her panic accelerated as each hour passed with no word from Eli.

Sam was stocking the cases in preparation for an early start the next day when Eli stopped by just before closing time.

"I have good news and bad news," he said.

The hopeful smile vanished from her face. "Give me the bad news first."

"Faith has disappeared without a trace."

She sighed. "I can't say I'm surprised. When Faith makes up her mind to do something, she doesn't mess around."

"We're not giving up, though. I blasted her picture out to my statewide network, which includes all the homeless and women's shelters. She won't get far without someone recognizing her."

Sam slid the last containers of lobster mac and cheese in the refrigerator case and closed the door. "I can hardly wait to hear the good news."

"In my opinion, it's great news." Eli held up the latest edition of *Lowcountry Living* magazine.

Sam's eyes zeroed in on the cover. "That's us," she said, pointing to the photo of Sam and Faith standing beneath the interlocking *Ss* on the wall. "I can't believe Janie gave us the cover." She snatched the magazine away from him and carried it over to show her mother at checkout.

"Isn't that something," Lovie said, marveling at the picture.

Sam flipped through the magazine until she found the feature. The title read: "Oscar Sweeney's Legacy Lives On." Beaming with pride, she read the two-page article out loud to Eli, Lovie, and Jamie, who appeared from the kitchen curious about all the commotion.

"Generations of vacationers have made Sweeney's a tradition, their last stop on the way to the beach for their family vacation . . . . The Sweeney family offers the largest variety of fresh seafood available in the state . . . . Served by a knowledgeable staff with a heaping helping of Southern hospitality . . . . Don't forget to ask for one of Lovie's top-secret recipes . . ."

Sam handed the article to her mother and engulfed Eli in a huge hug. "You did this for us. Thank you. You may very well have saved Sweeney's."

Eli grinned. "Does this mean I'm forgiven for yesterday, for taking my eyes off the ball long enough for Curtis to score?"

Her face grew serious as she remembered her ruined furniture. "None of that is your fault, Eli. You said yourself, the force doesn't have the manpower to offer personal bodyguards."

"If you're in the market for a bodyguard, I'd like to apply for the job," Eli said, winking at Sam.

"Ha. I'd hire you right now, except I can't afford to pay you."

He smiled, a naughty twinkle reaching his eyes. "I can think of plenty of ways for you to pay."

"Get a room, you two," Jamie said, and everyone laughed.

"When does this issue hit the stands?" Lovie asked.

"Today," Eli said. "Janie wanted to get it out well in advance of the holiday. She sends her apologies, by the way."

"I'm indebted to her for the rest of my life. What could she possibly have to apologize for?"

"She promised you a chance to preview the article before it

your sister, and your nephew. I'm committed to seeing this through. I won't stop until we have Curtis in custody."

"Assuming you catch him, how long can you keep him in jail?" Faith asked. "He threatened us with a gun the last time, and you were barely able to keep him through the weekend."

"We have plenty of charges to throw at him. And this time the judge won't offer him bail. Once he's locked up, he's not going anywhere for a long time, at least until Bitsy graduates from high school."

"But now we have Mama to consider," Faith said. "Where is she, anyway?"

"With Bill and Sean," Sam said. "They're taking Mom by her house to get her things, then picking the dogs up from the kennel before heading out to the farm."

Faith looked at her sister, then her nephew. "I love you all so much. It would kill me if anything happened to you because of me."

"How do you think we'd feel if anything happened to you?" This time, when Sam wrapped her arm around her, Faith did not push her away. "If you leave town, Curtis will follow you. You will be on the run for the rest of your life."

"Is there enough room for all of us at the farm?" Faith asked. "Jamie needs a first-floor bedroom."

"There's plenty of room," Sam said. "Jamie and I can stay in the guest cottage, which has a first-floor master suite."

"Bill described his alarm system to me," Eli said. "In addition to having all the windows and doors wired in the main house and the cottage, he has a variety of motion and light sensors positioned at various points on the property. I'm confident you will be safe."

"What do you think, Bits?" Jamie whispered to his cousin, loud enough for everyone to hear. "We're all going to Sean's for a great big sleepover. Wanna come?"

Bitsy removed her thumb from her mouth. "A sleepover?" she said, her voice soft and fragile.

"Don't get her hopes up, Jamie," Faith said. "I haven't made up my mind."

Bitsy crawled out of Jamie's lap and ran to her mother. "Please, Mama."

Faith reached down and picked the child up. Bitsy pulled her mother's head close so she could whisper in her ear, "Can we please go? I'm afraid Daddy will find us and shoot you. Then I'll have to be his little girl forever."

THIRTY-FOUR

SAMANTHA

S am beamed with delight as she counted the credit card receipts at the end of the day on Saturday. Sweeney's sales had exceeded her expectations for the first of the two big holiday weekends. She contributed a large part of their success to Janie Jasper's feature article. Throughout the day, she had spotted a copy of the latest issue of *Lowcountry Living* in more than one customer's oversize travel bag.

Roberto had planned well. Aside from a few of their more popular items, shrimp salad and gazpacho among them, they had plenty of inventory to open with on Monday. Same with the raw goods. In anticipation of a large crowd, Sam had overstocked, which should carry her through until a new shipment arrived late Monday afternoon. Jamie's sushi won the prize for bestseller. Every last package had been sold.

As she did every evening upon closing, Sam checked the temperature settings on the thermostats and made sure the doors on the refrigerated merchandizers were shut tight and the front door was locked. She flipped the Open sign to Closed and turned off all the lights on her way to the kitchen.

"If we want to have this cookout we've been talking about all day, I need to get to the grocery store before the beachgoers buy up all the hamburger meat," she said, hustling her family out the back door.

"I'll go with you, Mom." Jamie turned the key in the dead bolt. "None of us should go anywhere alone."

"That would leave these three damsels in distress," Sam said, smiling over at Faith, Lovie, and Bitsy.

"Sean's at the farm." Jamie removed his phone from his shirt pocket. "I'll text him, to let him know they're on their way home."

Sam cast a doubtful glance at her sister, who waved her on. "Go. Don't worry about us. You do the shopping, and we'll get the grill going."

"Okay, fine. I'm sure Eli is lurking around here somewhere, anyway," Sam said, wheeling Jamie toward the Jeep. "I've seen his patrol car pass by multiple times throughout the day."

Once they were buckled in and Sam had started the car, Jamie turned to her and held up his hand. "High-five. Today was a good day. Does this mean we're out of danger of bankruptcy?"

She slapped his hand, then crossed her fingers. "The jury is still out, but I'm definitely breathing a little easier."

Sam and Jamie daydreamed their way to the Harris Teeter. They talked about adding a butcher, maybe even an auxiliary food truck to hit different hot spots during the lunch hour. Sam even convinced Jamie to consider his education, perhaps culinary school if he decided not to pursue a degree in business management from Carolina.

Mother and son were so busy making plans for their future they hadn't noticed Curtis following them. He approached the Jeep as Sam was helping Jamie into his chair.

"Well, looky here. If it ain't the cripple and his sexy mommy."

When she heard his voice, Sam spun around to face him. "We don't want any trouble, Curtis. Be on your way, and I won't have to call the police."

"Fat chance, that." Curtis took a step toward her, reeking of stale cigarettes and alcohol.

Sam shoved Jamie's chair to the side. "Leave him out of it. He's just a kid."

"I ain't got nothing against the boy. It's you I'm after, bitch." He lifted a bucket of paint, preparing to douse her with it.

Jamie cried, "Mom, watch out!"

Sam's hands shot up, but her reaction time was too slow. She stumbled backward, clawing at her eyes and her nose and her mouth. The thick liquid clogged her air passages, preventing her from breathing. Suffocating, she panicked and opened her mouth to scream, but the sound that escaped was muffled.

"Next time it won't be red paint. Next time it'll be Faith's blood."

Although she couldn't see him, Sam sensed Curtis's presence in front of her, but when she tried to grab at him, she came up with a fistful of air.

"Hey! What the hell is going on here?"

Sam recognized Mack's gruff voice. She then heard the clanging of metal hitting pavement followed by the pounding of feet running away.

She swiped at her eyes. "I can't see! What's happening?"

"Don't do that, Mom." Jamie's hands were on hers pulling them away from her face. "You'll make it worse."

"He's right, ma'am," a strange voice said. "Try not to rub your eyes. I'll be right back."

"Who was that, Jamie?" she asked. "Where's he going?"

"He's the owner of the RV that was parked in front of us. He went inside his camper. I guess to get a towel."

Her eyes burned, her mouth was full of paint, and she worried she would be blinded for life.

Somewhere to the right of her, she heard Jamie reporting the assault to the 911 operator.

"Tell them to send Eli!" Sam said. "I need Eli."

"I'm texting him now, Mom." Jamie gave her hand a comforting squeeze. "Try not to panic."

"I'm a doctor. Let me help." The stranger was back, his gentle voice calming. "I'm going to guide you over to my camper."

She felt a hand on her forearm, a warm body at her side. She followed his lead, putting one foot in front of the other.

"Now, I want you to sit down in the doorway of my camper so I can look at your eyes."

When Sam felt the pressure of his hands on her shoulders, she bent her knees slowly and felt for the doorway behind her.

"Can somebody hand me that paint bucket over there?" the gentle doctor called out.

There was a long pause. "What's happening?" Sam asked.

"I'm just reading the label on the paint bucket, to see what kind of paint we're dealing with." Another pause. "Good, it's latex. Nothing a little soapy water won't cure."

She felt something warm and wet on her eyes.

"The soap may burn, but whatever you do, don't open your eyes until I say so."

Sam sat still while the doctor wiped at her eyes again and again.

"I'm going to splash some fresh water on your eyes, then dry them with a towel."

Sam leaned forward to allow for better positioning. She pressed her lids tight while the doctor splashed her face repeatedly.

"You can sit up now."

She straightened. When she felt a dry towel dabbing at her eyes, she grabbed it from him, burying her whole face in it. She pulled the towel away and blinked her eyes open. She'd never been so happy to see her son, no matter how blurry his face appeared. She closed her eyes, resting them for a minute. When she opened them the second time, Mack was bent over in front of her, taking big gulps of air.

"Did you get him, Mack?"

Mack inhaled another deep breath and straightened. "He got away from me, but the police are hot on his trail."

"Are your eyes still burning?" The hardened face in front of her did not match the doctor's gentle voice. She'd pictured a small-framed man with a crew cut and wire-rimmed glasses. This man, this so-called doctor, was bald with a round face covered in red whiskers, mustache and beard, and bushy eyebrows. Under normal circumstances, she might have mistaken him for one of Curtis's friends. She imagined him riding across the country on the back of a Harley Davidson—not greeting patients in an examining room.

"What kind of doctor are you?" she asked.

He chuckled. "I'm actually a veterinarian. I figured if I told you I treated animals instead of humans, you might not trust me."

"That explains your soft voice," she said. "Do your clients call you the pet whisperer?"

"I've been called that a time or two," he said, and let out a deep belly laugh.

From a distance, she recognized Eli's stocky frame approaching with a blanket in his outstretched hands. Once he reached her, he wrapped the blanket around her shoulders and helped her to her feet. "Let's get you home. I'll drive you and Jamie in your Jeep and leave Swanson to interview the witnesses."

"Thank you for your kindness," she said to the pet whisperer. "You have a better bedside manner than most doctors I know." She held her hand out to him.

"You're welcome, kind lady," he said, kissing the back of her hand. He slapped Eli on the back. "Find the bastard who did this to her."

"We're on it," Eli said.

Sam pulled the blanket up over her head and kept her eyes glued to the ground as Eli led her to the car. She felt like the

285

main attraction in the freak show at a state fair. Under Jamie's protests, she crawled in the backseat of the Jeep and curled up in a fetal position.

How could such a great day go south so quickly?

Her relief over being able to see gave way to rage as she listened to Jamie answer Eli's endless stream of questions. Curtis had changed the game rules. The stakes were higher than ever, and she didn't want to play anymore. He had destroyed her home and damn near blinded her. Next time he might douse her with gasoline and strike a match.

Next time he might go after her son.

※

Faith and Lovie were waiting for her outside the guest cottage, with a large container of dishwashing liquid and a stack of old towels.

Lovie wrapped her arm around Sam. "Come on, honey. Let's get you cleaned up."

"I've already got the shower running for you," Faith said, holding the door open for her sister.

"I don't need your help," Sam said, brushing her mother off. She grabbed the dishwashing detergent from Faith and a bottle of vodka from the fully stocked bar on her way up to her room.

"The booze will only make it worse, Sam," Eli called up after her.

She slammed the bathroom door in response.

Locking the door behind her, she unscrewed the liquor bottle's cap and took a long pull of vodka. She peeled off her paint-soaked clothes and tested the water before stepping into the shower, bottle in hand. In between swigs of vodka, she lathered and rinsed and repeated until the water ran clear.

Enveloped in the soft terry-cloth robe her sister provided for guests, Sam curled up in the corner of the bathroom, between the toilet and the window, with the vodka. The alcohol hit her empty stomach, making her feel woozy. She drank more, in desperate search for oblivion. When the room began to spin, she lay down on the floor, letting the cool marble soothe the raw skin on her face.

She passed out, only to be awakened a while later by Eli's persistent pounding on the door. "Open up, Sam."

"Go away!"

"If you don't open this door, I'll break it down. And I'm pretty good at it, too. I've had a lot of practice."

Despite her foul mood, Sam found this funny and covered her mouth to stifle a laugh. She crawled over to the door and opened it. "Leave me alone, Eli. I'm not in the mood for a sermon about addiction. Go find someone else to preach to about the virtues of your twelve-step program."

Placing one hand on each arm, Eli lifted her off the floor to her feet. "How about a hamburger, then? I have a fat juicy one waiting for you downstairs."

She didn't want food. She wanted more vodka. But if eating would get Eli off her back and food in her stomach, she would eat first, then have more to drink after he left.

He took her hand and led her downstairs to the small living area. Once she was settled on the sofa, he handed her a tray and sat down next to her.

"Aren't you going to eat?" she asked.

"I've already eaten, on the terrace with the others. We missed you. Jamie is quite the chef."

She pinched off a piece of hamburger and shoved it in her mouth.

"Why don't I talk while you eat? I'd like to tell you about my near-death experience with alcohol, if you're willing to listen."

He'd trapped her of course, but she couldn't very well say no. His patronizing attitude toward her drinking grated her nerves, but as much as she hated to admit it, she was curious about the events that had made him that way.

"I'm willing to listen. As long as you don't expect anything from me in return."

"Is it expecting too much for me to ask you not to judge me?"

"As long as you take your own advice and don't judge me." He shot her a gimme-a-break look, and she shrugged. "You backed yourself into that corner."

Eli leaned back against the cushions, pausing in thought before speaking. "When I was a junior in high school, I killed a kid."

Sam's sharp intake of breath caused her to choke on her food. Eli slapped her back, then handed her the glass of iced tea he'd poured for her. "You killed someone?" she asked when she was able to talk again.

"I now know it was an accident. But let me start from the beginning. I was the starting inside linebacker for my high school varsity team. It was my junior year, and college coaches from every division were recruiting me." Eli caught Sam sizing him up. "I may not be very tall, but I am strong and fast, even more so back then."

He took a sip of iced tea and licked his lips. "Anyway, we were playing against this prep school from North Carolina. Their quarterback handed the ball off to the running back, and I tackled him—a perfectly legal tackle. I didn't ram my helmet into his or anything like that. But the kid hit the ground hard, and the force of the blow killed him on impact. I learned later that he already had a concussion no one knew about. But at the time, as I watched the paramedics wheel his body off the field, all I could think about was that I'd taken another person's life, a kid who'd barely begun to live.

"My parents made me go to the funeral, which did little to ease my guilt."

Sam set her dinner tray on the coffee table, her appetite gone. "I can't imagine how hard that must've been for you."

"I started drinking any kind of alcohol I could get my hands on. I stole booze from my parents and my friends' parents, and when I still wasn't drunk enough, I paid the bums outside of the liquor store to buy me pints of cheap bourbon. I started skipping class, then I stopped going to school altogether, and before I knew it, I was flunking every one of my courses.

"My parents finally shipped me off to rehab, where I stayed for three days. I took money out of a nurse's wallet, got my hands on a bottle of booze, and hopped on the next bus headed to Nowhere, New Mexico. I passed out before I got to Atlanta and woke up in a dumpster in Nashville, Tennessee. I'd been raped and beaten within an inch of my life."

Sam's mouth formed the word *raped* but no sound came out.

He looked away in shame.

She placed a hand on his shoulder, encouraging him to continue. "What did you do then?"

"I called Kyle, who boarded the next plane to Nashville. He rented a furnished apartment, and for the next month, he stayed by my side. He nursed me while I detoxed, held me when I cried out in my sleep. He listened and he counseled. He helped me understand that Alexander Brooks's death was not my fault. He helped me find my way again."

Sam dabbed at her eyes with her napkin. "Did you ever play football again?"

Eli shook his head. "I never went back to high school. I got my GED, moved to New York City, and joined the police academy."

This surprised Sam. She'd always assumed Eli had gone to college before becoming a policeman. She had no idea he'd lived anywhere other than South Carolina. "Why New York?"

He shifted on the sofa to face her. "Over sixty thousand homeless people live in New York, many of them kids who have lost their way. As a police officer, I was in a position to help them, to keep them out of harm's way and find them shelter whenever possible."

"Why did you decide to move back to South Carolina?"

"I came home to be with Kyle after his accident."

"So you returned the favor."

"I didn't do it because of any debt of gratitude. Although I was plenty grateful to him for saving my life. We take care of each other. That's what families do. I don't need to tell you that. Look what you've done for Faith."

"I haven't done a very good job of taking care of Faith. I've basically fallen apart on her." Sam could admit it. She just couldn't stop it. She'd listened to Eli describe how alcohol had nearly destroyed his life, yet she still felt tempted by the bottles of rum and gin and vodka on the bar across the room.

"Don't you think some of what you're experiencing is fallout from Jamie's accident?" he asked. "Not just the surgery, but watching him suffer over the death of his best friend and seeing him struggle to walk again. You've been through hell and back, Sam. Most women in your shoes would've cracked a long time ago. All your life, you've been strong for everyone else. Now it's time to let them be strong for you. Let me help you, Sam." He tucked a stray strand of hair behind her ear. "I think your alcohol abuse is out of control."

She knocked his hand away. "I can quit anytime I want to."

"You're in denial," he said, shaking his head in disbelief. "You have no idea how many alcoholics have said that very same thing to me. Most of them have not lived long enough to prove it."

Sam jumped to her feet. "I plan on living long enough to prove it to you. But I can't prove it to you until you put Curtis behind bars. You do your job, Eli. Then I'll do mine." She stomped off toward the stairs, stopping long enough to grab her bottle of vodka from the bar along the way.

THIRTY-FIVE

FAITH

Faith woke from a fitful sleep to the sound of the dogs barking, relentless and ferocious.

Curtis.

She slipped on her robe and scurried down the stairs to the game room. Through the french doors, she spotted Mack, pinned up against the side of the guest cottage by the barking dogs.

She punched in the alarm code on the keypad beside the door. "Felix, Max, heel," she commanded, and the dogs darted to her side. She bent down to pet them. "Morning," she said to Mack. "I didn't know you were coming over so early."

He loosened his grip on the shotgun he clutched in the crook of his arm. "Actually, I never left last night."

She noticed his windbreaker rolled into a pillow on the wooden bench beside the door. "Did you sleep on that bench?"

He shrugged. "It didn't feel right leaving, after what happened to Sam yesterday."

"You mean you've been here all this time, and the dogs are just now noticing you?"

He chuckled. "Some guard dogs. They sniffed and licked me

291

all during the night, then for some reason turned on me this morning."

"They're just mad at you for not feeding them," she said. "Let me get them some food, and I'll fix us some coffee."

She was in the garage scooping dry kibble into giant-size bowls when Eli wandered down the driveway. "Out for a stroll so early?" she called.

He shook his head. "I thought I'd run Sam's car over to our shop to see if they can get some of this paint off." He ran his hand over the paint-splattered door. "You don't happen to know where I might find her keys, do you?"

Mack removed a set of keys from his pocket and tossed them to Eli. "I took these from her last night. Not that she was in any condition to drive."

"That was smart thinking," Eli said.

Faith replaced the lid on the dog-food container. "Mack and I were just going upstairs for some coffee. Care to join us?" she asked Eli.

He glanced at his watch. "Sure, why not? Technically I'm not on duty for another hour."

"Are you working the early shift this week?" Faith asked.

"No. I put in for overtime. Whether I get paid or not, I plan to work around the clock until Curtis is behind bars."

"That's awfully generous of you, Eli. I don't know how to thank you."

He smiled. "I'll settle for that cup of coffee."

"Then what are we waiting for?" Faith asked, and the two men followed her upstairs. When they each had a steaming mug in hand, Faith suggested they go out on the porch. "They're forecasting a scorcher. We might as well get some fresh air while we can."

Once they were settled in the rocking chairs, Mack asked Eli, "Any leads on Curtis's whereabouts?"

"Yes. Well, sort of." Eli glanced nervously at Faith. "We found

THIRTY-SIX

SAMANTHA

S am spent most of the day in bed, buried beneath a mountain of pillows, hiding from the bastard who continued to stalk her. It was late afternoon before she stumbled down the stairs to the bar.

"What the fuck," she said when she discovered all the bottles of booze gone.

She went to the adjoining kitchen to check the cabinets. She was so preoccupied with her search that she didn't notice Mack sitting at the bar reading the paper.

"What're you looking for?" he asked.

"A drink," she said. She opened the refrigerator and found the dregs of a bottle of Chardonnay on the door. She lifted the bottle to her lips, but only a few drops trickled out.

"That's not going to help your situation."

"You know,"—she pointed the bottle at him—"people keep telling me that, but so far everyone's been wrong. The alcohol helps quite a bit."

"Maybe in the short term." He came around the bar and took the bottle from her. "This isn't who you are, Sammie." He set the bottle on the counter. "Your father didn't teach you to solve your problems by getting drunk. Where's that spunky little girl who used to stomp her foot at her father, demanding he take her along on a deer hunt? Where's that brave girl who challenged the great Oscar Sweeney to shooting matches and beat him every time?"

Sam eyed Oscar's shotgun propped up in the corner. "That's what I need. A gun. Do you have one I can borrow? Curtis stole mine."

"If it'll make you feel safer, I have a handgun you can borrow."

Sam relished the idea of having a loaded pistol as protection against that lowlife son-of-a-bitch brother-in-law. "I better not," she said. "I might end up shooting my sister."

"You don't mean that."

"I do, actually." She held her thumb and index fingers up, about an inch apart. "At least a little bit. A part of me can't help but blame her for dragging us into her drama."

"Then why'd you stop Faith from running away the other night?"

"A moment of weakness, I guess."

"You promised Faith you'd do whatever you can to keep her safe. Now you have to honor that promise. She's not as strong as you are, Sam," Mack said, his voice stern. He'd never spoken to her like that before—like a father, reprimanding his daughter—and it got her attention.

"That's the problem, Mack. Everyone expects me to be strong, including you." Her eyes filled with tears. "But I don't have that kind of strength. How am I supposed to fight a slime-ball like Curtis? He sneaks around, hiding behind cars and bushes, destroying my house and throwing paint in my face. He has total control of my life right now, and I can't handle it. I feel so vulnerable. So alone."

Mack reached across the counter for a napkin and handed it to her to dry her eyes. "Come on in here, and let's sit down." He took her by the hand and dragged her over to the sofa. "First of all, you are definitely not alone in this. Your friend Eli is working on getting the paint off your car."

She jerked her head toward him in surprise.

"And I bet you didn't know I slept on the bench outside your front door last night, with only my shotgun to keep me warm." He chuckled. "But with your permission, I'll move inside tonight." He pressed down on the cushions. "This sofa would feel a whole lot softer to an old man's bones. I promise you, Sammie, I won't leave your side until this thing is over."

"Why are you doing this, Mack?"

"Because your father was my best friend, and I promised him I'd look out for his girls. You, Faith, and Jackie are like daughters to me." He let out a long sigh. "I love your mother, too. And I'm worried about her." His cheeks blushed. "Like a sister, you know." He'd tried to cover for himself, but Sam knew his feelings for her mother were far from platonic.

"I'm worried about Mom, too. Every day she seems more and more despondent."

"The sooner we figure out the secret behind that rusty key of hers, the better off we'll all be."

∞

After an alcohol-free evening, Sam woke the next morning with a clear head for the first time in what seemed like weeks. The aroma of coffee drifting up the stairs motivated her to get out of bed. She took a quick shower and was searching in her mess of a suitcase for a clean pair of underwear when her cell phone rang. Her stomach somersaulted at the sound of Roberto's disheartened voice.

"You better get down here right away, Sam. Someone broke in over the weekend and vandalized the market."

She threw on a pair of wrinkled khaki pants and her green Sweeney's polo shirt and hurried downstairs to the kitchen. Jamie was already showered and dressed and eating a bowl of Cheerios while Mack sipped on coffee at the bar.

"Curtis broke into the market. Eli still has my Jeep, Mack. Can you drive us? We don't have time to wait for Mom and Faith."

"I'll come back and get them later," he said, already heading for the front door with Jamie on his heels. "I'll help Jamie with his chair, if you'll alarm the cottage."

She poured herself a cup of coffee to go, then punched in the four-digit alarm code on the keypad by the door.

"When is this gonna end?" Sam said once they were on the road, heading toward town.

Jamie turned around to face Sam in the backseat. "No matter how bad it is, Mom, we'll sort it out. We can deal with anything as long as none of us gets hurt."

Sam kissed her fingertips and planted them on his cheek. "You have no idea how much I needed someone to remind me of that."

Maybe some good would come of all their troubles, after all. Maybe, just maybe, Jamie was finally putting Corey's death into perspective.

Three cop cars were parked haphazardly in the parking lot when they arrived at the market. Sam recognized some of the officers but didn't see Eli.

"Excuse me for a minute," Mack said, climbing out of his truck. "I need to have a word with Prospect's finest." He slammed his door and marched straight over to the group of policemen.

As soon as she entered the kitchen, she smelled disaster. Literally. The odor was worse than the inlet at low tide.

"Why is it so hot in here?" Jamie asked, fanning himself. "It must be a hundred degrees."

"Ninety-three according to the thermostat." Roberto pointed to the thermostat on the wall. "Whoever broke in here turned off the air conditioner and turned on the heat."

"That explains it," Jamie said. "It was hot as hell yesterday, and it's going to be even hotter today."

"The bastard flipped all the breakers except for the HVAC," Roberto said. "All our product is ruined except a few things we had in the freezer."

Willing herself not to cry, Sam turned to Jamie. He gave her a resigned shrug and said, "I guess we better get to work."

"I don't even know where to start." Sam was considering walking out the door and never looking back, when Jamie reached for her hand.

"Remember, Mom. None of us got hurt."

"Not this time, Jamie. Who's to say it won't happen the next time?"

"There are no guarantees in life. At least that's what Moses says. We do the best we can and pray it all works out."

"And Moses is right," Mack said joining them. "I read those officers the riot act. They assured me they haven't been slacking off but agreed there's room for improvement. They know they have to step it up if they want to catch the slimy little weasel."

"And just how are they planning to step it up?" Sam asked.

"By putting more men on the case for starters. And I've called in reinforcements as well. Bill is in surgery this morning, so I'm on my way back out to the house to get the others."

After he left, Sam ventured to the front of the market. Circling the showroom, she estimated thousands of dollars of ruined goods. She hoped the insurance premium wasn't among the past-due notices she'd received two weeks ago. As far as she knew, all their bills were current now, although they'd had to dip into their emergency funds to pay for them. Restocking their supplies would deplete the rest of that money.

If Curtis's goal was to ruin them, he was doing a damn fine job of it.

Sam, Roberto, and Jamie launched into action, emptying out

and throwing away. With all the starving people in the world, Sam hated to waste so much food.

Mack returned thirty minutes later with his troops. Faith and Lovie surveyed the damage in silence.

"Why don't we divide and conquer?" Mack said. "I'll take Jamie and Sean out in the boat with me to see what we can bring in while you ladies get things in order here."

"Be careful," Sam said with a look of concern.

"We can try our secret crab hole," Sean said.

Mack winked at him. "And I have a few secret holes of my own."

As they were leaving, Evan Brewster, the owner of the local hardware store, drove up with a truck full of fans in every shape and size. "Morning, Sam." He tipped his hat. "I understand you might be in need of some ventilation."

"How'd you—"

"Nothing ever stays a secret for long in Prospect. You of all people should know that," he said, smiling, his rosy cheeks glowing. Evan always played Santa in Prospect's annual Christmas parade. He certainly looked the part, with his white hair and beard. He reached in the cab of his truck for a bottle of cleaning liquid. "This here's the best cleaning product on the market—cuts through odors of any kind."

Faith and Sam helped Evan unload the fans and place them throughout the market. With the front and back doors open for ventilation, the putrid air began to clear out.

"Call me when you're finished with the fans, and I'll come back and get them," he said as he was leaving.

"Thank you, Evan." Sam stood on her tiptoes and kissed his cheek. "All I want for Christmas is a bushel of crabs."

He chuckled, his big belly shaking. "I'll see what I can do."

They worked straight through lunch, racing against the clock to sanitize the market before their new shipment of goods arrived around four. Sam was mopping the showroom floor when she noticed Donna Bennett's sleek black Jaguar pulling up alongside the curb out front. A WSTB van, the ABC news affiliate out of Charleston, slowed to a stop behind her.

"I need to get in there!" Donna tried to push her way past the policeman standing guard out front, but he held her off. "Sorry, ma'am. This area's off-limits."

"This sidewalk is city property." Donna jabbed her finger at the ground. "You can't stop me from being here."

"You're right. I can't stop you from standing there." The policeman pointed at her feet. "But I can, and I will, prevent you from going inside."

"Samantha will talk to me. We're old friends." Donna caught sight of Sam and waved. "There she is. Yoo-hoo, Sam. Do you have a minute to speak to the press?"

Sam responded by turning her back on Donna. She wheeled her mop bucket to the back and dumped the water. When she returned, Faith was talking to Mike Neilson, the emergency-room doctor who had helped their mother the night of her spell. He'd been in the market several times in recent weeks, but Faith had always been the one to wait on him. They appeared to have grown chummy.

"You remember Mike, don't you, Sam?" Faith asked when she approached them. "He has been my rock these past few days. He's the one who put me in touch with the shelter in Columbia."

"I appreciate you helping my sister. But for her sake, and ours, I'm glad the shelter thing didn't work out."

"I tried to tell her . . ." Mike winked at Faith. "If you're fortunate to have people who love you, letting your family support you is always a better choice. So many women don't."

Sam eyed the doctor closely. Could it be they were more than just friends? Sam would love for her sister to find a nice husband number two. But first they needed to get rid of husband number one.

Sam spotted Eli making his way through the throng of people gathering on the sidewalk. She was surprised at how happy she was to see him.

"Why didn't you come in the back way?" she asked, greeting him with a peck on the cheek.

"The trashmen are emptying your dumpster. I had to park across the street at the marina."

Sam wrinkled her brow in confusion. "But Monday isn't our normal trash day."

"Mack called them," Faith said. "I heard him talking to someone down at city hall this morning."

Sam shook her head in wonder. "Only a veteran boat captain would realize how rank the odor of rotting seafood could get in this heat."

"You really should talk to them, you know," Eli said, motioning at the press. "They're vultures. If you give them something to gnaw on, they'll go away. If you keep tempting them, they'll attract others from their flock."

Sam sighed. "You're probably right, but I have no idea what to say to them."

"I'll go out there with you. If they ask you something you don't want to answer, tell them your attorney has advised you not to comment."

"All right." Sam straightened, holding her head high. "Tell them I'll be out soon to make a statement. I just need a few minutes to get my thoughts together."

She started toward the kitchen, but Eli grabbed her arm, holding her back. "For what it's worth, Sam—I'm sorry we haven't arrested Curtis yet. It's not for lack of trying. I've been up all night, driving around, checking under every rock where he might be hiding."

This was news to Sam. After Saturday night, when he'd told

upstairs and into bed. Aside from the intense headache that plagued him, and an enormous amount of discomfort in his arm, Cooper seemed to grow stronger every day. The old Jackie would've worried that so many people living in the house might hinder his recovery. The new Jackie realized that family time was just what he needed.

"What're you looking for?" Bill asked when he found Jackie inventorying the contents of her refrigerator.

"I'm making a grocery list." She added sour cream and cheese to her notepad and closed the door. "I want to make a nice dinner tonight, something special, for Sam and Faith. For everyone, really. They've been working so hard to get the market back on track, I thought they deserved a break."

"That's awfully thoughtful of you," he said.

She ignored the surprise in his voice. The new Jackie understood how to hold her tongue when warranted.

"What can I do to help?" he asked.

"You can cook the tenderloin on your Green Egg thingamajig. I decided to serve beef, since I'm sure they are sick to death of seafood."

"I'll do better than that." He removed the list from her hands. "I'll go to the grocery store for you."

"I was going to ask you to stay here with Cooper."

He folded the list and shoved it in his back pocket. "You shouldn't go anywhere alone until Curtis is behind bars."

She started to resist, then stopped herself. The old Jackie would've resented the house arrest, but the new Jackie considered it a chance to reconnect with her family. "In that case, I'll take you up on your offer. It'll give me a chance to unpack and get some laundry started."

"Your sisters are not the only ones who have been through a lot in the past few days. The chores can wait, Jack. Why don't you take a bath and relax for a while?"

Jackie thought the idea of a hot bath sounded heavenly. "Maybe I'll just do that."

He headed for the stairs. "I'll let myself out and set the alarm behind me."

After checking in on Cooper, making sure he was asleep, Jackie readied her spa tub for her bath. She slipped out of her clothes and eased into the hot water. She leaned her head back against the marble and let the lilac-scented water soothe her stiff muscles.

She found comfort in the neutral territory she'd discovered with Bill. For the past two nights, they'd talked on the cell phone until the wee hours of the morning. He congratulated her when Finley Hall called on Monday morning and officially offered her the job as interim dance instructor. And he agreed to move back in the house with the boys so she could spend her weeknights in Charleston once school started. Not only did he support her plan, he helped her devise it. He would stay in the guest room, letting her keep the master bedroom for the weekends. She would come home after her last class on Fridays, so as not to miss Sean's football games on Friday nights. Cooper's skull fracture had ended his career as a linebacker, although he didn't seem too upset about the prospect of having more time to fish and hunt in the fall.

On the way home from Charlotte, she completed the first item on her checklist by calling Clara Graves, who sounded thrilled at the prospect of having Jackie rent her cottage. As soon as the Curtis crisis ended, she would focus on her second agenda item, which was finding a new housekeeper to help with the cooking and cleaning during the week.

Working part-time in Charleston would give her a chance to ease her way back into society, to reestablish contact with old acquaintances and make new friends. After her temporary dance job ended in December, she would move ahead with plans to start her own design firm if she felt the opportunity existed.

Somehow, someway, she would make it work.

She had yet to discuss the last item on her checklist with Bill. She would wait and see how the next few days went before she called Barbara the Barracuda to put the divorce proceedings on hold.

She had drifted off to sleep when the sound of the alarm chimes woke her up. She threw on a clean pair of shorts and a fresh T-shirt and went to help Bill with the groceries.

"Why'd you buy two tenderloins?" she asked, not in the old-Jackie accusatory tone but in the new-Jackie genuinely curious tone.

"One isn't enough, when you consider three teenage boys, plus Mack."

"Mack? You mean Captain Mack?"

"He's the one. He's been sleeping on the sofa in the guest cottage."

"Goodness. We really are feeding a crowd. I guess we'd better get busy."

Bill went outside to light the charcoal in his Green Egg while Jackie set things in motion inside. She put the potatoes in the oven for baking and set the dining-room table with her white china, royal-blue placemats, and red-checkered napkins. She sprinkled red-white-and-blue star graffiti down the center of the table and placed her flag-motif candles in her wooden pillar holders. She took her clippers outside and made Bill hold her bucket while she clipped red roses, white hydrangeas, and sprigs of lavender from her garden.

Jackie spent the rest of the afternoon in preparation for her dinner party. She was putting the finishing touches on her cheese platter when the others got home from work about six-thirty.

Sean came flying up the stairs ahead of everyone else. "Where's Cooper?" he asked, kissing his mother when she pointed to her cheek.

"He's been asleep all afternoon," she said. "Why don't you go wake him up?"

Lovie came around the kitchen island to give Jackie a hug. "I can't remember when I last saw you smile like this." Her mother whispered in her ear. "It's a good look for you. I hope you'll keep it."

"What's all this?" Sam asked, peeking into the dining room. "Are you having a party?"

Faith nudged Sam with her elbow. "A homecoming party for Cooper."

"And an overdue celebration of the reopening of Sweeney's, which I should have thrown for you back in June."

"I hope we're not having seafood," Sam said with the hint of a smile on her lips.

"Far from it. We're having beef tenderloin, garlic bread, a green salad, and potatoes." Jackie waved her cheese knife at the pan of twice-baked potatoes on the counter.

"If that's the case, I'm going to take a shower and put on a dress. I'm sick to death of these clothes," Sam said, and disappeared down the stairs.

"What can I do to help?" Faith asked.

Jackie glanced around the kitchen. "Everything's about ready. Why don't you get changed so we can catch up? A lot has happened around here since I've been gone."

THIRTY-EIGHT

FAITH

"She's been at it all week," Faith said under her breath, gesturing at Lovie, who was trying to cram her key in the lock of an antique pine hutch in the breakfast room. "You have a lot of things with keyholes, and Mom's tried every one of them. She's gonna drive us all nuts if we don't get to the bottom of this thing."

Jackie took a sip of her wine and nibbled on a piece of cheese. "I'm pretty sure your key doesn't fit my hutch, Mom."

"I know it." Lovie spun around to face them. "I just can't shake the feeling that this key belongs to something on this property. I've tried everything in this house at least once." She wandered over to the window and stared out. "Maybe it fits something outside."

Sean came barreling up the stairs, followed by Sam and Mack. Sean slammed a tumbler down on the kitchen counter in front of his mother. "Dad needs a refill. He said to tell you we're thirty minutes out on the meat."

Jackie went to their liquor cabinet and poured two fingers of bourbon in the glass, filling it the rest of the way with water. "Why are you so out of breath, son?"

"Dad made me go tie everything down on the dock and bring in the cushions from the boat. He thinks we might get a storm later. I'm tired of having to do everything by myself. When is Cooper gonna get better?"

"Aww, poor baby," Sam said, running her hand across her nephew's crew cut. "Are you worn out from so much hard work?"

"Where is Cooper?" Jackie asked.

"In the game room, playing one-handed Xbox with Bitsy and Jamie," Sean said before darting back downstairs with his father's drink.

"I think Bitsy and Jamie are afraid to let Cooper out of their sight for fear he might get hurt again," Mack said.

"They make for an interesting threesome, don't they?" Sam said. "One in a wheelchair. One with his arm bandaged like a mummy. And one so traumatized she can't stop sucking her thumb."

"The walking wounded," Faith blurted. "Oh . . . I'm so sorry, Sammie. I didn't mean . . ."

Her sister dismissed Faith with a wave of her hand. "You can't offend me. Jamie's on the mend. I feel it in my heart. His mood has improved dramatically over the past week, even considering everything we've been through. Maybe it's *because* of everything we've been through."

Hearing the reassurance in her sister's voice gave Faith hope that something good may actually come from the pain and suffering Curtis had brought on her family. She held up her wine glass. "Here's to hoping he takes those first steps soon." Three pairs of eyes stared at her. "Oh, dang. I did it again."

This time Sam burst out laughing. She grabbed the sparkling water she'd been nursing and held it up for a toast. The four of them clinked glasses. "I don't need alcohol to make a toast to that."

"The meat will be ready soon. We should think about getting everything else on the table." Jackie set her wine glass on the

314

counter. "Sam, if you and Mack will fill the glasses with iced tea, I'll get Faith to check on the potatoes while I toss the salad."

Bill came up a little while later, carrying a steaming pan of tenderloin beef. "This should sit a minute before I slice it. In the meantime, I'll go gather some flashlights. Looks like a storm's coming our way."

Faith was counting heads, to make sure she had enough potatoes on the platter, when she realized someone was missing. "Where's Mama?"

Everyone stopped what they were doing.

"She was here a minute ago," Sam said.

"Kids!" Jackie called down the stairs to the game room. "Is Lovie down there with y'all?"

The pitter-patter of little feet sounded below them, and then Bitsy shouted up the stairs, "She's not down here."

Despite the break-in at the market, Bitsy had relaxed considerably since they'd all been staying together at the farm. Much to Faith's delight, her daughter seemed downright giddy to have Cooper home.

Sam ordered Faith and Mack to check upstairs while everyone else searched the main floor. They looked in bathrooms and closets and under beds. With no sign of Lovie anywhere, they reconvened in the breakfast room ten minutes later.

"Let's approach this methodically. When's the last time you saw your mom?" Bill asked Jackie.

She thought for a moment. "Right before Sean came up to refill your drink. We were right here, in the breakfast room. Mom was trying to make her key fit the lock in the pine hutch."

Walking from the hutch to the window, Faith retraced her mother's steps. "She came over here to the window, then said something about her key fitting a lock outside."

All eyes darted to the windows. The sky had darkened, and the wind was whipping around in the trees. They heard the dogs howling to come in, terrified of thunder and lightning.

"Do you really think she'd go outside alone?" Mack asked. "We've told her a thousand times in the past few days not to leave the house unchaperoned."

"You know Lovie," Sam said. "She has a mind of her own."

Bill removed his iPhone from his back pocket and checked the radar. "Looks like the storm is still a ways away. Let's divide up and search the yard."

They flew down the stairs, one after another, to the game room.

"Cooper, you stay here with Bitsy. Jamie, Sean, let's go," Sam said. "We need to find Lovie before the storm comes."

Once outside, Mack and Sam headed toward the guest house, Bill and Sean to the garage, Jamie to the side yard, and Jackie around behind the house to her gardening shed.

Seeing the terrified look on her daughter's face, Faith had let the others go ahead of her. "Don't you worry, honey," she said, reassuring her child. "Lovie is here somewhere."

Cooper pulled his cousin close to him. "We'll be fine here, won't we Bits?"

Her eyes wide, she sucked even harder on her thumb.

Cooper winked at his aunt, his signal for her to leave.

Hunched over, Faith joined the search, fighting against the wind as she raced down the hill toward the water. From the dock, she had a clear view of the creek in both directions. She spotted Jamie and Lovie on the dock next door. Jamie's wheelchair had gotten stuck in the sand at the foot of the dock where the earth ended and the boardwalk began. Faith watched in amazement as he gradually stood, using the railings for support. He placed one step in front of the other, then another and another, making a slow and apparently painful approach toward his grandmother, who stood on the edge of the dock, facing the water, as if contemplating a jump.

Faith sprinted back up the hill, then along the sidewalk to the neighbor's yard.

"Can you stay for dinner?" Sam asked Eli when he was finally wrapping things up.

He glanced at his watch. "I don't get off for another hour."

"I don't imagine we'll be eating anytime soon. We're all too keyed up to think about food." When he hesitated, she said, "Please. I'd really like for you to be here."

"Okay, then." He leaned in and planted a kiss on her lips. "I'll see what I can do about getting off a few minutes early."

Not caring that everyone was watching them, she wrapped her arms around his neck and kissed him back, a longer lingering kiss, a promise of much more to come.

Eli had been gone only a few minutes when Moses's red sports car came to a screeching halt in the driveway. After struggling to get his long limbs free, he rushed over to Jamie and attacked him with a bear hug. "I knew you had it in you, little bro." He pulled away from him, then gave him another quick hug for good measure.

Jamie grinned. "Now you have to make good on our deal."

"What deal?" Sam asked.

"A friend of mine is the batting coach for the Red Sox," Moses said. "I told Jamie that as soon as he was on his feet again, we'd fly to Boston for box seats at a big game."

"You never stopped believing in him." Sam stood on her tiptoes and kissed Moses's cheek. "Stay for dinner. It's the least we can do to pay you back for all you've done for my son."

"I'd like that. I'm looking forward to getting to know the real Jamie, the wonder boy I've heard so much about."

A forest-green 4Runner pulled up behind Moses's car. Sam almost didn't recognize Mike Neilson, dressed in khaki shorts and a red polo shirt. It was the first time she had seen him wear anything other than scrubs.

"I hope you don't mind that I invited him," Faith whispered to Sam. "He helped me so much. I wanted him to be a part of the celebration."

Sam winked. "On a night like tonight, the more the merrier."

When the kids complained of hunger, they all moved inside for dinner.

"Let's clear the table for a buffet dinner since our party has grown," Jackie said. "I have some paper plates in here somewhere." She rummaged through a cabinet and emerged with a stack of patriotic designer plates.

"Looks like love is in the air." Faith gestured at Mack and Lovie, who were watching the sunset from the balcony, his hand placed loosely around her shoulders.

"Even though Mom solved the mystery behind the rusty key, I'm convinced there's something going on in her brain," Jackie said.

"I agree," Sam said. "After everything settles down a little, we can talk to her about going to Charleston for testing."

Sam saw the doctor smile at Faith from across the room, where he was comparing golf handicaps with Bill. "Looks like Mack and Lovie aren't the only ones bitten by the love bug."

Faith's face flushed bright red. "You're one to talk, Sammie. That was quite a kiss you gave Eli earlier."

Jackie loaded up their arms with paper plates and plastic utensils. "Let's go reset the table. I have something I need to talk to both of you about."

Sam and Faith followed their older sister into the dining room. "Have you and Bill made amends?" Sam asked Jackie. "Is that your big news?"

"Bill and I are friends again. We agree that's the best thing for the boys. I need to figure out *me* before I figure out *us*. Which is what I wanted to talk to you about. I've taken a job in Charleston."

A light bulb flashed on in Sam's brain. "So that's what you were doing in front of Finley Hall that day. Are you redesigning their cafeteria or something?"

Jackie shook her head. "I've agreed to be their interim dance instructor. But you're not far off base. My ultimate goal is to open my own design studio. Taking this temporary job at Finley Hall will give me a chance to explore my options." Jackie turned to Faith. "Which is where you come in."

"Me?" Faith placed her hand on her chest. "What do I have to do with you working in Charleston?"

"Everything, actually. There's no way I can commute every day, so I've signed a six-month lease on a carriage house in Charleston. Bill has agreed to move back in here with the boys. It's not what you think," Jackie said in response to Sam's raised eyebrows. "He will sleep in the guest room."

"I predict the two of you will be back together by Christmas," Sam said.

"I doubt it'll take that long," Faith added.

"Will the two of you let me finish, please?" Jackie said in an exasperated tone.

Sam pretended to zip her lips.

"Faith, I would very much like for you and Bitsy to move into the guest cottage. I know you are busy at the market, and if you don't like this idea, I totally understand. But I thought it would be good for the boys to have you here. I need someone to help with their laundry, get them off to school in the mornings, and cook them dinner a couple of nights a week. I will pay you, of course, and I don't expect you to do the heavy cleaning. I've hired a maid service for that."

Sam could tell by the twinkle in Faith's eyes that this was an answer to her prayers. Even if the judge sentenced Curtis to twenty years in prison, she had too many bad memories from her trailer to continue to live there.

"That would solve a lot of my problems," Faith said.

"And a lot of mine as well," Jackie said.

"I don't know what to say, other than thank you." Faith gave

Jackie a hug, then turned toward the stairs. "I can't wait to tell Bitsy. She'll be thrilled."

"Wait," Jackie called after her. "Before you go. We need to take a family photo."

The three sisters gathered together, and Jackie snapped a selfie.

"What are you planning to do with that?" Sam asked.

"I'm texting it to Donna Bennett." Jackie read the message aloud as she texted. "Headline for your morning paper. 'The Amazing Sweeney Sisters Survive Ordeal and Live to Tell About It.'"

After Faith disappeared downstairs, Sam helped Jackie stack the china plates on the sideboard and prepare the table for the buffet.

"You're doing a good thing for Faith," Sam said.

Jackie looked up in surprise. "One good deed can't compare to all you've done for her. You had your house destroyed, a bucket of paint thrown in your face, and thousands of dollars' worth of seafood ruined. And you never even complained."

"I internalized my problems, Jackie. I certainly didn't handle it with grace."

Jackie held Sam's shoulders in her hands. "After our argument in the parking deck at the hospital, you got me thinking about who I really am, and I realized one of the important qualities missing from my life is empathy. I'm a selfish woman, Sammie, but I'm doing my best to change. I took your advice. I put myself in your shoes, and I realized how much you'd sacrificed to help Faith. Then I put myself in Faith's shoes, and I asked myself what I could do to make her life easier."

Sam glanced down at her sister's feet. She hadn't noticed earlier that Jackie was wearing Sam's favorite pair of worn-out espadrilles, her bright-red toenail poking through the hole at the tip of her big toe. She looked back up at Jackie and smiled. "They're comfortable, aren't they?"

"And to think I've been cramming my feet into those bone-crusher heels all these years." Jackie drew Sam in for a hug, the only one Sam ever remembered receiving from her older sister. "I hope you don't mind if I keep them. For some strange reason, like magic, they give me confidence. I believe in myself when I'm wearing them. Just as you have always believed in me."

If you enjoyed the book and have a moment to spare, please consider posting a short review on Amazon to share your thoughts with others . . .

Please visit my website for more information about my novels
www.ashleyfarley.net

Sign up here for my newsletter

A NOTE FROM THE AUTHOR

I spent the summers of my youth on Murrells Inlet, in the upper part of the Lowcountry of South Carolina, at the tip of Garden City Beach where the mouth of the inlet meets the ocean. We dug for clams in the gooey black mud and caught crabs using hand lines—a piece of string attached to a chicken neck. Mostly, my friends and I raced our johnboats up and down the waterways —skiing and hydrosliding—annoying the weekly renters with our rambunctious behavior. Remember those days, Eve?

When the ocean was calm and the fishing reports promising, my father took us deep-sea fishing. We left the dock in the wee hours of the morning in order to make it to the Gulf Stream by sunrise. My favorite part of the trip was hearing the diesel engines rumble to life and vibrate beneath me as I slumbered away in the cabin below. Some days we never got a bite. Other days we returned with a cockpit full of tuna, wahoo, and dolphin.

I wrote this novel in memory of my father, Elbert, who shared his love of the water and taught me how to cook everything we caught.

For my mother, Joanne, and my brother, Miles, who share these sacred memories. And for my children, Cameron and Ned, and my husband, Ted, who have helped me make new ones at our river house near the Chesapeake Bay.

I am blessed with five amazing sisters-in-law who more than make up for the sister I never had. XOXO to Dina, Jody, Mamie, Katherine, and Tammy. Thank you for all your love and support and wonderful times.

I am thankful for my wonderful editor, Patricia Peters at awordaffair.com, who took *Her Sister's Shoes* to a new level with her amazing attention to detail and dedication to proper grammar.

Lastly, I'm indebted to my friends at the Yellow Umbrella in Richmond, who provided inspiration for Captain Sweeney's Seafood with their sleek market, fresh-from-the-water seafood, and expert cooking tips.

63797270R00203

Made in the USA
Middletown, DE
06 February 2018